DEADLINE

DEADLINE

BY

MARCY HEIDISH

Dolan & Associates, Publishers

This novel is for
the women of Rachael's
and for
Scott Wells

If you've ever been taken for money
If you've ever gone down with your pride
If you've ever stood up for a good friend and lost
Then you know that the river is wide.
But don't cry now, don't cry now... .
                    Don't Cry Now
                    J. D. Souther

The light shines in the darkness and the darkness has
not overcome it.
                    The Gospel of St. John 1:5

PART ONE

<1>

N0 SHOCK. No tears.

I was taught that first and I learned fast, and most of the time, I think I've got it. Most of the time, I think I mean it. And then something hits me, tugs me, snags me — and I have to learn all over again.

THIS TIME, it was outside a shelter for homeless women. A twenty-three-year-old volunteer, Meredith Crane, had just left for the evening. She was wearing a blue raincoat and carrying a yellow umbrella — the first things she had bought herself in Washington.

Recently arrived from Iowa, and recently en-gaged, she planned to study social work in the fall. Meanwhile, for the summer, there was the shelter. Once a week, Meredith would take off her small diamond ring, leave her fiancé, and head downtown. She looked forward to these Monday nights when she helped serve dinner at Mount Olivet, then stay-ed to talk with the women.

The last person to see Meredith alive was a wo-man named Carla. Sitting together on the shelter's stairs, they'd spoken of weddings and killed a roach. The insect remained on the fifth step, beside a rolled newspaper — ours, as it happened. At about eight--thirty, Meredith had gathered her things and said goodnight. The shelter's front door was already locked. She left, as usual, through the empty kit-chen at the rear of the building.

Outside on the front steps, she had paused, but-toning her coat. Perhaps she had peered through the fine rain toward her car. Before she finished the buttons, she was seized from behind. Before she could scream, she was struck; a blow to the head dazed her. I doubt she saw her attacker then, as she sank against the steps.

Perhaps Meredith Crane's last image was the steel tip of her umbrella, moving in and out of focus before her eyes. Abruptly, her head was jerked back, her mouth forced open. The umbrella was thrust down her throat, then her windpipe, before lodging deep in her thorax. A handle, blue plastic, was protruding from her mouth when police arrived — and when I did.

I'm a crime reporter, Metro section, big paper, Wash-ington, D.C. Six years of it: over a thousand violent deaths under my fingers, my keys, so to speak, into newsprint. Hundreds of nights, going out on violent stories. I should be used to it. I am used to it. But tonight, driving downtown, somehow I know: this one's going to hurt me. Mentally, I grope for the litany passed on to me by the last woman in this job:

No shock.

No tears.

Never let them see you react ...

By the time I reach Mount Olivet, the rain has stopped. The whole area is blinking like a star. Squad cars, detectives' cars; flashing blue lights, red lights, white spotlights. Radios crackle. Day-Glo yellow plastic tape cordons off the street. As always, the light is surreal. As always, in its glare, the tape seems to pulsate: Police line do not cross. Broken glass crunches under my high heels. No other media yet; I'd been nearby, driving home, when I'd picked up the call on my police radio. Opening my notebook, I walk into the glare. Detective Jed Jackson lifts the tape for me.

"My fair lady."

Jed says this every time, without irony — now. My first year, there was a lot of irony. Jed's been in Homicide almost two decades. He grew up in D.C.'s slums, got out, and became a football star before he became a star cop. First thing I heard about him was a simple epithet: "Son of a bitch." Second thing I heard was a nickname: "Deacon" — he's active at an A.M.E. Zion church. Third thing I heard, from Jed himself, was silence.

Pointedly, he ignored me for months. He didn't like women crime reporters and he didn't like my type: fair-skinned, small-boned, with a tendency to feminine clothes. The first time he addressed me, he told me so. But after a year together, working rough cases, things began to change. After five more years, we've formed an unspoken partnership. I guess we've helped each other out too many times. We've never discussed it. The closest Jed comes to praise is, "My fair lady" — without irony. And his frown at some rookie, staring at my legs as I step up to a corpse.

Tonight, though, there are no stares. Tonight I know the men out here, and tonight they are unusually silent. I look at the dead girl on the shelter steps. She is lit, over and over, by the bone-white flash of crime lab cameras. With each flash, the body seems to jerk, to lift, yanked from the dark by that eerie light. The medics have left;

the girl's been dead maybe an hour. Her blue raincoat seems new: clean, stiff creases, half-buttoned. She is sunburned; I can see a white circle on her left ring finger. I look at her face, her mouth — and look at Jed.

He nods. "What you think."

He means the umbrella.

"Pisses me off." He spits meditatively.

"And me." All we have to say.

I jot notes, then go inside the shelter. Jed's part-ner is questioning the director, Joan Kelly. Her hands shake. I talk with Carla, who shows me the roach and looks stunned. Some of the other women come forward; they smoke, they remember her, some cry. Ahead, I know, is the hardest part: the talks I'll have, back at my desk — on the phone. The call to the parents in Ames, Iowa. The call to the fiancé, here in D.C.

Outside again, I run into Sam, one of our photo-graphers. He shakes his head. We'll have art but proba-bly not till tomorrow's follow-up. Tonight, the paper's too tight. I know I'll get crime lab details, but not tonight. Not in time for tomorrow's editions.

Art.

Editions.

Easier to think that line. Easier than this line: this girl, this shelter — this bad-dream scene, lit up like a movie set awaiting the leading lady. As I turn away, Jed Jackson puts a hand on my arm. I always have to tilt my head to look up at him: huge hill of a man, creases start-ing to show in his dark face. We look at each other as we have, so many times, over police tape. Mostly, he just says, "Call me." Tonight, for the first time, he says, "Watch yourself."

"Call me," I say.

"My line."

Briefly, thinly, we smile. And then I walk over the street's smashed bottles to my car. As I open the door, I look back. The shelter is a dim, sagging shape against the sky. It stoops there, on a street of slouching, weary shapes:

Row houses. Warehouses. Storefronts. Half of them are vacant, boarded up. One store still bears the sign: Chix Wings 2 Go. Beyond, from the traffic circle, comes the sigh of tires, the sweep of headlights. The lights catch the street's broken glass, making it shimmer like water.

And within the shimmer, within the tape, within that dark-edged glare, I still see the blue of Meredith Crane's new raincoat.

■

<2>

THE LINE to Ames, Iowa, is still busy. Temporary reprieve.

Eventually, I'll get through. Eventually, I'll get her parents. Their line has been tied up for hours. Small wonder. They've already had their call from the D.C. police.

Waiting, I count the Styrofoam cups on my desk. Four. Not a good sign. It's only eleven the next morning. Last night, I wrote the story, in brief, for the late city editions; I filed at ten. A call to Crane's fiancé, for today's follow-up, turned into a call-back — and a visit. Back at my desk, to decipher my notes, I was too tired to go home. I've had some sleep, on the couch in the women's room off the vast newsroom floor. At 7:30 I was awakened by the cleaning lady, who keeps her coat there. My eyes opened on the umbrella in her hand. Somehow, I didn't get back to sleep.

Instead, I went to my desk. In the top drawer I keep a reporter's most precious possession: a Rolodex of contacts, sources, phone numbers. In the middle drawer I keep rubber bands, pens, peanut butter. In the bottom drawer I keep panty hose, an extra blouse. I keep rosewater soap and cologne. Some days the rosewater seems more precious than the Rolodex. This is one.

Now, as I drain my coffee, I can smell the soap on my hand. Inexplicably, this helps. I am not only waiting to dial Ames again. I'm waiting for my editor, Tom Nichols, to get out of a meeting. I'm waiting on calls from Jed Jackson and from Mount Olivet. The phone rings. I grab it.

"Bad girl," a voice whispers. "Out all night again. Don't think that went unnoticed. Don't think you aren't watched."

I sigh. "I'm going to have to report you."

"What was it this time ..." The whisper deepens. "Sex — or violence?"

"Sidney." I can visualize my housemate running a hand over her close-cropped Afro, her face the color of espresso — very good, very strong espresso. I can see her rich smile, her angular, elegant frame in a silk jumpsuit — not the usual image for one of D.C.'s public defenders. As an attorney, she is valuable enough to get away with jumpsuits. As a friend, she is valuable enough to get away with personal sass. She has taken it upon herself to worry about my romantic life. Sisterly, knowingly, she complains that I don't let myself have one. Until recently she's been right. I haven't had time, I say; made time, Sid says. She's right there, too. Until recently. Recently she's seen some hopeful signs, but this morning, I have to disappoint her.

"Sidney," I repeat now. "It was violence."

There is a pause on the other end.

"Murder. Young girl," I add.

"Shit," she says quietly.

"A shelter volunteer."

Long silence.

"Damn." Sid herself does pro bono work for the homeless. There is another silence before she goes on. "Bad
timing," she says, finally. "I'll be out of town a few days
on this case — you be okay?"

"I'll be fine."

Pause. No comment.

"Got some food in," Sid adds, then. "State-of- the-art
gourmet frozen dinners. You still remember the numbers
on the microwave?"

"One through five." I can't, don't, won't cook. I'm not
even great at heating.

"Be careful," Sidney adds.

"With the microwave?"

"I'll ignore that."

"Do good."

"No sweat."

"Get the stuff."

"Girl — get some sleep."

Even her hang-up sounds worried. Sidney hates this
beat for me. She grew up in Washington's inner city —
and escaped it. She knows what's out there. She said it
when I started, and she's said it to me since: Crime
reporting? Let someone else do that shit — Why you?

I dial Ames again. Still busy.

I glance across the newsroom. A huge space, it
reminds me of a football field with desks, a lot of desks,
close together, row on row. The newsroom is not yet at
high speed. It's too far from deadline, when the air gets
that charge, sometimes resembling that of an emergency
room.

Now: morning speed. Smell of coffee and carpet-
cleaner. People slouching at desks; people milling around
with cups. Vague tap-tap of keys, murmur of voices. I

look across the rows of lit computer screens, toward the
offices against the wall, offices fronted with glass.
Through one, I can see a meeting: Editors' meeting, half
a dozen people. I can see Tom, nearest the door, his eyes
on me.

I look away and dial Ames again. Again, busy. Crime
reporting? I get up for more coffee; let's make it five. Let
someone else do that shit . .

The police beat: Bad hours, nights, weekends; mostly,
little glory. Often, reporters dodge it, skirt it, leave it,
move on. I've thought of leaving. I still think of leaving;
and yet, somehow, I stay. In this city, lots of people want
to tell the stories of the living — the powerful, the famous.
Not many want to tell the stories of the dead — the
has-beens, the cash-ins, usually not powerful, not famous;
usually the average, the poor. Their stories interest me.
Their stories demand a teller. That's one reason I stay.

One reason. There are others, less lofty. As it
happens, I do this well — I've never known exactly why.
I know what I don't do well. I lack all political instinct.
I don't have an eye for or the interest in national news.
I'm drawn to "smaller stories" — stories without clear
endings. They make me want to finish them. Sometimes
I actually can. Some-times I just think I can. So many
unfinished stories here — each year there are more. Until
recently, that pulled me. Until recently, that held me.

Until this story. I think I know why it's differ-ent,
why it's got power over me, more than the usual hook. We
all get hook-stories, I've had them before. And God knows
I've had disturbing stories: they're axiomatic in this city,
and others, where the murder rate can outstrip the days
of the year. I've made disturbing calls before, like this one
to Ames. Like the one I made last night, to John McCall,
Meredith's fiance — a call that turned into a long visit.
Sometimes I've sworn I'll quit taping people cry. Press

Play/Record. Ask the questions. Press Stop. Return to
the office. Press Rewind; then Play. And listen to some
stranger sob his soul out. Hit Stop. Light a cigarette.
Take three aspirin. Have a Coke. Do whatever you do.
Hit Play again. Take notes. No shock. No tears. No
disgust either — at yourself, the intruder. Sometimes, to
me, that's how it feels.

Sometimes, though, it doesn't work that way. Sometimes, like last night, the bereaved is alone and needs to
talk. Sometimes, on the worst nights, and the best, you
become a companion in the dark: the stranger who is not
a stranger just then. It was like that last night, with
John McCall. For a few minutes I could do something —
some-thing small, that would never make the papers.
Now and then, that happens. But that's not the hook
here; it's some-thing else.

I go into the women's room and splash water on my
face. Standing at the mirror, I try to conjure the faces of
my friends: blessings, all. What would they say? Abruptly, their images fade. That sense of blessing fades. For
an instant, in the mirror, I see the dead girl's face. At the
time I thought she looked familiar, didn't know why. Now
I see the resemblance. To me. Same delicate bones, same
height. Similar face, similar auburn hair, hers, long,
pooling around her head — mine, short. But ten years
ago my hair was long. Ten years ago I was just a little
older than Meredith. I was twenty-five, working on the
paper and volunteering at shelters. An odd time for me,
a time of mistakes and transitions.

Like Meredith Crane, I had a white circle on my finger
from an absent ring. Unlike her, I'd just left a brief wrong
marriage — so brief it was like an extended date. Now I
see I was trying to run away from home. The attempt was
successful; the marriage too short to leave scars. I can
barely remember that tentative young man who dropped

the ring at the civil ceremony. A perpetual graduate student in botany, he must have gone on to teach. I've no idea; we've lost touch. It was one of those grad- school couplings, I guess, and I didn't struggle with it much. Perhaps not enough.

No, my struggle that year was with vocation. I knew I loved the taste and spin of words. I also felt drawn to some kind of ministry. I'd always been a dreamy, mystical child, a shy haunter of libraries and churches. Reading was a visible refuge — my spiritual life, a secret one.

At twenty-five, I thought I'd go public with it, and go to seminary. At twenty-five, naturally, I thought that might help change the world. I segued from Catholic to Protestant, and perhaps into the wrong denomination, the wrong school for me. I wasn't prepared for the gossip, the politics — and here too, I lacked instinct for it. Most of us got so wrapped up in our "process,"

I felt myself losing touch with the shelters, the jails, the very people I'd written about at the newspaper. Senior year I quit, disillusioned. I went back to journalism — and realized I had changed. I wasn't so shy, I wasn't so naive. I saw that storytelling was my call, my way to help. And in journalism, at least I knew where the land mines were. The city desk started me out again on the religion beat, thinking I had this great inside track. I stuck it out two years. In the end, I found that beat was mostly about politics too.

I decided to switch.

Something safer.

Crime.

•

THE PARTY in Ames has the phone off the hook, the operator verifies. I put a question mark next to Parents in my notebook, just as my line rings.

"Lady Nan." It's Jed.

"Nothing yet."

I picture our faces: controlled frustration.

"Brought some folks down for questioning," Jed says. "Joan Kelly, the director. Carla, that woman. A Dr. Heller, some shrink, he was at the shelter last night." He exhales smoke. "Nothin' solid."

"Terrific."

"Carla admits this much — "

I pick up my pen.

"She did kill ..." Long pause. "That roach." He laughs, wheezing slightly; smoking too much. We are doing this because we have nothing to do.

"No motive," Jed says, finally. "No evidence. No deep shit. Don't quote me." I almost never quote him. I tip him, he tips me, but it's off-the-record, unofficial. And Jed, with rare exceptions, only gets in print as "a department source" — just the way he wants it.

Jed sighs. "LaMarca's digging." His partner.

"Call me back if you get M.E. stuff."

"Let me know what turns up."

A pause. I wait.

"Meant it," he says. "Watch yourself."

He never says that. Now it's twice. Jed doesn't miss much. He must have noticed the resemblance last night, too. I think of that, off and on, till the phone rings again: LaMarca, with some "unofficial" preliminaries from the medical examiner's office and the crime lab. My pen begins to move.

Probable cause of death: asphyxiation and hemorrhage. Secondary contusions. Blunt force trauma. Ruptured larynx, esophagus, internal bleeding .. .

"How appetizing," says a voice behind me. "What are you doing for lunch?"

My editor, Tom Nichols, is reading over my shoulder. Shock ... I keep scribbling.

"Is that an answer?" His tie brushes my hair; he leans closer. I resist the urge to lean back. I can smell the starch in his shirt; he can smell my perfume. He drops a sample of it on my blotter.

A bribe? I write.

"A token. A remembrance."

Steel-tipped umbrella, I write, listening to the phone again.

"Oh Jesus." Tom's leaning so close I can feel his laughter: dark laughter, I know, because I know him and he knows this case. I know without looking up into his face. I try not to do that in the news-room, in encounters such as this. I'm still holding out. Tom makes no such pretense, never has. Now his lips graze my ear. "Really — early lunch?"

When? I write.

His hand, strong and square, appears over my notebook. Today, he scrawls. Two-inch letters.

"Before your phone rings again," he says.

His phone rings now, from the city desk. I wait till he's gone before I hang up. LaMarca already has.

·

"'RUPTURED ESOPHAGUS, internal bleeding ...'" I run through it, moments later, sitting by Tom's desk. "Let's talk about that here. The rest, over lunch."

"Or — other things." He tips back his chair. "Like — your life? My life? Instead of other people's lives? You know, transcend the genre?"

"Daring concept, for a journalist." I look up. Tom smiles. His gray eyes are serious, as they often are, watching me. Around him are packed shelves — books, periodicals: fiction, fishing, poetry. Every-thing is slightly askew, piled at odd angles. And all over the corkboard panel above his desk, there are photos of lakes: vast lakes, small pools, meadow ponds, patches of shining water. They always hold my eyes. None of Tom's awards are visible. I remember that impressed me at our first meeting. It still does.

"Okay," he's saying. "What's after `internal bleeding'?"

"Shock."

"Ah." Wry glance.

At forty, Tom can still look boyish, even with gray just starting to edge his dark hair. Tall and lean, he has a lean voice as well: he speaks with New England dryness. Years before, he started in the book review section of a Boston paper and, by some fluke, got drafted into Metro, investigative reporting. He worked his way through big stories, top prizes, to City Desk editing, and here, as assis-tant city editor, he is seasoned, respected, tough.

Too tough, we thought, when he was new. We didn't quite know how to take him, then: this Yankee loner, quietly observing, lunching alone, reading. Gradually, we discovered his deadpan humor; his willingness to fight the Metro chief for us. Gradually, too, I discovered his eye for social action stories, as well as crime.

Now it seems he's always been on the desk; I have to remind myself it's just a year since he transferred in from Chicago, after a divorce, and — rumored — a time out of work. Those first few months here, I noticed him watch-ing me. I chalked it up to professional appraisal, then to the divorce. I was wrong, both counts. He's never stopped watching.

I've always been amazed that someone so crack, so professional, would fall for one of his own reporters, and stay that way, steadily, patiently. It's a dilemma for me, this relationship. We have lunch. We have coffee. Occasionally, on some pretext, he drops over. I set limits — I'm not entirely sure why. In any case, he respects them. And waits. He is, I realize, waiting now.

"What's after 'shock?' " he's just asked.

"Death."

"Oh." Tom's faint, dark chuckle.

I flip through my notes. "No leads from Jed." "The umbrella — whose?"

"Girl-on-the-Go Rainwear."

Tom looks at me. His eyes glimmer. Some stories, no matter how you try, you keep edging up on laughter. Especially the bizarre stories. This certainly fits that description. Tom tries again. "Drugs? Theft? Rape?"

"None. No prints, no motive."

"Dare I ask again — the umbrella?"

"The victim's."

"Family? Boyfriend?"

I tell him: an August wedding planned.

Tom pauses. "Hate to say it, but from our standpoint, it's a grabber. Definitely front page, Metro."

"Above or below the fold?" I can't help asking.

"That I don't know — you reporters — "

"You editors — you care just as much."

"You're right." Tom comes around the desk, leans over my chair, glances at notes. "After this follow-up story, can you do a mood piece? Reaction from the shelters, the homeless women?"

I look up at him, thinking. Abruptly, our faces are close; too close. Our lips could brush. It takes us both by surprise. His eyes on mine turn a deeper gray. For an instant he lets himself touch my hair — just an instant;

the briefest touch. Then he moves back, leans against his desk, reaches for a cigarette. I look at my notebook, focus in again on the story. I've been brewing an idea all morning.

"I'll go you one better," I say. "I'll go undercover — as a shelter volunteer. Best way to catch the mood, maybe some leads. Look, the cops have nothing, but they know something's there. So do I — and I know shelters. Tom — I want to go inside this story."

His lighter pauses. He watches me over the flame.

∎

<3>

ILIFT THE taper. For a moment, I watch its small light. Over me the church arches, dim and protective. Small, low-beamed, it lacks the Gothic reach of the cathedral that soared through my childhood. Even so, it's good to be here; here in one of the few downtown churches that remain unlocked. It smells of tallow, flowers, incense — perhaps the incense is only a memory from long ago. I light one candle, then another; one more. Always three: a childhood custom, passed on to me. The saints' statues seem to bend and shift in the flickering light. I come here during tough stories. I come alone. This, I know, is part of my preparation for tomorrow.

Suddenly, behind me, the heavy door slams. A spiral of wind enters the nave. The candle flames dip. My hand pauses, holding the taper. There is no step, no sound; only a presence — strong, dense, tangible. Slowly, I turn, my back to the candles.

The church looks empty. Pillars are in shadow. Confessionals, across the back, are dark, vague. I don't wait to see if I'm imagining; you develop a sense about danger, from covering it. Holding the lit taper, I walk swiftly from the church. Outside on the steps, I blow out the flame — and keep walking.

Behind me, footsteps, maybe twenty feet back. I pause, as if to check my purse. The footsteps pause. I start walking again; the footsteps resume. Now I move fast and deliberate, right into the heart of Dupont Circle. In the twilight, this is a good place to lose pursuit — traffic, street musicians, panhandlers, people walking home, people feeding birds, people sitting all around the fountain in the circle. I mix with the crowd, thread past a flower seller, past a peddler of burritos. By the time I near our town-house off Connecticut Avenue, I know I'm clear. The foot-steps, the presence, is gone.

I must remember not to tell Sidney or Tom. He is embroiled at the office. She is embroiled in Memphis. For an instant, just inside my front door, I feel a brush of fear, like the wind in the church. Forget it. I flip on lights. The living room springs up before me in its familiar colors, Sidney's peach golds, my blue greens. Our books glow faintly from floor-to-ceiling shelves. I shoot the dead bolt on the door behind me and busy myself with small, ordinary things: mail, music, microwave.

The house feels slightly different without Sidney. During her many trips, I often relish the total privacy — but not quite, tonight. I remind myself how many weirdos follow women in big cities. Why am I dwelling on this? I'm tougher when the story isn't mine.

I move upstairs. My floor is the second, Sid's is the third — a sloping garret, done in black and cream and chrome, Italian high tech. My area, with a hall and two rooms, is a contrast: all natural woods and Shaker furniture and the watercolors I used to do — five, ten years ago? The whole arrangement, with its pondlike blue rugs, reminds Sidney of an electrified dock. Electrified, because my workroom houses a computer, stereo, and three tele-visions with three VCRs. I may work at a trestle table, but I'm an incurable gadget lover, a media freak. I tape three networks' daily coverage, keep up, catch leads. Now, I check the six o'clock local news. There's a shot of Mount Olivet's back doorway, followed by a comment from Joan Kelly outside the shelter. Her hands still shake. The Crane story runs first on one network, second on the other two. I watch the footage carefully. Something about it tugs at me. I can't pinpoint it, let it go for now.

.

I'VE ALREADY taken the messages off the answering machine. Another form of electrified Shaker, set in an antique dry sink, the phone is rigged up with call-waiting, call-forwarding, speed-calling, two lines, and a feature known as Caller-ID, which shows the incoming number as the phone rings. Actually, I haven't kept that last one hooked up and I'm about to dispense with call-waiting. However, in principle, the phone system's up to workroom tech.

Now, as I pass it, the phone rings: it's Tom. He might stop by. If it isn't too late. If it's okay. If he untangles some editorial mess.

I want to tell him about being followed. "No new stuff on the networks," I say instead.

A pause. "Later?"

"Well — if you can."

"Well — if you're up."

Our games.

"Don't forget your umbrella." I can't resist.

"I was trying. Bye, darlin'." A slip.

As always, I find myself looking at the phone after one of these conversations. Perplexing. Probably shouldn't be. There is a sudden sound downstairs: a small explosion. For a moment I freeze. Then I move toward the steps. The smell cues me. Once again I have blown up something in the microwave.

.

TAPE RECORDER. Later, I run bathwater. Batteries. Add rose oil. Notebook. Scented soap.

Necessary preparations.

All is arranged for tomorrow at Cana Place, a day shelter, and for tomorrow night at Susanna House. The contacts are made; I'll act as volunteer at both. Only the shelters' managers will know I'm a reporter. Only Tom will have their numbers.

My clothes drop to the bathroom floor. The soap and oil scent the room. I intend to soak for a very long time. I am watching the tub fill as the phone rings again. I hesitate. I could let the answering machine get it. Then again, it might be Tom, saying he's on his way. I don't want to be in the tub when he arrives. Or maybe I do. I sigh — at myself, at the dilemma, at the phone. I turn off the water, cross the hall, and answer.

On the other end, a strange, live silence. I listen to it. Someone there, listening to me listen. I hang up.

If it weren't for the church, the walk home, that call would have less power. I know that. I know that, even though I'm on this story. Even though we rarely get hang-ups. But that's probably what this is: random wrong number, no more.

I cross back to the bathroom; look at the half-filled tub. The faucet, not turned tight, is dripping. The sound is loud in the quiet house.

The phone rings again. I stay motionless. The answering machine comes on after the fourth ring. There is a silence; then an audible click. Another hang-up. I listen to its echo, and to the dripping water. For another instant, I pause.

I will not let this bath be stolen from me. I step into the tub, lean back into the perfumed water.

Abruptly, the phone rings again. I sit straight up.

Four rings. The machine gets it. I hear the answering message play, then silence. That same live silence. Then a click.

Another four rings. Another pickup, by machine.

For a moment I hear an intake of breath, as if someone is just about to speak, before the connection is broken again.

I can see my wet hand gripping the side of the tub. Skidding across the hall to my office, I run to the phone. I hook up the Caller-ID box and, dripping water on the rug, I stand watching the small screen. Now of course, the phone does not ring.

Back in the bathroom, I let the water out of the tub. I dry off, put something on. Walking through the house, I try front and back doors. Both are bolted fast. I realize that I am still listening for the phone — which, now, is mute. When Tom knocks moments later, I jump and glance out a window. Distracted, I break one of my general rules for this relationship. I open the door in my nightgown.

Tom looks rather pleased, actually, but politely does not comment. On the coffee table, he spreads before me the early edition of tomorrow's paper. There's my follow-up story — page one, Metro: above the fold, the lead.

"Terrific play — how'd you do it?"

"The story did it." He looks up at me.

"Great."

He hears some note missing from my voice.

"Something happen?" He studies my face.

"Oh — just some crank calls." I try to sound light and don't, quite. "Before you came, nothing really, it hap-pens. . ."

"Sidney — "

"Away. Really: okay."

Tom's eyes deepen in color, as always, with emotion; a range now — tenderness, worry, ache. So much unspo-ken between us. For the first time, he draws me to him.

"Hard not trying to protect you." His lips against my hair. "Constant struggle."

"Hard sometimes not letting you." My voice sounds shaky; I let myself lean against him. After a long time, he tips my face back. Our lips brush, linger. And he kisses me soft and he kisses me deep and it is a long time before we can let go.

We do not mention this other constant struggle — mine, holding back, holding out. Nor do I mention my walk home this evening. That would only worry Tom more. And it would wreck tomorrow's assignment. If not the day's plans — the night's.

■

<4>

THROUGH THE dusk, through the rain, I watch the women gather, a straggling line down the street. I draw nearer. Heads begin to clarify: heads in scarves, bandanas, visor caps, a head tented in an orange blanket. Shoulders shift and shrug, some wrapped in dry cleaners' plastic bags to keep off the rain. Below, in line, a long row of restless feet: slippers and high heels, rubber thongs, battered shoes and broken boots — swollen feet, tapping feet, shuffling feet, and beside the feet, the bags.

In my jeans, I walk toward the line and take a place. I look up at the door of Susanna House, a night shelter for women, about to open for dinner. I've been at another shelter for lunch. I've been on the streets with the women all day. I'm tired, but not as tired as the people around me. I remember now, from ten years ago, the women's fatigue at dinnertime, and the memories that flood in at this hour. Memories of other dinners; memories of kids, of home.

My own memories come as I stand here, my own defenses down from fatigue. I see an elegant apartment overlooking Central Park; I see silver on the sideboard, and the darkness under the Steinway piano, where I often hid as a child. I remember lying in bed at night, listening to my father slamming doors. I remember, after their perfect dinner parties, the sharp sting of voices: my parents' fights. I remember wondering, at six and at sixteen, if it would all come apart. What would happen to me then, an only child? Would I slip, alone, through this secret crack in our lives?

At six and sixteen, I wondered sometimes if I'd become one of those women who lived on the streets; one of those women who lived out of bags, who lived out of nowhere. I knew, somehow, this could happen; it was some time before I felt free of that fear. I was free by the time I went to college, and soon after, when my mother died, swiftly, gracefully, at the hosiery counter in Bonwit Teller — a heart defect, undetected. I knew I would be all right, but I never forgot my sense of connection with homeless women. Maybe that's why I don't feel alien here, now.

Now I watch a hand try the shelter door; a green door in a brick wall. Other hands thrust deeper into pockets, armpits. Heads bend against the rain. I wonder if these women are thinking about murder. Everyone spoke of it today. But these women live with it — every day.

Suddenly, the door swings open. Light spills down the steps. The line starts to move. For just an instant I feel apprehension. And then I am moving with the line. I am climbing the steps, walking into the shelter.

Susanna House: 5 P.M.-8 A.M. Women Only
No Drinking, No Drugs, No Children

The building was once a private grammar school. The neighborhood changed; the school stood empty. And then, nine years ago, Zoe Heywood appeared on the shelter scene, altering it with her presence. She raised funds to open the school as a shelter and named it for a woman in Luke's Gospel. Susanna House is the biggest, best-run shelter in town and a model for others — the reason I've chosen it tonight. It also has an air of the school it was. Kids have painted on these walls. At the right angle, in the right light, I can see vague outlines on the windows of paper leaves, long removed.

Past the paintings, past the windows, now, the women trudge. Some lug bags, others push carts. The regulars, I know, have left more bags by their cots. I wonder if this shelter is too big, too well run, for a killer. Or if it might be a new target.

I am watching, making notes, as a figure rises before me: Zoe herself, in the office door. Tall, angular, with long, curling, prematurely gray hair, the figure is striking, as is the face. High forehead, high cheekbones, chin held high; it is the face of a model or a debutante, at forty. In fact, Zoe was a debutante from Manhattan and Sag Harbor. I try to recall what I found on her in the back files: some interview, Trends section, two years ago:

Old money, old family, dating back to the Revolution. Her father, rich, restless, roving into various radical causes: the Spanish Civil War, socialism. Ruined by McCarthy in the fifties, became a recluse, eventually a suicide. But somehow his fire passed to his daughter, who used it differently. The best schools in social work gave her skills. Travels in India and South America gave her vision. Years with missionaries blended action with spirituality. Zoe brought all this expertise to the D.C. shelter community, enriching it, training volunteers, inventing programs, drawing money and attention to the homeless as no one else could. I left the shelters just as Zoe arrived in them. Still, I always hoped to meet her. And now she stands before me looking vaguely like Katharine Hepburn in loose trousers and sandals; she beckons.

In her office: chaos. Messages for women tacked all over the walls. Boxes of supplies: paper, pens, tampons, soap, roach spray. A blackboard with volunteers' names, their assigned days. We look at it together. I copy it, she copies it, and erases it with one sudden sweep.

"Shit," says Zoe. With her offhand elegance, in her society accent, the word sounds as if it's culled from Jane Austen or Tiffany's catalog. "Stupid," she says, "considering.

"Any special problems here?"

"Overtly, no, except with the volunteers, who, I'm afraid, have been dropping in droves since things got, well, scary. Actually, I do need you tonight. My assistant director's sick, I've got one girl doing dinner, and God knows that's not enough, shelter this size."

"You said `overtly.' " I'm writing. "You pick up a change ... undercurrent? Mood?"

She nods, twisting her pencil. Before she can speak again, she has given out six bars of soap.

"It's tense," she says, finally. "Murder's everyone's nightmare. I mean really, homeless women are attacked so often on the streets. Shelters, though, they're supposed to be safe, and so — "

Suddenly, in the doorway, a man appears. I had not heard him approach, and involuntarily I start. It is a man who looks oddly familiar, and yet I know we have not met.

"I'm about ready to wrap up," he tells Zoe. His eyes shift to me; he offers an expansive smile as we are introduced.

"Dr. Heller is the psychiatrist who rotates among the shelters. He can tell you about mood," Zoe says.

"Very apprehensive, very `who's next?' " he says quickly. Too quickly? "I was at Mount Olivet the night of Crane's murder."

"That must have been disturbing," I say.

There is a slight pause. "Naturally," he says, then. "Disturbing for all of us."

"Who is next?" I ask fast, to catch him off guard.

He smiles disarmingly. "Maybe I am. If I have a psychotic patient who's homicidal."

"Do you?" I look at him.

"Too soon to tell." He leans in the doorway, watching us both for a moment. "Even so," he says finally. "Take care, won't you? You're both too damn good-looking, and so was Meredith Crane."

That smile again. And then he's gone. I turn back to Zoe.

"A special friend — to me, to Susanna House, to the whole shelter-providing community," she says, nodding after Heller. "You can cross him off your list. Now what was I — "

Before she can go on, we are interrupted by the shelter itself. Through cracks in the floors, through cracks in the ceiling, through stairwells and hallways and wallboard and plaster, it rises like a spirit — the smell of two gallons chicken, one gallon onions, one gallon celery, two gallons rice, six pints raisins, ready now to feed the women of Susanna House. And then we hear shoes on the stairs — the click of them, the rap of them, the clatter and shuffle and patter of them. The rhythm becomes a rumble; the building shakes.

Zoe and I move toward the kitchen. By the stove is a big-eyed girl, her face shimmering with sweat and her mouth tight with fear. She is leaning over cauldrons of food. "Ready," she says, fast and breathy. She's from a Quaker high school, she says, in response to my question; she does this as a class requirement and her mother is waiting outside in the car. "Bye, see ya."

She's gone.

Zoe looks after her and looks at me.

Together, we lift the heavy cauldrons from kitchen to dining room. A serving stand gleams at one end; fifteen round tables seem to float beyond. They are covered with blue plastic cloths and they blend with the shelter's walls, also blue. The women's artwork hangs there above the women themselves, who form another growing line now. There is a smell of wet clothes, wet hair, as the line moves toward us. Ladles in hand, Zoe and I wait behind the serving stand and listen.

"Who you pushin'?"

"No one pushin' nobody."

"Someone got the time?"

"Dinner time."

"Shit."

"You pushin' me."

"Unusual here." Zoe ladles rice.

"Unusually edgy?" I ladle stew.

She nods. I watch an older white woman move along the line. Fork. Spoon. Knife. Paper cup, blood-red Kool-Aid. Her hands are full, a cigarette clamped between her teeth, one eye shut against the rising thread of smoke. She looks wizened, wary, wise. I watch her carry a full plate to a table where she sits alone. On the tablecloth's plastic surface, someone has written in ink, two words: Find Me. Swiftly, deliberately, the old woman covers the words with her plate.

A black woman, ancient and gnarled, raps with her cane against the floor, three times, as if summoning a genie. Her face, deeply furrowed, is the color of rich soil.

White hair sprouts from her chin. The hairs quiver with indignation. Everyone calls her Ma'am. She raps the floor again, beside the seated woman.

"That my place."

Silently, the other woman slides into the next chair.

Ma'am looks down at the words on the table; she too covers them with her plate. Another woman sits beside her: Angel, they call her. She is almost entirely en-shrouded in a blanket, tented over her head. A delicate, veined hand emerges from the folds.

The old woman passes a fork to her. The blanketed form bows. Rocking, humming, Angel begins to feed herself — and the shelter cat, a striped tabby, who jumps on her lap. Gold feline eyes peer out of the blanket. Angel croons softly. I can hear the cat purring from where I stand spooning stew, making a series of mental notes. The old white woman holds my eyes: she has an Irish face, an Irish brogue. For a moment, it seems she has walked out of my childhood.

But before I can get hooked there, a new woman sits at that table. I feel the room's tension rise, as if a weather front were passing through. The woman runs a hand through faded blond hair. She looks around; her eyes seem dazed, unfocused. One hand fumbles with her plate, one moves to her pale face: a bruised face with a gash over an eye. There is a brass key pinned to her white blouse. Her skirt is neatly tailored, her shoes not yet run down. She looks around again and shakes her head.

"Here — " she says to the room.

No one says anything.

"People get killed ..."

"Shut it," says Ma'am, sharp.

"Now I'm here."

Silence.

"Anyone else been killed?"
The air seems to thicken.
"Who did it?"
"You lookin' at me?" Ma'am half-rises from her chair.
"No. Yes. I mean — "
Ma'am reaches across the table and grabs the new woman by her blouse. Rolls scatter. Zoe is starting to move. The new woman's blouse rips. She stands, but Ma'am won't let go and drags her swiftly across the table. Plates of stew and rice skid with her, and there is a quick red flash — spilling Kool-Aid. The new woman swings at Ma'am, hitting her across the mouth. Saliva and blood spray across the table. Ma'am swings back; the new woman twists away. More blood, abrupt and brilliant, pours over her blouse. She looks down at the key pinned there, splattered crimson now — and then she is at Ma'am, the two of them rolling onto the floor.

Suddenly Angel shrieks — her blanket is caught in their thrashing. With a jerk, as if sucked into complex machinery, she is pulled into the struggle. The rest of the room is silent. No one moves, no one but Zoe, diving into the center of the fight. Rolling with the women, she grapples with shoulders, arms, separating the figures. In moments, it's over. Zoe raises one bleeding woman to a chair, then another. She signals for me to call an ambulance. She restores Angel's blanket and speaks quietly to everyone. And then she is behind the serving table again, breaking the room's taut silence.

"Seconds?" She lifts her ladle.

·

LATER, AFTER the ambulance has come, after the shelter has calmed, after dinner is over, I stand in the kitchen, mopping the floor. I've already done the dining room: sponged down the bloodstained table, mopped the blood from the floor. The kitchen is quiet and brightly lit and I am alone. The blue floor is wet, shining. I look down: there is blood on my white apron. For a moment I think of Meredith Crane cleaning up after another dinner in another shelter. I check the back door: it's locked. I glance through its glass panes. Across the street I see an empty row house, a doorway. And then, in the doorway, I see a man standing very still. His face is in shadow but I catch its angle. He is watching the shelter. He seems to be watching the kitchen, with its many windows and its windowed door. I try to get a better look at him: a man in an expensive raincoat, half touched by streetlights. I cannot make out his face.

I move away from the door, wring out the mop and empty the bucket down the steel sink. Watch yourself; I hear Jed Jackson's voice. For a moment I hesitate, then move to a window. The man is still there, still motionless, still watching from across the street. Now I feel a rush of adrenaline. I glance at the phone. I could call Jed and stay here, visible and solitary, behind the kitchen windows

A sudden sound behind me makes me wheel around.

A figure stands in the kitchen door, a figure hooded in a blanket. Angel's eyes gaze out at me; from within the blanket's folds, a cat purrs.

"Sorry — " Angel says.

She takes a large tray down from a shelf: a tray of fruit, already arranged. "Zoe sent me for it," she says. I nod; the hooded form bows and leaves.

Instantly I am back at the window. The man across the street is gone.

■

<5>

AMAN SITS in the dark on the steps of my house. I see him half a block away. My step slows; I watch.

His cigarette glows. Drawing on it, he gazes down the sidewalk. I move a few steps closer. The streetlights catch him now. It's Tom.

It's Tom and it's good to see him, so good that for an instant I want to run like a kid. I don't. I keep pace; look ironic. Walking toward him, I remember I'm still wearing my stained apron. At the bottom of the steps I pause.

"Happened to be in the neighborhood." Tom's voice is wry.

"Funny — so was I."

He puts his cigarette out and comes down. I feel the strength of his relief as he lifts me into his arms.

"I'm filthy, really filthy," I murmur in his ear. He holds me still, then out at arm's length.

"Tomato sauce becomes you," he says, looking closer. "That is tomato sauce, isn't it?"

"I think we better go inside."

Inside, I pour myself a beer and offer one to Tom. He declines — never drinks; unusual in a newsman. I drop the apron on the floor. He retrieves it, holds it to the light and looks at me.

"A fight," I say.

"Jesus, Nan."

"The women — Susanna House. Some tension around the murder, it just exploded at dinner. All I did was mop up afterward. And get your mood piece," I add dryly. "Good stuff. Dynamic. Plus — " I take a drink. I know it's premature to say this; I say it anyway. "I think, at the end, just possibly, I might have got a glimpse of ... well, let's just say, a key player."

Tom leans against the counter, my bloody apron still in his hands. I tell him about the man in the doorway. "If someone hadn't come into the kitchen, he might have made a move. He could see in; he was definitely watching. I wonder if Susanna House could be a lure."

"And you could be the bait?"

I nod.

Tom drops the apron back on the floor.

"Nan, for Christ's sake." His voice is sharp now. "You're not a cop, you're a reporter."

"You're right, Tom — on the first try." He won't laugh with me; he's getting that stubborn look I've sometimes seen in the newsroom.

"Don't kid around with this. If anyone's bait it's un-dercover cops." His tough-editor voice. "Probably just who that guy was tonight. A narc. Check it out."

"It just happens I did check it out," I flare up. "Called Jed from the shelter before I left. No flares, no plain-clothes, not there. I know what I'm doing, and I'll go back."

"You saying this just to get a rise out of me?"

My voice is sharper. "I never say anything just to get a rise out of you.' This is an important story, something we care about." I set down my glass. "A good story too, you know that, you've been with it right through."

"I seem to remember." His wry half smile now. "Well — are we going halfway?"

"Halfway? Or taking wild risks?"

"Wild meaning stupid? Have I ever done that?"

"No. I have. Always mistakes."

"Is that really it? Or something else?"

For a moment, silence. Tom turns, pours a glass of soda. He sets it down, watches it a while, turns back. "Something else," he says quietly. His eyes, shifting grays, are on mine.

I touch his face; his hands are in my hair. It is a long while before we speak again.

"Tom," I say at last, against his shoulder. "Does this mean we shouldn't work together?"

"No." He smooths my hair. "Just means I smoke more. Sleep less. We fight. You sleep less. You start smoking — "

"Oh, well, if that's all ..."

•

MO M E N T S LA T E R, upstairs in my workroom, we're watching coverage of the Crane murder. Three VCRs. Three networks. Shots of Meredith's graduation pictures. Shots of the shelter, by night, by day. Shots of the shelter's women. Interviews with some. Interviews with Joan Kelly and with Dr. Terrence Heller, the psychiatrist; I remember him from Susanna House. A sandy-haired, lanky man, his face is long and serious. He sucks on a pipe, offers theories. "Didn't know Meredith well."

"Pompous," Tom comments. "Maybe it's the pipe. Do they all get pipes with their couches or what?"

"Defensive, I think. All three interviews, he hammers that same point: he didn't know her well."

"But — no motive."

"That we know of."

"And no evidence."

I fast-forward to Joan Kelly. We study her face: thin, nervous, big-eyed. She talks fast, too fast. And she too seems defensive. "Never happened before ... I wasn't anywhere near the kitchen."

"Bad line," Tom observes.

"Scared." I flip through notes. "Her background's good, she's been a rape counselor, she directed a program for homeless kids ..."

"Good on paper. You never know."

"And she's got a good assistant director ..."

"Even so — "

"You never know."

I rewind to a crowd scene outside the shelter and freeze-frame. "See that man's face? Just behind the police line?"

"A little wild-eyed. Who is he?"

"No idea." Tall white man, thirties, haggard country face, bad teeth, blue windbreaker. "Look at this." I fast-forward now to the interview with Joan Kelly. Over her shoulder the same man's face, same rumpled dark hair.

"Again." Tom looks closer.

I fast-forward to the interview with the psychiatrist — another network. We scan the faces in the crowd.

"There." Tom's finger taps the screen. Same man, same blue windbreaker. "Not the guy tonight?"

I pause, looking at the face, the build. "About same height, build. But the man tonight was well dressed. Good raincoat. Seemed ... different. But I couldn't see his face ..." I trail off.

The Crane story plays out. On one screen a blonde anchorwoman, glossy-lipped, goes into a promotion piece for the new Humanitarian Awards coming up next week at the Kennedy Center. A dazzling evening. An important evening. The presenter, a nun renowned for her lifelong work with the poor in Africa. The award's recipients are also impressive: a scientist, a missionary, a physician. Their faces fill the screen, one by one. The physician is last, his name a white line of print beneath his head. Abruptly I click off the VCR and stand staring at the screen.

"Sorry," I say. "Went past the story."

"You all right?"

"Just ... a surprise." I hit Rewind.

Tom does not press. For an instant the remote-control gadget trembles in my hand. Tom, behind me, draws his arms around my waist, and I lean against him.

"Tell you sometime," I say after a while.

"No rush." His cheek on mine.

My hand steadies. Once more we run through the story's coverage. It snaps me back: here, now. I remind myself to dig more on Kelly, on Heller, and especially on that man in the windbreaker.

The tapes run at normal speed. And now I see what I'd missed before. I see the faces of the homeless themselves. They crowd the screen, they crowd the room. Their eyes, stunned, scared, staring out at us. Their silent, riveting faces.

Freeze-frame.

Tom looks thoughtful. "You know," he says. "It could be any one of them."

■

<6>

IAM DRIVING to the paper at 7:30 in the morning, and I knew I shouldn't have turned on the police radio. I'd planned to come to work early, to get a jump on the follow-up story, to get going before interruptions start. But at 7:36, I hear, "Calling Homicide," and then, "We have a fatal." I catch the location and run a yellow light. I'm driving away from the office now, driving, still listening.

Washington's pale monuments seem to flash past, shimmering, unreal, in the morning light. Soon I am beyond those marble corridors and through the worst traffic, over to northeast D.C., where brownstone replaces marble. I'm almost there — a place that is not a shelter, not a back alley, not the usual scene of a crime. This is a convent, built around a courtyard and crowned by the dome of an old Spanish-style church. Clear June sunlight floods the street and the convent's stucco walls. The dome glistens. But just beyond it, just to the convent's left, there is also the red-blue flash of squad cars.

As I park I see a crowd has gathered. A network truck is already on the scene with other reporters. Still, I can't see what forms the core of this circle, what's pinned this crowd in place. Finally, threading my way toward the center, I see the still-point:

A car. A fairly new Ford: plain and gray, neatly parked in the convent's lot, open to the street. The Ford's window on the driver's side is rolled up; that door is locked. On the passenger's side, the window is rolled down halfway. That door is not locked, not tightly shut.

I lean forward and, without touching it, peer into the car. On the front seat I see a woman's form, a woman lying on her back, her legs half-tucked beneath the steering wheel. A woman — a nun. The short gray habit is smooth, covering her knees. The short gray veil is askew above short white hair. The nun's face is aged, lined, thin. Blood has congealed on her chin and on her collar and spattered the cross at her neck. Her skin has turned bluish. Projecting from her mouth is a dark shape: an umbrella's curved black handle.

I make quick notes, just before the cops push us all back and restore the yellow tape around the immediate area. Beyond the photographers, beyond the journalists, there is another circle: a silent one, motionless and gray. It is a circle of nuns, the dead woman's community, standing like a frieze of figures, heads bent. I look at them and ache. I think of all the candles flickering in churches, all the candles I have ever lit. I see all the churches that have ever arched over me, comforting, protecting, and I see nuns moving through them; I see them stooping, whispering to me. I never went to parochial school, but there, on the street, I remember the sisters who took time with me, in naves and transepts — all the sisters, now in one mosaic. I snap myself back from the image and find my best source: Jed Jackson. The former tackle is easy to spot.

"Who is she?" I ask as I uncap my pen.

"Sister Josephine Sullivan."

"How old?"

"Sixty-three. Same M.O. as Crane."

"Except the shelter," I add.

Jed flashes me a look. "She was a volunteer at Saint Claire's — a day shelter, northwest. There yesterday. Went one afternoon a week."

I look at him and start writing again. The crime-lab guys, dusting the car for prints, beckon Jed away. I find Jed's partner, a guy my age — another tall one, easy to spot in a crowd. Olive skin, black hair. Frank LaMarca.

"Shit," he says to me. "A nun." Shakes his head. "My kids go to this school. Shit."

"Was she killed in the car?"

"Looks like it. One of the sisters saw her pull in last evening, cut her lights. They all figured she'd come in, skipped dinner — went to bed. Not unusual for her. They missed her at Mass this morning, found her right after."

Jed drifts back. "No prints. Again."

"The umbrella?"

"Not hers."

"Theft, rape?"

"Neg-a-tive."

"Again. Like Crane."

Both detectives nod.

"A serial pattern?"

"Could be." Jed spits meditatively: his custom.

"Shit," says Frank again.

A woman is breaking through the police lines. There is a flurry of cops. The walkie-talkies crackle louder. The woman, weeping, wants to see the body. A detective leads her away, and I follow. Within instants I discover that the woman, Nikki, is homeless and a regular at Saint Claire's shelter. Between her and Reverend Mother Margaret Moore, the convent's superior, a picture of the victim begins to form. It still amazes me, how that happens at a murder scene: like a painting on the air.

Sister Jo had been a hard worker: always mopped the shelter, washed windows — even at her age. An ordinary woman, no great gifts, skills. Peppery at times, could be stubborn. A strong shoulder to cry on — Nikki remembers putting her kid into foster care, then weeping on that shoulder. Now and then the nun would do quirky things: on a cold day, warm the women's shoes up — wrapped in foil, under the broiler. Josephine Sullivan had entered the convent at eighteen. Next June she would have celebrated her forty-fifth anniversary; in six years, her Golden Jubilee. She had no known enemies or, for that matter, close friends. Listening, I feel that ache again.

Beside me, LaMarca is back; keyed up, chewing gum. The smell of spearmint fills the air. The medics are sure Sister Jo has been dead over twelve hours. Odor. Rigor mortis. LaMarca speculates: did she roll down the far window last evening for air — or to chat with someone? Someone who became her assailant? Did she open the door to comfort someone — or to invite a killer into the car?

There are, of course, no answers. I shut my note-book. LaMarca shoves more gum in his mouth. The smell of spearmint is too sweet; I turn away.

I'll make a quick stop at Saint Claire's Shelter, then to Police Headquarters. Eventually, there will be some leaked "preliminaries" from the crime lab, maybe the M.E. Across the street, I call Tom from a phone booth, sketch the story, and promise it by deadline.

And then I turn back toward that crowd around the car. The circle has thinned; I pass through easily now. I pass through in time to see a priest lean into the car to anoint and bless Sister Josephine Sullivan. "May light perpetual shine upon her ..."

Behind the priest, the Mobile Crime Lab guys drive away. The medical examiner's white van pulls up; a small team of men climb down and approach the car.

" 'Tag'n Bag,' " says LaMarca. "About time."

A gurney rolls forward. The church bells ring the hour and then they start to toll. They are tolling still as the white van moves slowly away.

Only bells on the air.

No sirens. No need.

■

<8>

Deadline. OLD prison term. There used to be a line outside prison walls — an invisible line, some yards out. Within that line, a convict could be chased but not shot. Over that line — he was fair game. Good as dead. Dead meat, as Jed Jackson likes to say.

Deadline.

Now, a news term. It's another invisible line: a time line. Within it, a reporter can be chased — by editors, sources, whoever. Within that line, you file your story. Beyond it — your story's good as dead. You are too, on some papers. Figuratively, at least.

I happen to like writing on deadline. It concentrates my mind, gets the words rolling. I like the feel of the newsroom on deadline: the build of energy, the sharp air, tap of keys, rapid-fire. Phones ringing. Ashtrays filling. Editors pacing. Computer screens flashing green words. Hundreds of stories forming in that heightened, sharpened air. Hundreds of minds spinning sentences into the system. Controlled hysteria if the system chooses, just then, to go down. Sometimes not so controlled. Deadline: a catalyst that brings out the best and the worst in us.

It's 4:15 and we're moving toward it now: deadline's 6:30. The tension's still building in a slow wavelike swell. Hysteria, controlled or uncontrolled: not yet. The phone is just starting to bother me. I look up, it rings. "Nan Skillen." I'm cool.

Another paragraph; another call. "Nan Skillen." I'm abrupt.

Three more sentences. A call. "Skillen." Sharp. Six words. The phone. "Nan." Exasperated.

Partly, I don't like what's coming through the line: Sidney, my housemate, will be away all week. Jed Jackson has no leads, no motive, no evidence. Much of his "unofficial" preliminary stuff is a repeat of Meredith Crane's: asphyxiation, ruptured esophagus, larynx, internal bleeding ...

And then a call-back: an added twist. Literally. The umbrella, askew, pierced a ventricle in the heart. I've never known how Jed gets his info from the M.E.'s office; a pipeline somewhere, but I don't ask where and I don't need to: I just write it in — attribution to reliable sources. I am writing as I get a series of return calls from shelter directors. All express shock.

No one, by the way, has seen the man in the blue windbreaker. No one has anything but praise for Dr. Terrence Heller. All I can glean is his shelter schedule — interesting. Yesterday was his afternoon at Saint Claire's. Inconclusive, though, Sister Jo's death occurring elsewhere. I pass that along to Jed, anyway, and turn back to my computer screen. No more unprofitable calls. Deadline is closer. I'll get this piece done, and done right, only without more interrup-tions.

Instantly the next interruption appears: Sam Wile, one of our news photographers, who ambles over and perches on my desk. Sixtyish, still among the best in his field. Sam sometimes gets past news, with artistic photo exhibits. You'd never know it to look at him, this bear-like, rumpled man with graying tufts of hair on his head, his hands, his open collar. He's been a friend for years; I went to school with his kids in Manhattan, where I grew up.

For some reason, he has always taken a special interest in me. When I moved down here, he got me a job on this paper — in Obits. My illustrious start. He helped me get back again, after I left seminary. I've been out with him on so many stories, I can't remember them all. It was his camera flashing, that last murder scene and the one before it. Sam — I love him. But why, near dead-line, he'd perch on a reporter's desk — I can't fathom. And because it's Sam, I won't ask. I stuff the irritation. Whoever calls me next, no doubt, will catch it instead.

"How's it going?" Sam seems to search my face.

"Good, fine. On this shelter story now."

"Yeah, that Crane girl — blew me away. And I don't blow away easy." He runs his hand over his face and glances at me again. I start to wonder if this is about something else. "Anything up with you?" he asks, search-ing my face again.

"Just the usual ..." Over Sam's head I can see Tom, watching us from the city desk. "How about you?"

"Oh, I worry about my kids — y'know?"

Sam, Sam. "They're never too old, right?"

Tom is walking toward us.

"You're like one of them, Nan. Know that?"

"Sure do." Why is he saying this?

"Just so you know."

Tom is by my desk now. I see the blur of blue oxford cloth shirt to my left; the rolled-up sleeves, the loosened tie. Glancing up, I also notice he looks faintly annoyed.

I wonder if he dislikes deadline interruptions — or if he can be jealous of this grizzled, aging, fatherly man.

"Nan ..." Sam's voice hesitates. "You heard about ... these Humanitarian Awards coming up next week?"

"Yeah, I did." I hear the tightness in my voice now. Both men, no doubt, hear it too. I go very still; can't quite hide it.

"Well, good, just so you heard. Talk to me, if you need."

"Sorry ..." Tom, polite, firm. "I need her."

Sam tips an invisible hat to me and ambles off.

Tom looks after him. "What was that about?"

"Not sure ..." I think I know.

"Saw him settling in."

"Is this a rescue? Or — you really need me?"

"Really." His lips at my ear: "Need. You."

"You have to jazz my pulse on deadline?"

"Did I?" Tom looks pleased, surprised.

"Story's coming." A stab at professionalism.

"Ready to show?"

"Needs another draft."

"May I?" He looks at the screen.

"Not quite how I want — "

I scroll up to the lead anyway. He reads over my shoulder, making suggestions, on target, as always. As always, I can't quibble. Much. And as always, we're aware of being close.

"How many inches you going to take off this one?" I tease; half-tease. Tom's a sharp editor, despite his feelings. In fact, I think he's sometimes tougher on me, to compensate. "How many? Two? Six? Twenty?"

"None. Powerful stuff."

"I need to rewrite."

"Not too much."

"An hour."

•

AN HOUR later the newsroom has hit high deadline pitch. I'm ignoring it, and the tap of keys around me, and the tightness of the air. I stay in my story, wrapping it, feeling it come right, and by deadline it's at the copydesk; the story clears, I sit back. By seven Tom has wrapped up the other pieces he's editing.

Someone flips on the big TV, overhead, against the wall. As if we haven't had enough, most of us drift over to watch the evening news. Sister Jo's murder is the lead local story on the network we watch, and then the programming moves on. There's a cut to commercial, and to another promo for the upcoming National Humanitarian Awards. Once again the recipients' faces begin to flash on the screen.

Swiftly, I gather my things, grab my briefcase — and glance up at the wrong time. The TV footage has passed the scientist, the missionary, and moved to the physician. "Dr. Karl Gordon, pioneering spirit ..."

I glance away; slip out. Behind me, I hear footsteps. At the elevator, I turn.

It's Tom.

•

WE STOP in some Polynesian place; actually, the first place we see. We sit at a rattan table, on rattan chairs. Behind us, a parrot squawks from a cage. Overhead, a ceiling fan squeals. Bongo drums dominate the Muzak. Our drinks arrive — for Tom, ginger ale; for me, something with rum.

He lifts his glass.

I stare at mine. It is huge, frosted, and shaped vaguely like half a pineapple. Floating within it — a small paper umbrella, handle up. Silently, I pass the drink to Tom.

He looks at it. He gets the check.

"I think," he says, "we can do better than this."

We can; we do. We pick up cold salads, bread, fruit, take them to my house, and out to its small back patio. Tom takes off his tie, we take off our shoes. For a few moments I lean against him, and we just stand there by the table looking up, and out.

It has become apparent to us that we are standing in the midst of a warm June evening with a breeze, with stars. It has become apparent that we forgot it was out here.

Tom turns to me; I see his smile, white in the twilight. He kisses my forehead. We light candles, spread the food on the table. For a while we don't need to talk at all.

From someone's window, music floats down: Hey Jude ... don't make it bad ... The Beatles. Twenty years ago. "High school," I say.

"College."

"Danced to this." I wince. "Wrong guy."

"I never danced."

"Hard to believe." I look at Tom.

"I was one of those quiet types. I watched."

The music shifts in the dark. Nobody does it better... Carly Simon: a little over a dozen years ago.

"I remember this on the radio when I was first at the paper ..." I think back. "Starting to work in the shelters, wondering about seminary. That age. Trying to figure it all out — my life."

"And I was fucking up mine."

I look at Tom. Unusual tone, for him.

He pauses. "Got married."

We've never talked about it.

"Mistake. Bad one. Bad years." He pauses, as if trying to decide something. "Something else ..." he says, finally. "It ... went with the marriage." He takes a breath. "My father ... brilliant architect. Brilliant alcoholic. And I — " He tries to sound wry; cannot. "I began ... to follow my father's second pattern. Brilliantly." He waits, stops; goes on. "It was easy — in the news business. The drinking never showed at work, I always functioned, performed, even won prizes. And — got worse. Got worse for six years."

He watches me. In the candlelight, I can see his eyes. Somehow I know he's never told anyone. And I know he fears I'll pull back now.

"Tom ..." I touch his face, take his hands. It is a while before he speaks again.

"My father died then, drunk, car accident." His hands tighten on mine. "I quit cold, alone, no help. Not the best way — my choice. I didn't talk about it, didn't grieve, left the marriage. And worked it all out in my mind, very carefully: What happened. What would never happen again. For a long time — it was better, alone."

I press his hands. Watching him, my eyes fill.

"You understand this," he says, amazed, moved.

"Different shadows, same dark." I hesitate; let it come. "Summer nights, as a kid, I used to sit out on the back steps and listen to glass smash inside. The perfect summer house, the perfect city apartment. The perfect family. And ... my father's rages. I was always running from him; always got away somehow. It was easier for my mother not to see. For a long time I thought it was my fault, all of it. I haven't seen my father since college. I haven't had the bad dreams since."

Tom's arms come around me; I go on.

"And there was Nora, Nora Callahan. Irish, from Dublin, she worked for us. She cooked, cleaned, took care

of me, sat with me, nights like this, on the back steps.
We'd watch the fireflies . . . and I'd see all the candles,
hundreds of candles we lit together in churches. Always
three candles at a time: one for her, one for me, one for
blessings to come . . ."

Summer. Air the color of plums. Dimming grasses, lit
screen door behind us. Fireflies rising in the air; fireflies
like votive candles. The garden winks with them, as if it's
floated out among the stars. Someone in the doorway
then: shadow of his figure, falling over me. I fix my eyes
on the glimmering lights: light that lifts me from the
man-shaped dark . .

"What happened to Nora?" Tom is asking gently.

"She stayed. She stayed and loved me — stayed just
long enough, I think. I remember sitting in the kitchen
with her during the afternoon, listening to the scrape of
her knife on potatoes, the snap of beans in her hands —
the lilt of her voice, singing, praying, telling stories . . ."
I pause. "Somehow, her power was stronger than my
father's. And he felt it. He fired her when I was nine, I
never knew why. I just remember coming home and finding her gone, bed stripped — "

"God, Nan." Tom smooths my hair.

"For years I'd catch glimpses of her in the park across
from my school. As if she were still watching over me,
somehow. And after a while — I stopped seeing her. By
that time I was strong enough. There were other things.
Summers in Maine. Other people. Teachers — "

"Teachers — for me, too."

"English? Newspaper?"

He nods. "And a wrestling coach. You?"

"Same. Minus the wrestling coach."

"Oh?" Tom smiles.

"I do wonder, though ... if it's still Nora, giving the shelters their spin for me. She was an immigrant, poor. Sometimes I wonder if I'll find her in a shelter."

"Maybe you already have." He looks at me. "In all those faces I read about today."

The music in the air changes, becomes all twangs and chimes. I turn on the radio behind us. We find opera. We find heavy metal. We find easy listening. Finally we settle on some country station: soft melody, soft voice. The song changes. Another comes on, then another. And after a while, we don't notice.

Sitting on the chaise lounge together, we lean back and look at the sky, the city's glow; at the lights and the dark and the stars. And then, for the first time, we are lying in each other's arms. I feel the whole length of Tom's body against me, and his fingers trace my shoulders, his mouth on mine. After a long time, he looks at me.

"I'm dancing," he whispers.

He presses me close again, and we are lost in that dance a long while, till the music stops, and abruptly a newscaster's voice crackles on. Reflex: we both look up — then laugh. The stories seem to pass over my head now. The announcer's voice flows ... an advertisement; another promo for the upcoming Humanitarian Awards. The date. The recipients. Scientist. Missionary. And — "Karl Gordon, pioneering physician ..." I stiffen in Tom's arms.

His eyes search my face. I take a long breath. "That's ... my father."

■

<9>

FACES IN my mind. Faces on the wall. On the shelter's wall, in the common room, the women of Susanna House have put up faces. Faces from newspapers and magazines. Faces layered, overlapping, glossed over so many times with paste, they have taken on a sheen. Women's faces gaze from the wall: women advertising soap and cigarettes, hair oil and hot tubs; women in aprons and G-strings and fur coats. The Breck Girl and Miss Black America. Mother Teresa and the Maidenform Woman and the Supremes. The faces appear to scan the dingy room, the faces of women's dreams.

I stand looking at them, making notes.

It is before dinner the next night, and I can't figure out where everyone is. There is an odd silence in the shelter. Zoe is not in the office. The women are not in this common room, with the television chained to its table, nor are they in the dorms.

I'm late getting here from the paper; I missed the dinner line outside. In fact, I'm here, with a reluctant go-ahead from Tom, only because the Metro chief is still intrigued. That could or could not last. Depending on what happens.

And now I don't know what's happening. All I know is that the silence is strange. The office is empty. I start toward the kitchen, the dining room. They are empty. An uneasy feeling comes over me. I pause, listening, and glance behind me, out a window. No one on the street.

I move back toward the front hall, and look out another window. Abruptly, then, I see him — same man, I'm sure. Same man I saw outside Susanna's the last time. Same height, stance, build. Same coat. Again — I can't see his face. He is in an alley this evening, in the twilight, half hidden by a dumpster. For a moment, as he gazes at the shelter, he seems to look at me. I move back before he can see me too clearly. Swiftly, then, I start for the office, the phone. Jed Jackson's number is repeating in my mind. But halfway down the stairs, I hear a wail from the shelter's second floor. Instantly, I'm running that way.

The second-floor bathroom seems the source of the wail. The place is huge, institutional, and tonight, crowded. This is where everyone is — amid the six sinks and six stalls and the stained tub.

Here, ranged around the tile floor, the women of Susanna House have formed a loose circle. Their faces, like the knuckles of a hand, seem somehow connected — by expression, tension, angle. Six mirrors reflect the faces back into the room. From the doorway I cannot see what lies within that circle, what connects the faces.

I move forward; no one seems to notice. Finally, I see what holds the eyes: A towel covering a still form. Something with contours; something, I know by the shape and odor, that has been alive. Something about the size of a baby.

No shock. No tears.

My notebook is out, pen moving. The old Irish woman is stepping forward. She lifts the towel. There is striped fur; there is blood. The curve of a cat's head. It is the cat I saw at dinner, in Angel's lap. The shelter's cat, with her spine wrong and her neck wrong and the light coming through her ears. The cat on her side — dead.

I see tears on the faces around the circle. Tears glinting on tough faces, in tough eyes. And beyond the circle, from a jagged hole in the wall — another pair of eyes.

Tough eyes. Dark eyes, in a dark face. Not an animal's. A woman's.

"Ma'am," Zoe says, from the doorway.

Silence.

"Come out," Zoe commands.

"Noooo." The wail I heard from the stairs.

The hole is womblike and large — kicked-in, bashed-in plaster, tufted with insulation fiber. Ma'am has crawled in there. Crouches there now. Zoe glances at Ma'am; surveys the room. A faint smell of burning food is in the air.

"Fifteen minutes," Zoe says. "Then dinner. You'll be out of there by then, Ma'am." Encouragement. Command. Warning. Zoe is gone — toward the kitchen.

For a moment, no one moves. Ma'am's eyes stare out from the wall. The faucets drip and whisper. Angel cries out from the depths of her blanket, "She kilt Penny."

"Never meant to, Jesus God." Ma'am's voice rises from the hole. "Was feeling down, so I hold her tight, too tight, oh God. I take her down here, give her water, hope she be to rights — she ain't." Ma'am's eyes glint, wet. "Knowed you'd all kill me. I fucked up. Fucked up again."

The women, as if one, shift forward a step. The old Irishwoman is ahead of them. She is reaching into the hole, she is touching Ma'am, drawing her out, easing her forth; rocking, holding her like a child.

I watch. Make notes. And remember another Irish-woman with a frightened child. I remember. And I keep watching.

The old woman is leading Ma'am to the bathtub now. They are both covered with soot and insulation and plaster dust. Someone turns on the tub's faucets. Hands reach out. Many hands, lifting Ma'am.

And then, for moments, she is lost from my sight. She has shattered into the shelter's many faces; the women surround the bathtub. I hear water running, weak at first, then strong and full. I move nearer, watch hands reach out. Strong hands. Gnarled hands. Calloused hands. Hands with the streets under the nails. The Irishwoman's hands among them. Her profile layered amid others until I cannot make it out. Ma'am's voice has quieted now. Now there is only the sound of water. The women of Susanna House are washing one of their own.

.

SUNLIGHT POURS through the room: early afternoon light. It is the next day and Susanna House is empty, the women out in the parks, the day shelters, women still talking of death.

"I knew Sister Jo; I trained Meredith." Zoe is patching the bathroom wall. "It's a shock for everyone here. I hope to God it's stopped."

"What's your guess? Serial killings? Coincidence?"

She puts down her tools. Again I note how striking she is, even as she pushes back her long hair and frowns, thinking. "Let's hope — coincidence."

"Have you ever noticed a well-dressed man watching the shelter? A tall man, expensive dark rain-coat — " She looks at me sharply.

"Never." Her voice is abrupt. I move on.

"Could the killer be ... one of the women?" I expect a reaction. I get it.

"Probably what everyone thinks." Her voice sharp again. "Crazy women. Drunks. Sure — blame the homeless, probably what the police think, too."

"I understand that's offensive." I'm brisk. "It is to me, I know. But can you say — what percent of homeless women are mentally ill?"

"Maybe ... sixty." Zoe glances at me again. "My estimates tend to be lower than others. Doesn't take that much to put a woman on the streets, and it doesn't have to take mental illness. Old age can do it, a fire, a husband's death. For someone with no money, no family, it's not so hard to get knocked flat by one job loss."

"I understand." I'm writing. "But is there anyone who stands out for you? As dangerous? As especially angry?"

"Everyone's angry." Zoe keeps working at the wall. "Everyone's angry here. I mean homeless women get killed, beaten, and no one pays attention ... until it's middle-class volunteers. I live here, I see it, I hate it." She sighs and lifts her long hair off her neck. "People aren't angry enough."

She steps back, surveys the wall. "Look, if you want to hang around here, today — that's fine. In fact, I'd like that. Show the public there's nothing to find. Not among the women." She looks at me again and lays down her tools. There is a sharp clink. Her anger is attractive, her face somehow luminous. Suddenly she smiles. "God — what a case." She shakes her head. "You know where I'd look if I were you? I'd look for angry men, the ones who attack women on the streets. Or I'd look for some man who got turned away from a women's shelter, some night, by a volunteer. Maybe there's someone raging mad about it — try that."

And soon after, I'm alone. Zoe has gone off on a series of errands and, as promised, left me to wander Susanna House. The shelter branches over me, oddly quiet without the women. I move up and down the stairs, peering into the dormitory-style rooms. Red plastic milk crates marked Sunnyland Dairy hold a few possessions. Army cots with green army blankets form dim rows. From a light fixture, a torn pink blouse swings from a wire hanger. In one room, on an old green chalkboard, some long-gone teacher etched the words Welcome, new day. Under that, in Magic Marker, someone has scrawled more recently: New day sucks. I am inscribing this phrase into my notebook when abruptly there is pounding on the door below.

Zoe's last directive to me was not to open the shelter, except to leave. I move to a second-floor window and look down. On the street below a man steps back, gazing at the shelter — a man in a windbreaker. I shift to another window for a better angle. The pounding resumes. The man on the videotape?

I run downstairs to see his face, eye level. From the hall window, I can. The videotape speeds through my mind. That face. This face. That windbreaker: this one. Yes. I'm certain now — same man. And the man is shouting.

"Want my wife, you bitches. I know she's in that hell-hole, let her out." He waits a moment. "God damn you — took my wife." He kicks the door — a boot, by the sound, Another kick. I hear the door shudder. Then, red-faced, he's wheeling around, he's heading for a pickup truck double-parked out front. Tan and brown two-toned Ford — I get the license number. He lays rubber, screeching away.

Quickly I turn toward the office, the phone. Jed can run a make on that license: West Virginia. The story is alive again. I dial — but Jed's away from his desk. I decide to wait here. I move about the shelter again, wander through the dining room, the kitchen, the supply room. It has a back door — I make certain it's locked. I climb up to the third floor, where Zoe lives. Her door is prudently locked. She's compassionate but she isn't stupid. I'm alone in the shelter maybe a half hour, then I go down again to the office to try Jed.

As I approach, the phone starts to ring. I grab the receiver.

"Susanna House."

"Nan?"

Tom's voice; he kept the number.

"You just caught me."

"Good." He speaks fast. "Something's in motion. Jackson called a second ago, I happened to pick up your line. Inside tip, he said. On his way. Something urgent, big — all he'd tell me." Tom pauses a second. "I'll say it this time: darlin' — careful."

An instant later, I'm jotting an address.

A minute later, I'm the one laying rubber.

■

<10>

Running LIGHTS, darting lanes, I get there fast, ditch the car out front, and flash my press ID. The doorman's hands fumble. The Marlowe Hotel, the city's most elegant, is on alert. I count two squad cars, empty, flashing, in the drive, behind a stretch limo. I spot Jed Jackson's unmarked Buick. More on the way, no doubt. No other media — yet.

Through the lobby past the palms, the azaleas. Past the concierge's desk with the single rose. Past the huge Ming vase, the orchids. Past the gilt-edged mirrors, the antique clock, to the left, down the curving staircase. On the deep carpet my heels make no sound. My dress is already sticking to my back. I reach the lower floor, glance around. To the left, the ladies' room. To the right, the exclusive restaurant, La Reine. The maitre d', looking ashen, is already being interrogated. This whole plush, beige level is tense, transformed. They've just strung up the yellow tape — in front of the ladies' room. An officer recognizes me, lifts the tape, looks at my legs. I open my notebook.

Pushing open the ladies' room door, I see floral wall-paper. Expensive wallpaper: mauve roses on gray. There is elegant lighting, scented air. There is a marble counter, marble floor, a spray of fresh roses, a basket of soaps. And beyond the roses, amid mirrors and marble and mauve — men: three crime lab guys, two uniformed patrolmen, a police lieutenant, two detective teams. They look off-scale: excessively large, excessively male, some-how, in this setting. Their radios crackle. Mobile Crime Lab is dusting for prints. Jed Jackson, beside me, jerks his head toward four stalls at the room's far end. "Go ahead."

Heads turn at the click of my heels. I reach the farthest stall. The door's open, scuffed, kicked in. I don't touch it; my pen lifts. First thing I notice is the blood. It forms an uneven pool on the stall floor, where a blue handbag lies on its side. Next I notice the blue shoes: high-heeled pumps, matching the bag. My eyes move up, to the toilet seat, and the figure sprawled there — a blond woman, her head flung back, arms limp at her sides. Her ivory linen dress is drenched in blood. A diamond wedding ring shines from the left hand. The woman looks to be late thirties; hard to pinpoint age, though, given her pallor. A gash in her throat must have opened the carotid artery. Her skirt is down. The blood-spattered commode is closed. In silence, I take notes.

"Jeez." A mutter behind me. Without turning, I know it's Sam Wile. I step out of his way. The crime lab photographer is already in action. As always, the camera's flashes make the body seem to move, to jolt. I turn away. Jed and Frank LaMarca are leaning against a long marble slab indented with three sinks; pale rosebuds are painted on each bowl. The cops' sleeves catch in a basket of delicate linen towels.

"Big time," LaMarca says. "Congressman's wife." He fills me in: Sharon Welch, thirty-eight, mother of two, was the wife of the Democratic representative from a large Ohio district. She had come for a late lunch at La Reine, with two male friends, to plan a fund-raiser for AIDS. They lingered over coffee; the dining room emptied. Before departing, Welch excused herself to go to the ladies' room. After twenty minutes her friends were worried. One summoned the maitre d', who in turn summoned the concierge. After no response, through the ladies' room door, the concierge finally went in. At first he saw nothing. Hesitantly, he moved toward the stalls — under the last one, he saw the blood. The stall was kicked in. Mrs. Welch, clearly, was dead. Leaving everything untouched, the concierge ran for a phone.

"No weapon found." Jed frowns. "Looks like a stab wound from a blunt knife. Hard to say exactly what, how without Dr. Death." He means the medical examiner.

"She died in there?" I ask.

"Yeah, fast." Jed frowns again.

I keep writing. "In a stall, locked from inside?"

Jed is unfazed. "Coulda been shut from outside with a belt, a string."

I nod. "Any link to the other murders?"

"Don't look it. Different M.O., locale. This killer's bolder. Ballsy. No dark streets for this one."

"This one's got major ego, maybe digs risks," LaMarca says.

"You mean someone just walked in that door — " I say.

"Uh. That door." Jed points to a small white louvered door at the back of the ladies' room, in the wall behind the stalls. "Supply room back there, linen, soap." LaMarca goes on. "Unlocked. Opens out onto a hallway, accessible enough, but safer. Traces of blood on the supply room floor, oh yeah, and vomit."

"Charming." My pen moves. "Related?"

"Gotta wait on the lab."

"Family — "

"Husband on a plane to Dayton, he'll hear it when he lands," Jed says. "Two kids, ten and twelve, still in school, they don't know." A pause. Jed's jaw muscles work.

"His office — " I ask, finally.

"Got to them. They're working up a statement."

For another moment we say nothing. Often, at times like this, Jed will talk about the Redskins, or a baseball team, a basketball star, depending on the season. Times like these, he likes to remind himself of sports, his first love — and remind us both there's something beyond the police tape. His silence now is ominous, odd.

"What do you think?" I say, after a while.

"I think there's a fried-chicken dinner after church this Sunday," Jed says, slowly, deliberately, his eyes on the painted sink. "I think I'll take my kids, you know my boy, he's ten, same age as — " He breaks off.

"I know," I say quietly.

"Damn." His eyes remain on the sink another moment. Then he turns to LaMarca. "What you starin' at?"

Frank goes to bug the crime lab people. Jed drains his Styrofoam cup of coffee. I take it from him. "Go to that chicken dinner," I say.

"Don't go to the can in hotels," he says.

"If your guys are done, I'll try her friends." I slip him the license number I got earlier, and explain.

"My fair lady," he says, as always. We look at each other. For the first time in all our years together, we do not smile. And then I am out through the doors, I am ducking under police tape again, I am watching a gurney roll up on the plush carpet outside the ladies' room of the Marlowe Hotel. Beyond it I see two pale young men sitting motionless on a striped couch. The dining room, across the way, is empty. There is a smell of stale perfume and carpet cleaner in the air.

I wrap up in an hour. Nothing unusual has been seen. The concierge has noted that anyone could slip into the hotel, though not everyone would know about the supply closet. Who would? I ask. Employees, he says, hesitating slightly. Frequent female diners, or guests familiar with that ladies' room. "Women who could afford La Reine, women of our clientele wouldn't — " He trails off and glances at Sharon Welch's friends. They look slapped, shocked, but have little to add — only Sharon's unhappiness with Washington; a developing Valium habit. No serious depression, however; certainly no thoughts of suicide.

"I could kill myself," says the maid, behind us. She services the ladies' room, but saw nothing. However, she just came on her shift; her predecessor has gone home. I get names and numbers for both maids, then head back upstairs.

In the lobby, I duck into a phone booth and dial the paper. I expect Tom to be in a meeting, but he grabs the phone on the first ring. I tell him where I am, give a brief rundown; he whistles.

"Got what I need, I think." I glance out the booth's glass doors. "Looks like the troops are rolling in." Reporters, video cameras, photographers have just hit the lobby. "We've got a jump on this, bless Jed."

"I'll get our stringer in Dayton."

"I'll try the Welch house?"

"Good. I'll send someone to the Hill."

"Remind me later: a lead, today, on the shelter thing."

"Any tie-in with this?"

"Doesn't look like it."

A pause. All that's unspoken between us has been moving under our words; we hear it now, in the silence. I hear it in Tom's voice more clearly as he asks when I'll be back.

"Maybe two hours. Wrap it by deadline."

"I'll tell them. Bye, love."

.

BUT BY deadline, it is not wrapped. By deadline, things are different. And I am still leaning over the computer. Deadline passes. Information trickles in. People go home. I keep writing. Tom is behind me, one hand on my desk, reading over my shoulder. The newsroom quiets. We won't make the first edition; but we'll make the rest. We'll make it — with a changed story.

A change I can almost chart.

At one o'clock this afternoon this piece looked pretty straightforward. Congressman's wife found killed in hotel. Grisly. Unsolved. Tragic. But straightforward.

By 1:40, as I left the Welch house, the story had taken a twist. I had found no one at the Georgetown residence except the housekeeper. A pleasant, heavy-set Jamaican, she had been with the family six years and was used to the press. I sat with her in the kitchen; she was snapping green beans. I remember the beans scattering across the floor as I told her. Too shocked to cry, she talked: knew of no enemies, no threats, no unusual calls or visitors. I turned off the tape recorder. And, as often happens, then came the tears. And more details; I took out my notebook. Sharon was homesick, the housekeeper said; at loose ends here. Such a fine person. The only thing, lately, that seemed to lift her — volunteering at a shelter.

My pen paused, skipped. Moved.

The shelter was called Haven Place: a small house, for pregnant homeless women. Sharon Welch had been there just yesterday.

By 1:50 I was heading for the shelter. I tried Jed on my car phone. He'd just left the hotel; I couldn't get through to his cruiser. I reached Haven Place, downtown, and found myself in a tiny row house, in a shabby sitting room, surrounded by six pregnant women, one volunteer, and the director, Sue Merino. A television murmured in the background. A fan moved smoke-filled air. A woman's head, painted in watercolor, held my eyes. Beneath me, the couch sagged.

At my news, the women wept. The volunteer dropped a plate of brownies. Sue Merino sat down, hard. Sharon had been so loved here. She'd come twice a week; was about to add a third day. She'd baked these brownies, these brownies on the floor, and told them all about her lunch today. She was going to bring back matchbooks, souvenirs from La Reine.

I turned to a fresh page. More questions. Did anyone mention Sharon's lunch — beyond the shelter? Sue Merino thought. She had, in fact, at a local shelter providers' meeting, last night. Bragging a little, she said, about their VIP volunteer. Other volunteers were at the meeting. Also social workers, shelter directors, physicians, and that rotating psychiatrist, Heller. Some of Haven Place's women had mentioned the lunch too, this morning at Resurrection Baptist Church, which served breakfast to the homeless. The women had been talking about La Reine matchbooks. And about Sharon.

My hand kept moving across the notebook. Inside, though, I was getting that crummy feeling that sometimes comes. I looked at the scattered brownies. I thought of the scattered beans. I thought of the housekeeper, even now nearing the Welch kids' school. No shock. No tears.

I got back in the car. This time, I reached Jed Jackson at his desk.

"Christ," he said. Unusual. Religious man.

"There's an umbrella in that hotel. Somewhere."

"Be back to you."

Our phone connection broke up.

By 3:30 I was walking onto the newsroom floor, and Tom was walking toward me. As always, he could read my face. No exhilaration there over exclusives, scoops. I must have looked as I'd felt at the shelter.

"Food," he said firmly.

"Deadline — "

"A break."

In the elevator, a crowd pressed me against him. His hands touched my waist. Even amid this story, this grim day, it was impossible to ignore the impact of seeing each other, of being close. His hands lingered. The elevator doors opened. The cafeteria, ahead, was almost empty.

At a back table, over chicken salad, I told Tom every-thing in detail, from the beginning. These stories, for some reason, never interfere with my appetite. After the hotel part, Tom was chewing Maalox. After the shelter part, he was smoking. After the food, I was feeling much better.

And after thinking it out together, we got a strategy. I'd go with what we had, to start; within an hour we'd have a report from Dayton. If Jed and the hotel came in with more, we'd add, and file at deadline. If not, we'd still file what we had and do a more extensive follow-up tomorrow.

By 4:30 I'd written a lead we could go with and about twelve inches. Tom was reading the story, as it grew, on his screen — but then he was beside me. Gelson, the Metro chief, wanted the story more "fleshed-out," more complete; we could have till 8:30. The managing editor had "requested" this: they wanted "full," not "sketchy"; they wanted first editions to carry it. "They want a Pulitzer," Tom muttered. "Not to mention the feeding of the five thousand." This story was front page, above the fold. And this story, we knew, had too many missing pieces. The whole damn thing could change.

And did.

By 5:30 we had reaction from Welch, we had a decent draft. Straightforward — and, we knew, incomplete. I stalled, an hour from deadline. I tinkered, I made calls, I double-checked facts. We watched the clock and watched the phone and still there was nothing. Nothing yet.

And then, at 6:20, Jed Jackson was on the line. The police had found the umbrella. The morning maid at the Marlowe Hotel had checked the ladies' room just before going off her shift, in a rush, to pick up a sick child. Rita Marcos had found a burgundy umbrella, stained with vomit, behind a cabinet in the supply room. She had also noticed traces of blood. As a trained Marlowe employee, she had thought a guest had become ill, perhaps too much to drink — and covered her embarrassment in the supply closet. Marcos had cleaned up the vomit, feeling nauseated herself. Hastily she had washed off the umbrella in the supply room's industrial sink. She knew she hadn't been thorough enough; she knew she had rushed. Again, she mentioned her own nausea, as she wrapped the umbrella in plastic, left it at the front desk — and went to get her child. Jed Jackson, not pleased, had brought Marcos in for questioning. The crime lab, not pleased, had the umbrella: steel-tipped, bamboo handle — not the victim's. Jed dodged the term serial killing, but was quite forthcoming on body fluids.

"Lab guys rushed. Traces of gastric juices, vomit, blood, on the umbrella," I told Tom by phone across the newsroom. I could hear a Maalox packet opening.

A pause. Another packet opened.

"More to come," I promised.

"Make sure I have a Danish in my hand when you tell me.

I scrolled down on the computer and started to rewrite. Five minutes to deadline. I called Jed back and tried, one more time to get an answer: serial or copycat pattern?

Serial. I scrolled up, added it. He'd said the M.E. might rush an autopsy report. Special case. Big time. But by deadline — nothing. Tom decided to hold the story. And wait. If we had it by 8:30, Tom said, we could make the first editions by a hair.

Six-forty. Seven-ten. Seven-twenty: the autopsy report filtered through Jed, was in.

Cause of death: massive hemorrhaging, shock, convulsions. Initial blunt force trauma to the head, not fatal, not quite hard enough. Some object not unlike a blunt knife had entered Welch's mouth and throat, leaving marks. Before it could penetrate further, however, the weapon had apparently induced vomiting. There was evidence of repeated reverse peristalsis. Abrasions on Welch's hands indicated her struggle to remove the object. A shred of burgundy nylon was found caught in her diamond ring.

Tall, athletic, Welch was stronger than the two preceding victims. It was assumed she dislodged the weapon. Once more, it was rammed into her mouth — differently this time, perhaps deliberately; perhaps botched. In any case, the weapon had pierced her throat from inside, nicking her carotid artery, and breaking through exterior flesh. Again Welch summoned strength to wrest out the weapon, flinging it from her — perhaps in convulsive spasm. This effort had elevated her heart rate and accelerated the fatal hemorrhaging. Sharon Welch died in the stall where she was found. The stall door had been locked perhaps by a tool or a belt from the outside; the lock was scratched. For ten minutes, a hotel customer later complained, the ladies' room door had been stuck shut.

"Got your Danish?" I phoned Tom across the news-room.

"The M.E. came through?"

"Jed just called — and there's more."

"Be right there."

I put in a call to Haven Place, to Welch's friends, and started writing, once again. In moments Tom was beside me. "If we can get it by 8:30, Metro will be happy."

"We'll make it."

I rubbed my neck, my shoulders. For a moment the green letters on the black screen scrambled before my eyes. Tom turned up the television in Metro; in silence, we watched Representative Pete Welch weeping in an airport. And then we were back at my small screen again.

•

IT IS 7:48.

Calls are still coming in. Haven Place. One of Welch's friends. My pen scrawls a few sentences. Sharon had a bladder condition, which caused frequent trips to ladies' rooms. She was open about it, matter-of-fact, like the athlete she was. Everyone knew. Including, it seems, her killer.

It is 8:10. Tom rubs my shoulders. He is leaning over, editing as we go, and it goes smoothly. One more call comes in: Jed, again, with a definite from the M.E. and

Crime Lab. Traces of blood and body fluid on the umbrella match Sharon's. I scroll up, we find a place — insert. Scroll down. I glance for an instant at the clock, then at the screen again.

I'm writing faster now, seeing the images through the words. The dead woman in the elegant marble room. The weeping women in the sagging shelter. Beans scattering in a Georgetown kitchen. Brownies scattering in a downtown row house. And moving through every scene, the invisible figure who knows the story as we do not — and who has killed three people. I see their faces now, in rapid succession. And, abruptly, the faces on the wall of Susanna House.

It is 8:28. The story's wrapped. Tom sits down at the terminal, going through the copy once more, squinting through his cigarette smoke. He makes a change here and there; nothing major. I flip through my notebook double-checking facts, quotes, making sure nothing's missed.

Nothing is. The story clears. It's going to press.

And we are going to dinner.

·

THERE'S A fish place we've come to like in Washington Harbor. It's warm enough to sit outside at small white tables; we overlook boardwalk and river. Behind us a huge fountain plumes. The place almost feels like Europe; it feels far away, and that is how we want to feel just now. We don't talk murder. We don't talk story. We both feel relief — but not relish, not triumph. We sit in the warm June night and eat crabs and don't talk much at all. We don't need to. It's enough, being together.

After dinner we walk by the river. A path runs from the boardwalk, along the Potomac. On one side there's water and the dim bulk of Roosevelt Island. On the other, grass and foliage; ahead, the glowing white cube of the Kennedy Center. We lean against the rail by the river. Tom turns my face toward him; his lips linger on mine. After a while, we walk back.

It is only then that I hear someone behind us. And even then, I don't think much about it. Others walk this path; sometimes there are joggers. It is when we reach the boardwalk again that I hear the footsteps cease — a bit too deliberately, a bit too abruptly. A biker streaks by, a runner trots past. The sound of those footsteps is lost. We stroll back toward the outdoor tables, the fountain — and only then I spot it: the figure I've seen outside Susanna House. On the other side of the fountain, the silhouette pauses; turns. Cascading water blurs it, screening the face. But the figure's stance is tense, alert. The blurred gaze seems trained on me.

I turn to Tom. He looks at me, questioning. I turn back to the fountain.

The figure, again, is gone.

■

<11>

WATER: RIPPLING, cascading in tiers. I watch it objectively, clinically. I note how water, spraying, falling, blurs and yet reveals a form — though the form, now, is mine. I stand in the shower and think of the figure behind the fountain. I still see it as I step out, dry off.

I am in my house alone, earlier than expected: just past ten-thirty. On the boardwalk a half hour earlier, Tom mistook my expression for a crash: fatigue. I hadn't realized how tired I actually was, with the start of a headache — not till that moment, that glimpse through the fountain. Concerned, Tom drove me home. "Get some sleep. A lot of sleep." He'd smoothed my hair. "If I come in, I'll be tempted to keep you awake."

"I'll be fine."

"I'll be home."

His eyes, again, held shifting grays, showing what he waited to say. I felt bad, letting him go, making him wait. Making him worry. But if he'd known my other thoughts, he'd be far more worried. The last time I'd been followed,

I'd had phone calls. A series of silent hang-ups. I wondered if the pattern might repeat tonight. If it did I wanted to be there at home to catch it. Because I knew, this time, what I would do.

Wrapped in a towel, now, though, I feel dubious. I wish this gamble hadn't hooked me. My headache is gone. I gaze out over the patio. I can see the chaise lounge where we were last night. The air is warm again tonight; I think of Tom — and then the phone begins to ring.

I'm beside it in three steps. I watch the number coming up on the Caller-ID screen, still hooked up. Grabbing for a pen, I take the number down. No number I recognize. I wait another ring and answer. Again, on the other end, that live, listening silence: someone on the verge of speech. I hang up. A minute passes. The phone rings again. Again my eyes are on the screen. The number comes up. The three-digit prefix, the next four digits. The same number. This time I let the answering machine get it. Once more, I hear it. That same silence. And before the machine clicks off, I am pulling on clothes. My short hair is drying. I can be out in five minutes.

I dial the number I took down. I'm still not sure if I'll try to draw information or do a trace — possible on my phone system, with its two lines. I'll know when I hear the voice. The call goes through. I hear the first ring; the second. The pickup: a receiver smoothly lifted. "Good evening, the Marlowe Hotel."

I pause, off guard.

"Good evening?" Polite repeat; desk clerk.

"Yes, good evening." Reporter's practiced calm. "I've received an incomplete message leaving this number ..."

Not one that ends in double zeros; not institutional. I gamble. "One of your guests."

"Yes, ma'am."

I know damn well he won't give a name. "I wonder if you might ring my friend?"

"I'm sorry ... that guest has just turned his line to Secretarial. That's why your call came in to the desk. Would you care to leave a message?"

"Thank you, I'll try back later." I stand looking at the phone. "He," the clerk had said. The guest might have gone out. Or to sleep. "Just," the clerk had said. I had a hunch it was the former. I could be wrong, of course. It could mean a wasted trip, possibly a long night. But wasted trips, long nights, aren't anything new. And I usually go with a hunch.

Ten minutes later I am stepping into the Marlowe's lobby. It's the second time in twelve hours I've run lights to get here. The concierge's desk is empty; the red rose, still fresh. In the quiet lobby, an elderly man in a deep chair reads a paper. Not ours. The main desk is at the far end, near the elevators.

I position myself. A comfortable chair. A magazine. I deliberately do not face the doors. If this guest is the caller and out for a walk, I don't want to be seen as he returns. This time I'll do the watching, and the calculating. I open my magazine. Behind me I hear the lobby doors open. A couple in evening clothes breezes past; perfume, like some notes of jazz, drifts by and is gone.

Fifteen minutes later, twelve people, by my count, have passed through the lobby. I begin to have some second thoughts. Maybe this is the wrong way to do it. Maybe tomorrow I should just ask Jed Jackson to call the desk, demand the name. He can, as a homicide detective on a case here. The trouble is, I want to do this myself. I remain in my seat. The elderly man across from me must think I have a reading disability.

Again I hear the lobby doors open. I glance at my watch and then up, and almost miss him. He is walking fast, but — that's the one. After a moment I stand casually; I follow at a measured pace. The man moves down the curving stairs I trampled earlier today. His step is still quick. Keeping my distance, I stay behind him, the deep carpet muffling my tread.

The man reaches the second level, passing the huge floral arrangement at its center. He moves toward another flight of stairs leading down to the hotel's lowest level. I watch: no sign he senses anyone following. Keeping the same distance, I trail him down the steps. No mirrors. No glass anywhere. No reflections. No way I can see his face — or he mine.

The third level, also beige, plush, branches off into conference rooms. In the far wall one door is different: black, marked Garage. The man heads there directly, as if familiar with this route.

Damn, I think. I don't know where my car is. I let them valet park it. If he drives off, I can't follow. But I can get his license number. And I can wait.

He opens the garage door, passes through. I let ten seconds pass by, then crack the door. The garage is dim and shadowed. The lobby's light is also low; no brightness flashes as I ease the door wider and slip into the garage. Cement columns rise up at intervals; the garage is full. My shoes in hand, I duck past cars; pause behind one column, then another.

The man is moving toward a dark green Thunder-bird. I shift one column closer but cannot make out the license plates. A noise; I stop short. The man, his back still turned, is opening the car's trunk. In this light his form is vague; I hear my pulse.

The trunk rises. The man, leaning forward, removes something. There is the slam of metal: trunk closed. He is ahead of me now, moving back toward the hotel. I wait in the dimness, listening to his quick footfalls. Halfway

to the door, he passes briefly under a light. His back is to
me, I still can't see his face. But in that light I can see
what he took from the trunk. I can see what's in his
hand.

An umbrella. A black umbrella; steel-tipped.

I stand absolutely rigid behind the column. The door
opens, clicks shut. Glancing out, I make sure he's gone
through. Now I'm running, now I'm at the door — I slow
down to open it; open it with care. A crack; wider. He's
ahead of me, moving toward the stairs at a slower pace.
I put on my shoes again, following, keeping a good distance. I can still hear my heart. Now I follow with different steps, cautious, on guard. As he goes up the stairs,
I find my eyes transfixed by the umbrella's steel tip.

He reaches the lobby. I pause on the steps. Now,
somehow, I have to find out. A name, a room number,
some fact — something to give Jed. And I know I cannot
allow myself to be seen.

I slip behind a screen of palms that fringes the discreet cocktail area at the lobby's far end. I wonder if he'll
get his key from the desk or if I'll have to trail him
upstairs. He does not go toward desk or elevators, but in
another direction, nearby. In the light I can see the
expensive cut of his dark raincoat. I see his hair is gray.
I see the strength of the body; a fit body, not an old man's
body. I see it even beneath the coat.

The man steps over to the newsstand. I shift closer,
down the length of palms, close as I can without being
seen. If he turns left from the newsstand, I'll miss his
face. If he turns right — I'll see him, straight on.

He buys a paper. I see it slide across the counter. It
is tucked under his arm, beside the umbrella. There is
the sound of coins on the counter's top. And then,
pocketing his change, he turns; turns right, not glancing

toward the palms. He doesn't see me. But I see him; I see his face.

He turns toward the elevator. I remain motionless.

The man is my father.

■

PART TWO

<12>

I'VE BEEN sent out: Another story.
I reach the scene. Night: hot, oppressive dark.
I see the police line, the flashing lights. The area cor-
doned off — black tape this time. Strange. The cops'
faces: strange, too. "Way to go," they say. "Good tip." I
duck under the black tape. I seem to move in slow
motion. Through the lights' bong-white glare, I look down
at the victim: a man on his back in the street. A man in
an expensive dark raincoat, strong body, gray hair. Blood
on his coat, blood on his chest. I look at his face. My pen
lifts. I cannot write. I cannot breathe ...

.

COLD SWEAT. Racing heart. I grope for the light.
Across the room I see my oak dresser. I am awake now,
I am in my own house. That crime scene was a dream
and has not happened, and still I can't stop shaking.

I look at the clock. Three in the morning. I get up and walk through the dark house — exactly what I did when I returned from the hotel, and exactly what I made myself stop. Shut it off. Wait till daylight. Wait till the shock wears off. Firmly, I'd forced myself to bed — and paced through my sleep right into that dream.

Downstairs now, I see the blur of my white nightgown in a mirror. My eyes adjust to the dark. In the kitchen, my hand brushes something on the counter: a pack of Tom's cigarettes. I light one. The smell makes me feel he's near. Again I think of calling him — don't want to wake him. Don't want to tell him. I go into the living room, walk its length twice. The cigarette glows in the dimness. My mind works over everything I swore to leave alone till tomorrow.

My father.

In town to accept a coveted award. In town ahead of time, for some reason: lecturing, visiting, meetings; anything. Then again — he is also watching a shelter. Watching covertly. Watching at a time of murder related to shelters. He is calling the reporter of these murders and hanging up. Perhaps he is only calling because the reporter is his daughter, estranged — and it is too hard to speak. Perhaps he was only getting his umbrella tonight in case of rain. There is a chance of rain in the forecast, I've checked. Many people have steel-tipped umbrellas. Among them, my father. And the murderer.

No apparent motive. Not enough information. Not enough to tell anyone. Or so I tell myself, knowing damn well that if this were a different man I'd tell Tom, I'd probably tell Jed. After all, I've been followed; I've had a series of hang-up calls, calls that could be considered harassment. Maybe my father only wanted to hear my voice, I don't know. I light another cigarette. I quit smoking five years ago. Amazing: you can just pick some

things up again. Amazing: after all these years, after all
my childhood pain, I still want to protect my father. This
father I scarcely know anymore. If I ever did.

I go upstairs again, into my bedroom. At the back of
a closet, on the top of a shelf, is a hatbox. I haven't looked
in it for years. Now I stand on a chair and pull it down.
In the lamplight, objects spill on the bed. A faded Playbill
theater program: Camelot. My first Broadway show; my
father had taken me. I'd been eight years old and
entranced. We had bought the soundtrack album. The
music had filled our big Manhattan apartment, I remember. Our time at that matinee is one of my few good
memories of my father.

Under the program, there's a letter written on a
prescription pad. August 1969. The only letter he wrote
me, my summers in Maine as a teenager. My mother
traveled. And my father, already a renowned visionary
physician, went to Appalachia alone. There he founded
and directed a pioneering medical-outreach clinic for the
rural poor, a clinic that kept growing, branching, spawn-
ing others.

During the winter my father maintained his fashion-
able East Side practice in pediatrics and shuttled back
and forth to the clinic. Summers, he was always in West
Virginia, except for a weekend or two. I remember his
shadow, those weekends, falling over me and Nora as we
sat watching fireflies on the back steps. I remember him,
brooding, angry, those weekends. I used to wonder why
— and stay out of his way.

Now I look down at an old photograph. My father,
mother — and I. One of those summer weekends; I must
have been five; my father the age I am now. Our faces
look tense; my mother's, already absent, aloof from the
scene. In the child's face I can see my own, the woman's.
In the father's face I scarcely see the one I just glimpsed

at the hotel. My father has aged in the fourteen years since we last met. Not through the vigorous body, but in the lines of the jaw, the mouth, around the eyes. The last time I saw him, his hair was full and dark.

I study the photo. The perfect family. The beautiful family: Everyone would say that. "Smile," I remember my beautiful mother whispering just before that shot. I was a serious child, big-eyed, listening; always listening. Listening for the next rage. Rages no one else knew or spoke of. I never understood what caused them; gave up trying. Gave up when I left home — and gave up on him.

My father. Sleeping tonight a few floors above that marble room where a woman, today, was killed. My father: successful, charming with clerks and patients and strangers. And guests.

Each evening from September to September...
I go downstairs, holding the theater program.
before you drift to sleep upon your cot ...
In my dark living room, I see another.
think back on all the tales ...
I try not to think back.
that you remember ... of Camelot ...

·

A PARTY. MANY parties, filling the spacious apartment overlooking Central Park. A cook would come in, working magic in the kitchen. Under her hands, butter became shells; lamb bones a crown; chocolate, snow. Enchanted parties, hanging on the dark, above the glimmering city ...

Tinkle of ice cubes. Murmur of voices. Scent of fresh flowers, perfume. Nora, in lace apron, passing a tray among the guests. Light: amber, peach, gold, spill-ing over abstract paintings and intent faces. In the mirror, shifting silks. Women like long-stemmed flowers; I peer at them through the stair rail. Below, in the duplex apartment, I watch my lovely mother's hair. She moves easily among the guests; she flows through the room, a trail of sea-green silk. There are important people here tonight, I know. People from the arts, and medicine, as always, but also people who have come from Washington, D.C. — from President Kennedy's White House. They are here to help my father start his new dream — a free hospital in Appalachia. "Vision": the word floats up to me, and "birth."

I am a child crouching, I feel, on the edge of something miraculous and unrepeatable. I stay, though I have already been presented to the guests and sent to bed. I stay, disobedient and hidden, unable to sleep. I stay, listening to my father's voice telling of his dreams for the new project. Tell them loud and clear ... deep voice like a stronger colored thread than the others in the weave ... there was a fleeting wisp of glory ...

He stands on the coffee table, suddenly, in a leap. His eyes are bright, his presence commanding. The room quiets. He makes a toast with no glass in his hand. "To all of you here tonight, bearing this vision forward ... and to all who are not here, and yet who move among us, the nameless, faceless poor ..."

The voice of a preacher in the mouth of an atheist. The voice of a poor boy from the Bronx, the son of immigrants who ran a dry-goods store. The voice of a young man who worked his way through medical school — and worked his way up to the East Side, the society wife, the daughter with the private schools and the art lessons. And the fear.

He sees me now, through the banister's railing. He sees me and his face changes abruptly. Others are making toasts. He steps down from the table, smoothly excuses himself. I am rising and the room below is

blurring, I am running and the hall streaks past; I've defied him, disobeyed him again, all I can do is outrun his rage, his step behind me on the
stair ...

.

I AM ON the stairs of my own house now, all these years later. And all these years later, I am shaking. It is a long time since I have let myself remember. Back in the bedroom I open the box again. Now I lift out other tokens, counter-weights ... a broken rosary, worn brown beads. Missal markers, ribbons: green, purple, white. A ticket to the ferris wheel at Coney Island ... saving tokens, hopeful relics, Nora ...

I close the box, set it back, and move to the window, where I look out at the patio below. After a while I go downstairs and unlock the back door. The patio is hushed and dim; warm air touches my skin. The sur-rounding walls are high; the gate, secure. I lie back in the chaise lounge where Tom held me — was it just the night before?

I look up at the sky as we did, and remember the feel of his arms. I do not want to need this man. I've tried not to need this man. It seems I do, even so. I sit smoking his cigarettes and holding Nora's rosary, until the cigarettes are gone and the beads dangle from my fingers. At last, in the chair, in the dark, I fall asleep. And do not dream.

.

A FACE HANGS over me. There's sunlight in my eyes. I sit bolt upright.

"Little early to get a tan?" Sidney's voice: ironic, hip.

"God, you scared me to death." I stare at her.

"Glad it was me," she says, ominously.

"What time is it?" I blink, disoriented.

"Eight-thirty in the A.M."

"What are you doing here?"

"Live here, babe." She grins.

"Don't smile so big — so early."

"Early plane. Told you, left messages."

I rub a hand over my face. "Right." In the kitchen, I make coffee. Sidney, a cook in her mother's tradition, pro-duces a full breakfast. "That shit they serve on planes ..." she mutters.

I've never understood how she can get up at five, make an early plane, and materialize like this: rested, slick, articulate. I've seen her do it before, and if I didn't love her I'd hate her for it. I feel hung over, disheveled, slow. Good to see her, though, even through my daze. Even good to see the lawyer in her, which, at the moment, is cross-examining me.

"When did you start smoking?"

"Last night, at eleven fifty-one."

"Uh-huh." She looks at me. "Tough story?"

I shrug. "How was your case?"

"Long. Dull. The story?"

I pause. In the patio's sunlight, last night seems a hallucination. Then, for a moment, it comes back: the man turning; the face. I decide then, firmly: I'll tell no one. Not till I know more. And I'll start practicing right now. I tell Sidney about Sharon Welch — guessing she's read about it.

She has. And frowns — hates to see me in the midst of this. Hates my being on the crime beat more, I think, each story. When Sid was ten she saw her father shot to death on the street in front of their house; he was caught in cross fire — drug wars, even then. Sid also has a mother who until recently worked three jobs, and who told Sidney over and over that she could be anything she wanted. Sid's learned from both parents. And has a well-developed sense of evil — a word she's not ashamed to use. A keener sense of it than anyone else I know.

Now Sidney's large silver earrings catch the morn-ing light. Her jumpsuit today is burgundy. Listening, she twists a spoon in her long fingers. I'm finishing my catch-up report. "Some volunteers dropping out, scared. I feel partly responsible. All this coverage. It's never been dangerous for volunteers before, and shelters can't run without them, you know that ..."

Sid knows. She knows from all the pro bono legal counsel she's given shelters over the years. She knows from her mother, who occasionally volunteers at the Eighth Street Shelter, in her neighborhood. And Sid knows, from me. But instead of mentioning fear, Sidney does what I've learned to do: she switches gears, turns professional. She speaks as a lawyer — about the shelters' liability for suits. She makes a note on a pad. I make a note on a paper napkin.

And then we are both standing, clearing the table, moving inside. We are both switching gears once again, getting ready for work, for the day. Real life appears to take over, on one level. On another, moving just beneath the surface, there's a darker current. I'll feel it, I know, till I've stepped in deeper. As I dress, a plan begins to form in my mind.

Ten minutes later I'm running out the door.

"What's the rush?" Sidney looks clairvoyant.

"Stop to make." I look inscrutable. "House-keeping," I add. And dash.

■

<13>

HOUSEKEEPING IS here. Housekeeping has hit the Marlowe Hotel.

Across the top floor: maids and carts, brooms and bottles and Breath O'Pine, Tilex and towels. And through the cans, through the bottles, over the towels, behind a cart — I watch.

From the lobby's phone booth, I've called my father's room: no answer. At the desk, I've left him a folded note: blank. Watching the desk clerk file the note, I caught my father's room number. And so I've found my way here, to watch his door, which happens to be open. There is a sound of vacuuming within. Perhaps I'll slip in if the maid leaves for more supplies. I could also enter boldly while she's there, as if that's my room. Inwardly I debate, unsure. But I am absolutely sure of something else. However this has to do with my father — I want to know. I want to find out for myself. And maybe find out it's nothing.

The vacuuming has stopped. The maid comes out, goes to a cart down the hall. Quickly now I slip through the door and into the center of my father's hotel room. A quick scan: what you'd expect of the Marlowe. French Regency writing desk. Upholstered chairs, muted paintings. The credenza that conceals TV and bar. King-size bed, just made. The drapes are open; ivory curtains billow toward me. I part them, slide a glass door open, step out onto the balcony. Far below is the green, intricate sweep of Rock Creek Park. For an instant I see the apartment of my childhood, overlooking a different park, a different city. I defer the memory. As I turn I hear footsteps in the room: through the curtains, for a moment, I see the maid. And then she is gone. The door clicks shut behind her.

Immediately, I go to the desk. On the blotter there is paperwork. Familiar crabbed handwriting. Looks like a speech — the handwriting stops me. For a moment I see the letter on the prescription pad, the face of the father in the old photo. The father writing at his desk at home, late into the night .. .

Again I push, lure, yank my mind back. The only way I can do this, I know, is to treat this room as a stranger's. To treat this whole scene as — story. Someone else's. The key to that is simple: move fast and do not think.

I open the center desk drawer. Room service menu. Hotel stationery, sewing kit, all untouched. Right-hand drawer: a folder, not the hotel's. I flip it open: a typed, official letter. National Humanitarian Awards heading. Standard welcome. I skip down to the signature: Representative Peter R. Welch, Chairman.

My notebook is out. For some moments, journalist supersedes daughter.

I shuffle through the folder: a schedule of events planned for recipients prior to awards. I copy the schedule

in a hurried scrawl.   At this moment my father is
addressing medical students at Georgetown University.
Later I'll check out where he's been — and will be.
Another sheet of paper: instructions for recipients the
night of the awards, still five days away. The schedule of
events extends back only three days. That's all.

The other drawers in the desk yield nothing. Bracing,
I turn to the bureau. This will be personal, difficult. Top
drawer: cuff links, tie clasps, pennies — his top bureau
drawer always looked like this. He always saved pennies,
from the time he was a child during the Depression. Now,
under the pennies I find a small photo. There we are, the
perfect family, in a snapshot just like mine.   Swiftly,
before it can snag me, I replace it under the pennies.
Beside them a manila envelope, unmarked, unsealed. I
open it — and see my name, my byline, on a series of
clippings: every story on the shelter murders, plus the
follow-ups. The papers seem to tremble slightly —   a
breeze from the balcony, I tell myself. I know it's my
hands.

I drop the clippings back in the envelope, drop the
envelope back in its place and move to the bedside table.
Its single drawer holds a Gideon Bible, slightly dusty, untouched. Beside it there's a prescription bottle — I note
the medication, a mild one, for sleep. I almost pass over
a small hotel notepad, blank except for one nameless
phone number. I recognize it immediately. It's mine.

For an instant the numbers swim before my eyes. I
flip to the next page in the notepad. Two more phone
numbers, vaguely familiar, can't quite place them. I take
them down and flip through the pad.   The remaining
pages are blank.

Back to the desk. I wasn't thorough here, I got too
shaken by that first glimpse of handwriting. Now, with
forced detachment, I lift the legal pad, scan the speech.

Nothing catches me. I am more interested in what's underneath.

Tucked in a corner of the blotter, more photos. Snapshots of the Outreach Clinic in Appalachia. The clinic itself. My father before it. Photos of children, parents; more children.

I put the pictures back and turn to the blotter's other corner. Tucked there is another schedule, this one not official, not typed — in my father's crabbed writing. The list outlines a series of speaking engagements, dinners, luncheons, meetings. It explains what he was doing here prior to the awards committee schedule. I scribble this new list down, and as I reach the earliest entry, my pen skids.

The date of his arrival in Washington holds me. My stories' datelines flash in my mind. My father arrived the day before the first murder.

Again, numbers, letters, blur in my sight. Get a grip. No shock, no tears. Ever. Under any circumstances ...

Damn it — even these? Especially these: I know.

I make final notes. Time to get out of here. Time to get back to the paper. I replace the schedule just as it was. I check photos, making sure they're in the right order. I set the legal pad back in place.

Scanning the room one last time, I pick up my briefcase. Just as I turn to leave, there's a knock at the door.

"Valet," a voice calls.

In two steps I'm out on the balcony. I listen; in moments the door clicks shut again.

Coming in through the curtains, I hear my heart-beat. I glance around the room. It is empty. And yet it is changed. A dark suit hangs on the outside of the closet door. A dark suit wrapped in plastic. My father's suit, like all the ones I remember. I know the cut. I know the faint pinstripes. It is as if, somehow, he is standing before me.

I leave the room. I leave the hotel. And still I see it: that dark form, shrouded in plastic, hanging on the air.

■

<14>

T HE NEXT time I see that suit it is passing through a metal detector. Instantly I recognize it. And I recognize my father, in an unlikely place for him. Still, I knew he'd be here — here in this cathedral.

It is two days later and ten in the morning and Mass is about to begin: a memorial Mass for Sharon Welch. Her body has already been flown back to Ohio. This service is for those who knew her here; for those who know her husband. He sits in the front pew with his children, across the aisle from the president of the United States, who has been whisked in through the sacristy.

The cathedral is packed. There are Congress people. There are various political types, social types, Washington types. And, in drastic contrast, shelter people: directors, supporters — women. I see the resi-dents of Sharon's shelter and other faces I have come to know: Ma'am from Susanna House. Carla, who knew Meredith Crane at Mount Olivet. And halfway down the aisle I spot an elegant explosion of long gray hair: Zoe Heywood. Near

the front, in a black dress, sits Sue Merino, director of
Haven Place. Papers tremble on Merino's lap; the program cites her as eulogist.

Notebook in hand, I roam the nave's edges. My
father's suit keeps slipping into my line of vision, whatever angle I take. I take yet another. I make a long circle
around the cathedral. Other figures appear to me —
suspects in the shelter case. Joan Kelly from Mount
Olivet; she looks shaken. Dr. Heller, the psychiatrist,
looking impassive. Jerry Silver, a rotating physician for
the homeless; not a suspect yet, but could be. Hadn't
considered him before. And again I catch sight of my
father. This is the closest we've come, in daylight. I shift
my eyes away, and roam.

The cathedral echoes. There is an expectant hush as
the processional begins. Light, through stained glass windows, spills colors over the pews, over bent heads, raised
faces, over my father's silver hair. Again I look away, look
elsewhere. One of the bent heads, I see, is Sidney's. She
is here with her mother, sitting to one side. One of the
raised faces, I notice, is Tom's: he's on an aisle, toward
the back, and he is watching me. Sidney lifts her head
now, also glancing my way. They both look slightly
worried. They both know, these last two days, something's
not right with me. And they don't know what.

I keep moving slowly, observing. The TV networks are
here, their lights bathing the altar in a surreal glow not
unlike the light at the scene of a crime. The priest,
concelebrating with two others, looks washed out. His
white chasuble seems to vibrate in the glare. I see Sam
Wile edge forward to get a shot of the altar, then, through
a series of columns, the president and Welch. Behind
every column, every pillar, there are photographers,
Secret Service, police, and, of course, reporters. I see
people from the wire services, from various Washington

bureaus; the guy from the New York Times, the reporter from our own Trends section. We pass, she and I, and smile; we often lunch together. Gina is doing a personality piece on Sharon Welch: an Appreciation. We move on, circling in opposite directions. Mass has begun.

"Lord have mercy ..." The priest's voice, miked, echoes.

"Enjoying yourself?" A hiss in my ear.

"Christ have mercy." I make the next response with the congregation — and give it an edge. Blondish, bearded Matt Kress is beside me — a Capitol Hill reporter, he's assigned to cover this with me, and doesn't like it. Especially because he was told by the Metro chief not to "cover" — but "contribute."

"Your story, Nan — right?"

I ignore him.

Matt looks at me. "This setup sucks."

"Nothing we can do about it, Matt."

"Maybe there is, maybe you could just — "

I am too wired for games. "Forget it."

"Your story," he says, "for just one reason."

I know what's coming. I don't need this either.

"You're fucking the deputy city editor," he jabs.

The Old Testament lesson is being read.

"If I were," I say evenly, "I'd be covering the mayor." That shuts him up for a second. I'm not finished. "You must not be fucking anyone, Matt," I add quietly; he stares at me. "Otherwise, you'd be covering the Senate."

Voices rise and fall: a responsorial psalm has begun.

"You bitch."

"Thank you."

"Glory to the Father ..." The priest's voice echoes.

I really must be wired. I don't talk like that to colleagues, as a rule. I don't talk like that in church —

the residue of seminarian in me. I've been holding myself
too tight, too controlled for days. No shock. No tears. No
sleep, either. Not much. What there is — flashing with
strange dreams, can't remember them in the mornings.
I've traced all my father's appointments, from the day he
got to town. He checks out on them all. But at the time
of the murders — no appointments. Not that I know of,
not recorded. Not that it necessarily means anything.

I've called the two phone numbers from the note-pad;
called at different times of day. No answer. I'm stymied:
can't make a case — or break one. Meanwhile, I've held
out on Sidney. I've held out on Tom, who seems
increasingly concerned. I overheard a whispered discussion in the kitchen, last night after dinner: Tom and Sid.
It made me feel rotten then and it makes me feel rotten
now. I glance at Tom. His tan suit is visible on the aisle.
He's still watching me. Editors seldom see their reporters
in action, but his glance holds more than appraisal, more
than concern. We haven't had time alone for two nights.
I try not to think about that, either. I hope I look cool,
detached, professional; my press ID clipped to my white
linen suit. I smile at Tom and know the smile is strained
and he's not fooled. Everyone is standing for the Gospel
reading.

"I am the resurrection and the life ..."

Jed Jackson sidles up to me. I've been holding out on
him, too. We've concentrated on the guy with the truck,
the West Virginia plates. They check out to an
unemployed miner named Fred B. Dade, whom no one can
find. Now, his eyes on the crowd, Jed leans closer to me.

"See him?" His voice is low. He means Dade.

I shake my head. He moves on, scanning, watch-ing,
intent.

A long slow rustle now, as everyone sits again. The
Gospel has been read. Sue Merino, from Welch's shelter,

steps up to the lectern: this will be the eulogy. I move in close for the heart of my story. News photo-graphers are also moving in. Sam is beside me. The net-works shift their cameras. Sue, flooded in light, blinks. I'm close enough to see her hands shake. She is an attrac-tive woman: tall, dark, about my age, broad shoulders, masculine. If I'd been paying more attention, I'd have checked into her more thoroughly. I make a note and watch, crouching just beyond the communion rail, as she begins.

"I'd like to open with a prayer ..." The prayer of St. Francis: "Make me an instrument of your peace ..."

The cameras are rolling; my tape recorder runs. I make notes anyway as Merino starts to speak. And then, suddenly, my pen has skidded into a long inky line on the page, as she goes on:

Sharon Welch was a caring person. Sharon Welch was a risk taker. She worked faithfully at Haven Place, and elsewhere, in service, last month. Last month, at a special workshop.

In Appalachia. With Dr. Karl Gordon. At his Out-reach Clinic for Children.

Crouching by the rail, I am absolutely still. I let the tape recorder get the rest. Now there is a connection, a thread between my father — and a victim. And I don't know what or how much it means. Only one other person here knows I'm feeling hit: Tom. But he doesn't know how hard — he doesn't know the rest. My tape recorder keeps running. I do not hear the eulogy's end, or part of the liturgy.

"On the night he was betrayed ..." The priest's voice finally comes through to me. In the cathedral now, most people are kneeling. At the altar, the bread and wine are being consecrated.

"Do this in memory of me ..." As if from a great distance, I watch the priest elevate the chalice. In my head I hear the Sanctus bells of my childhood. For a moment, just a moment, I let my mind run like a child to Nora. And then everyone is standing, the cathedral is echoing with the Lord's Prayer. Holy Communion is about to begin.

I force myself back — here, now. Attentive. Alert. On the job. I move closer to the altar rail to watch the faces at Communion. As a Protestant seminarian, I had often served the chalice, moving behind the rail myself, in fieldwork parishes. I know how faces can look at that time; how revealing, each one, in its own way. Today I want to see what the faces will tell of this story. Certain faces in particular. I know my father's face will not be one of them. In a way, that frees me to focus.

As the Communion line forms, I move nearer. For an instant I feel like an intruder. I push past the feeling and scan the line. For a moment, an usher holds it back. The Secret Service snaps into new positions. The presi-dent moves toward the rail. A non-Catholic, he simply bows his head, receives a blessing — and is whisked out a side door.

The line begins to move forward. To its left, in the nave, there is another, noticeable movement: Someone rising, moving swiftly — away from the altar. Dr. Heller slipping out. Across the nave, Jed's eyes follow him. Heller is through the doors and gone.

Welch is approaching the altar rail with his child-ren. They kneel, receiving bread and wine; today, Com-munion is in both kinds. One of the kids starts to sob; the little girl. Her father's arm comes around her; the priest touches her head. Still she weeps into her father's shoul-der. I swallow. I keep writing. Welch and family are escorted from the cathedral.

Now the ushers let the line inch forward. People fan out along the altar rail. I move in closer. And it is then that I see him down the center aisle: the man from West Virginia — Fred B. Dade. No windbreaker today; clean white shirt, dark pants. Why didn't I spot him before? Circling the nave several times, I'm sure I would have picked out his face. Maybe he was behind some column too. I begin to feel uneasy. The man looks agi-tated; his jaw works, an eyelid twitches. He is still about twenty people back, his gaze fixed straight ahead — an odd, lit gaze. Too lit — too fixed.

Swiftly, I move toward the priest. Leaning over the rail, I give a brief, whispered warning. Then, standing, central, visible, I flash a sharp look across the nave to Jed, who starts to move.

But before he can get there, Dade is moving too — he is rushing forward, he is breaking through the line, plunging toward the altar rail, toward the priest, toward me. Dade reaches the rail, grabs it, rattles it. People scatter. I am so close I can see the veins standing out in his neck as he turns, shouting. "No one listens — think I'm scum. Took my wife — them shelters, took her off me, bitches treat me like dirt. I want my wife — you give her over. Give her to me, or I'll get you all

The priest touches Dade's arm. Dade shakes him off, swings wide, and knocks the full chalice from the priest's other hand. Red wine plumes upward, seems to explode in the air. People scream. I feel the wine hit me, I taste it on my lips. The priest looks as if he's been shot; so do I. A crimson pool drips down the chancel steps.

The chalice is rolling and the cameras are flashing as Jed dives forward, wrestling Dade to the floor.

■

<15>

RED STAINS on my white suit. Spilled wine; conse-crated wine. And now, in addition, cherry soda. Sam, a can of it in hand, collides with me in the news-room. Again, bright crimson liquid pluming in the air; again, spattering me.

"Sorry," we both say.

"Just a little jazzed up," Sam adds; grins. Tom looks at me and does not grin.

There is a little too much adrenaline around here, in Metro, in the atmosphere, in the aftermath of that arrest, that chaos at the altar rail. From a distance — to Tom, to Sidney, to half the congregation — it looked as if there'd been an attack, a knifing, something. Murder in the cathedral, right before their eyes. The cameras caught it all, including swift crowd control by the police. I'd kept writing as videotape kept rolling, and after some minutes, order restored, the priests had continued with Com-munion.

And then it was over. Reporters raced to phones, com-
puters, bureau chiefs. The network video cameras rolled
away. The bright lights went dark. Tom drove me back
to the paper. Outside it was overcast, cool. As he threw
his jacket in the car, I saw his shirt sticking to his back.
A block from the cathedral, he pulled over, pulled me into
his arms. "Thought you'd been hurt," he said, finally.

Now, as I stand by my desk, doubly stained, I know
he's remembering that moment. Everywhere else around
us there is elation: one of those newsroom adrenaline
highs. Metro chief bragging. Managing editor beaming,
circulating. City desk celebrational. Everyone seems to
know one of our reporters tipped the police — earlier,
then on the scene before a thousand people, on videotape.
Everyone seems to conclude that one of our reporters
helped crack this case.

"Way to go," says Sam, lifting his soda can.

"Way to go," says Sidney, by phone.

"Way to go," says Gina, passing through on her way to
Trends. Petite and fair as I, she thrusts a fist over her
head. One for the women, it says. "God," she adds, low-
voiced. "Thought you'd been stabbed."

"Way to go," Matt Kress says, with some effort.
"Thought you'd been killed."

"Disappointed?" I sit down, sign in on the computer.

"Sorry about all that." He leans over me. "How do
you want to do this?"

We confer. He'll try to get Welch and reaction from
Congress types, then try to get a quote from the cathedral.
I'll run down the police angle, background on Fred B.
Dade, include what I've already got exclusive, and draft
the actual story.

Matt's eyes move over my body.

Can it, I think.

"Great," he says.

Damn it, I think.

"Hey." He says. "Glad you're not fucking your editor."

"Dinner tonight, Nan?" Tom is right behind him. "Of course."

Matt vanishes. I start to work. And then all the static, the stains, the splatter vanish. An image begins to emerge. The image of a man. A man who is not Matt, not Sam, not Tom. Not Dr. Terrence Heller.

And not my father. Above all, not my father.

An image of Frederick Beale Dade, thirty-seven, born near Wheeling, West Virginia. Son of coal miners. Unemployed two years. Frequent participant in mining strikes prior to that. Married to Johnice Taylor twenty years earlier. Five children. In May of this year his wife left home, accusing him of beating her repeatedly. She said she was going to Washington, D.C. She knew about some shelters there, shelters for homeless women, battered women.

He thought she'd be home in a matter of days. When the days grew into weeks, he came to find her. Slept in his truck, tried different shelters. Got turned away by volunteers at Mount Olivet, Susanna House, and Saint Claire's; two of the three shelters related to the killings. Dade's description of the volunteer at Saint Claire's fit Sister Jo Sullivan; at Mount Olivet, Meredith Crane. But he denied murder, insisted he just wanted his wife. I think of him pounding on the door of Susanna's the day I was there alone. I wonder if I have seen Johnice Dade there at dinner. No one seems to remember the name. Johnice, at present, is nowhere to be found. I want my wife ...

I pull Dade's quotes from my notebook. I pull out a new quote, from a call this afternoon to Joan Kelly at Mount Olivet. I wonder why she didn't tell me this before, when I first asked; why she didn't tell me a volunteer had turned him away. I let it go for now and call Jed Jackson again. I talked with him earlier — Jed was on adrenaline himself, then. He still is.

"Way to go," he says, again.

"You got him."

"We got him."

"One thing, Lady Nan," he adds. "Next time a man runs at you, story or no story, get the hell away — hear me?"

"Hear you." I smile.

And now he hears me probing for more information, trying to get him to draw some conclusions; make some statement on Dade that I can use. Here it comes:

Dade's history shows a pattern of abusiveness to women. Not only his wife, but a waitress who dropped charges and a neighbor in his trailer park. He admits his anger at shelter. Volunteers who turned him away. Frederick Beale Dade is now the prime suspect in the case.

"Thanks, Jed."

"My fair lady."

"You locate the trailer park?"

"You folks haven't?"

"Our stringer's on it."

"But we're faster."

"Some of the time."

He laughs, gives the address.

And leaves me there, staring at it. I am still staring at it as the line goes dead. I have forgotten to hang up the phone.

The address of Dade's trailer park is adjacent to the Outreach Clinic for Children; director, Dr. Karl Gordon. I feel some of my relief slipping from me. Amid all the action, all the sure things, I realize I discounted that connection in the eulogy — between Sharon, victim three,

and my father. This new link has brought it back into
focus.

Matt is hovering at my shoulder.

"Got Welch, got reaction."

"Good — there's the story." I scroll up on the screen.
"Feel free." He stares at me. I'm already on my way to
the library and the back files.

Everything on Welch is out.

I remember Gina, working up a profile for Trends. I
stop by her desk; we're far enough off deadline, it's okay.
I'm just out to confirm Sharon Welch's presence at the
workshop. Gina shows me; I note it, go back to my chair
and sit down hard. Across the way, Matt is typing away
on our piece, pulled up on his screen. As it turns out, I'm
glad he's there — working, driving. For the moment, I
cannot.

"How's the story?" Tom's voice behind me.

"Prince Charming's got it."

"I'd better take a look." He sighs.

"Not a bad idea."

"Meant it about dinner." Tom leans close. "We'll celebrate."

He moves in Matt's direction. I feel tears forming
behind my eyes. They think it's all tied up. Maybe it is.
Tom wants to celebrate, maybe we should. I don't know
why I can't feel everyone's relief. What's wrong with me?
I won't, can't spoil it, this high Metro mood; this dinner
tonight.

Damn it.

Two more calls to make. The two numbers from my
father's notepad in the Marlowe. I wait till after five. In
the rush of deadline, I haven't tried these numbers after
that hour, only during the day. One more try, once again.
I dial the first, hear the call go through, count fifteen

rings, twenty rings. I'm about to hang up when someone answers. Female voice, unfamiliar. "Susanna House."

I stare at the phone. Susanna House clicks off; maybe a volunteer, a resident.

For another moment I just look at the phone. Then I dial again, the second number this time. I count four rings, five, ten. Again I am about to hang up. And then, on the eleventh ring, there's an answer. A familiar voice, this time, slightly out of breath.

I hesitate. "Zoe Heywood?"

"Speaking." Must be her private line upstairs. I give my name, the paper's name — she remembers, remarks on the day we've had. Cutting her off, sounding cryptic, I talk low. "Zoe, look, no alarm. Just a caution, be careful, okay?"

An odd pause. "Okay," she says. No questions.

"Okay," I echo. Another brief pause. An uneasy one. We hang up.

·

IN THE women's room, I splash water on my face. I glance in the mirror. My suit looks bloodstained. My face looks pale, strained. Glimmering in my eyes are tears I've been holding back for two days.

Way to go...

For a moment I hear the nightmare voices again, see the dream: the man lying in the street, the man with blood on his chest. The man with my father's face.

Way to go, Nan ...

Tears in my eyes. Blood on my suit.

My blood, given for you ...

I turn from the mirror.

Be a pro...

Swallow tears.

Think back on all the tales …
Almost deadline.
That you remember … of Camelot …
Almost time to go home.
Hold it together.
Dinner, celebration.
Way to go.

■

<16>

O START with, this evening ... may I recommend ..."
The waiter, in black tie, speaks softly. "The poached
asparagus in basil butter ..."

Tom and I sit on a plush banquette behind a perfect
table.

"Or perhaps the medallion of gingered salmon ..." We
listen to a series of bulletins that sound nothing like
news, nothing like murder, nothing like Metro — nothing
like anything we've heard this past week.

"Also a chilled melon soup with creme fraiche ..." We
are sitting in a dusky, elegant restaurant. The colors are
muted, gentle sea greens. The lighting is subtle, con-
cealed. A garden-like space appears to float along one
wall — slim trees, flowering shrubs, bending palms, and
from somewhere, the faintest splash of a waterfall. We
sit, it seems, in some moonlit realm, remote and silvery as
an enchanted forest. Voices are low. Steps are silent. We
are together, held by quiet magic, as if airlifted from our
normal terrain.

But for moments here and there, that terrain breaks through, if only to me. Suddenly I see again my image in the newsroom's mirror, stained, stressed. To erase it, I glance down at my black cocktail dress: low cut, almost baring my shoulders. Different image. Different reflection.

It is a reflection that shows in Tom's eyes. He has never seen me like this and does not make games of hiding his reaction. Nor have I ever seen him in this handsome suit, this finely cut shirt. We are like two kids on a first date, stealing looks at each other — and yet my mind jumps backward. Today. Yesterday. The past three days. To information, old and new, and to that night of discovery at the Marlowe Hotel. This restaurant, this enchanted realm, also happens to be in a hotel; not the Marlowe, I remind myself. Absurdly, I feel tears gather again behind my eyes.

"And for the entree, may I recommend ..." I finish a glass of very good, very chilled wine. "The rockfish with cream ..." My glass is quietly refilled. The tenderloin of lamb with madeira ..." The waterfall murmurs; the palms bend and whisper. "The warmed salad with feta cheese ..."

I finish another glass of wine. Our dinner arrives in discreet stages. The garden floats, silvery, before us. Under the table, Tom turns my hand in his. The spell of the enchantment grows stronger.

"We should make a point of doing this," Tom says. Tomorrow night."

"And the next, and the next ..."

"I could acclimate."

"So could I." His eyes are serious.

We have promised not to talk shop. We talk, instead, of many things, and amid the palms, behind the gracious table, within the dusky, gentle realm, we talk of books. Obscure books we both have read and loved. Old dogs we have owned and lost. Music we drive with and read with and fall asleep with; much, the same. We speak of light-houses, which we both love. Between us we know all the working lights in the country, and don't know why we know.

And, over coffee, we talk about lakes. The cold clean Maine lakes that filled my summers and chilled me into swimming, as a child. The New England lakes that filled Tom's sight as a boy, as a young man, and still adorn his desk. He talks of those lakes as refuge from his father's alcoholism, from his family's conspiracy to cover it up. Tom used to row out to a lake's center and sit there in his dinghy for hours, books and apple cores piled around him — he was often alone, preferring that. The person closest to him was his grandmother, Elizabeth Nichols, strong-spined matriarch, who understood her quiet grandson.

"She'd come out in the boat with me sometimes. Sometimes we'd talk, sometimes I'd watch her fish. At eighty, the year before she died, she was still catching bass. One time I sat scribbling some description of her, the way she looked. Big hat. Straight back. Cigarette. Fishing rod. She reached over and impaled my paper on the rod. She read what I'd written. And told me to keep writing.

Everyone wanted me to be an architect like my father. Not Gram. When I decided on journalism school, her gift to me was tuition. And later, in her will, her house — by that lake." He pauses, thinking. "I dream of living by water again," he says. "I'd love to run a small paper — obscure, unimportant. In some obscure, unimportant New England town. Near a lake. And probably never will. But I keep the photos up to remind me: 'They abide.' My grandmother's phrase for certain things. Lakes. Hills. Some hymns. Some faces. Stars. Deep love. And for her, rocking chairs."

I smile. "They do abide, those things. I like that word;
it's old and strong and right."

Tom smiles at me. "What abides for you?"

I pause, thinking, letting the wine and the enchantment float me the rest of the way out. It isn't far, it's easy
now.

"Lakes — for me too. Books. Churches. Certain kinds
of hands, work-worn, weathered, old. Words. Light-
houses. And when I was growing up — there was another
kind of lighthouse, for me." I pause; haven't told this
before. "This lighthouse was really a hotel, of all places.
A grand hotel in New York City."

Tom nods.

Suddenly I feel shy, shy as the girl I was there. "When
I was fifteen and sixteen and seventeen I used to sit in
that hotel lobby and look into the Palm Court. I'd stand
behind one of the columns sometimes and listen to the
music. In the evenings I'd watch the candlelight on the
tables. Most of all I'd watch the women going in. Women
laughing. Beautiful women, I thought, in such beautiful
dresses, with men who were in love with them — I was
sure. I used to wonder if I would ever be one of those
women, beyond the palms."

"And were you?" Tom touches my face. "Did you ever
go back?"

"You know, I never did. I covered a story there once,
some freelance magazine thing. I stood behind that same
column, those same palms — taking notes."

Tom looks at the foliage before us, then back at me. I
think you're there tonight," he says quietly. "You've gone
beyond the palms, to the table that's been waiting." He
takes my hand. "The beautiful woman in the beautiful
dress. With a man who's in love with her."

"Tom ..." Under the table, our fingers twine and turn.
Maybe it's the way he has touched the fragile body of that

dream. Maybe it's the enchanted place, or maybe it's the wine, or something more; something I can't yet say. But, against all my rules, all my upbringing — there in the dusky restaurant, I brush Tom's lips with mine; light, lingering, and for a moment, bolder. Then, remembering myself, I draw back a little, but Tom's eyes hold me; his hand tilts my face toward his again.

"Excuse me ... may I offer something more?" The waiter, discreet, gaze lowered.

Tom looks at me. I don't have to speak. The check is requested. And I am still with Tom, beyond the palms, as the check comes and goes, and we move through the en-chanted restaurant.

•

ABRUPTLY, OUTSIDE in the lobby, cameras, press, people. Our Trends reporter, Gina, and Sam taking photographs, and just beyond, through arched doors, a cocktail reception. At first I am able to stay within the magical isle and see it all as if through some invisible screen. If we can just float past it, and keep on floating, I feel the spell will hold.

But then I see a sign that reads Reception: National Humanitarian Awards. I glimpse a face, a figure, that snaps the spell — Tom sees it too. We both see my father, in profile, in conversation; we see him at the same time. And abruptly it is all rushing back, all crowding forward — all that I've held within, these past three days. Rewind. Fast-forward. Freeze-frame. Play ... I can't seem to breathe.

I start through the lobby, almost running; I sway. Tom's hand is at my back, steadying me, and he is with me as I move toward the main doors, and outside in the air, at last, he is finding me a place to sit — a bus stop, a bench: I feel its roughness under my hands. Knees weak, I sit; it's still hard to breathe.

Tom bends over me. "Your father ..."

Tears behind my eyes. "Not just my father ..." I manage. "Oh God, Tom — I don't even know what I'm thinking anymore. I don't know what's true, what's not, I'm afraid he's — "

I can't say it. I can't do anything but break more rules. No shock, no tears, but I am shocked and it is showing and now tears are streaming down my face. I am sitting at this bus stop crying in front of strangers. I am crying in front of my editor, after all, who could turn professional, who could make me take a rest from this story. Who could make me take a rest from all stories, period.

But who is also Tom. "It's all right," he's saying, quiet, steady, drawing me from the bench now. And we are walking, my face streaming, and all I can think is how awful, the evening ruined — "All right, darlin'," he says again, his arm around me, and we are at his car.

•

BY THE time we've reached Tom's apartment, I've soaked his handkerchief; I've cried myself out. Still shaky, I start to apologize. He takes my hands, very firmly, in his. "Stop."

"I don't know ..." My voice trembles.

"Tell me ..." He smooths my hair.

We are sitting on his couch. Dimly, I am aware of a dusty wall behind us, and clutter: piles of books, magazines, unhung pictures, boxes of more books, never unpacked. His apartment looks vaguely like his desk. Obscurely, this helps. I take a breath. And tell him. All of it: from the first sense of pursuit, to the Marlowe

Hotel; from the hang-up calls, to Sharon Welch. Every fear, every suspicion. Hearing them aloud, in my own voice, in words, in sentences — this seems to sap some of the fear, some of the power. The crying has lightened me; the telling lightens me more, though nothing has changed. My voice, starting shaky, steadies now; as steady as Tom's eyes on me. "No wonder," he says, at last. "Look at it one way, it's almost the worst nightmare. Yours. Mine, too — once."

He knows, really knows, I can see.

"I used to be afraid," he says quietly, "Afraid every time someone was killed by a drunk driver. Afraid my dad was the drunk. And — one time he was. Got it hushed up, paid off, bad stuff." Tom's jaw tightens, remembering. "And finally he was the driver again. And the victim." He looks at me. "That nightmare. I know how it looks."

"I should have realized ..." I lean my forehead against his. "I haven't talked about my father to anyone in fourteen years — until you, until a few nights ago. I never thought anyone would know ..."

"I was the same, kept it in ..." He tips my face back so I can see his eyes. "If it really is the nightmare, Nan ... and I won't brush that off, it's possible ... I'm with you ..."

I take his hand. "Tom. Should I quit the story?"

"No. It's yours. And I know you can tell it — however it plays out. You can tell it like no one else."

I feel lighter still; light enough, almost, to smile, and that amazes me, this night of tears. Tom sees the smile's beginnings, traces it with his finger.

"What about — " I have to ask. "The police?"

He pauses, thinking. "Let's hold off another day or so. See what comes from Dade. We'll watch it ... together ... okay?"

Again I nod, relieved. I can breathe. "Is there ... another angle on this story?" I ask then. "One I'm missing?"

"Yeah ..." He pauses, thinking it through. "Another angle — same facts. Okay. Prominent man comes to town alone. Wife dead, daughter estranged. He's lonely, wants to catch a glimpse of his child. Watches — from afar. Wants to talk to her — loses his nerve whenever he tries. Even gets the number of a shelter where he's seen her, where she seems connected. Still, he can't quite speak to her, maybe afraid. He clips her stories — after all, she's his kid. He happens to hit town just as this serial killing starts — coincidence.

Like thousands of men, he owns a sturdy umbrella. Like thousands of well-to-do travelers, he stays at the Marlowe. Happens to know Sharon Welch, she was at one of his workshops. He knows hundreds of other people too, from clinic workshops — they're alive. No motive for him to murder Sharon — tactical error, in fact, since her husband's chairman of this big awards committee. But to the daughter, he looks suspicious: the following, the lurking, the calls. Because she knows him, knows him as no one else does. Knows the rages, the violence — sure, she sees it through that lens. And through that lens, it looks like a nightmare."

I feel the relief fizzing through me now, cautiously at first, but building, lighter — lifting me past this shadow. I let out a breath.

Tom smiles. "That angle play?"

I nod. "Like other stories: they talk themselves out."

His face is serious now. "Don't stop talking to me, Nan — please."

"I won't." My voice comes out a whisper.

"Need to know where you are."

"I'm here." I touch his chest.

He wraps me against him, and it is a while before we look at each other again. Slowly, then, I unknot his tie. He has always waited for me — to be ready, to let him know. This is the night of breaking rules and feeling freed.

For another moment he looks at me, questioning; deepening grays in his eyes. I kiss his eyes, and all their colors, and drop his tie to the floor. His mouth is on mine then, tender and sweet and deep; his hands on my bared shoulders, and softly, he slides my dress down till he can kiss between my breasts. I hear the whisper of silk as the dress slips off under his hands, and I feel his lips warm against my skin, against lace. His arm is under my knees then, and he is lifting me, carrying me to bed. Our mouths cling, even as he unbuttons his shirt, and then we are lying in each other's arms, pressing close, his fingers gentle and his body hard, and we are lost in this dance that is ours; ours alone. He whispers my name as he fills me, and we move into a dance that is new, that sweeps us, rocks us, bends us together, till there is nothing but this.

Later, we cannot sleep for the nearness of each other, and for the hold of gaze on gaze — strong and sweet as the dance. Tom runs his fingers down my cheek, across my lips.

"Nan — how I love you." His voice is rough from feeling it so strongly, from waiting so long to tell me, and after I tell him too, we do not speak anymore. We are lost in each other again, found in each other again, and we are a long time together in this deep lake; this lake beyond the palms.

■

<17>

B AD GIRL." A whisper through the phone. "Out all night. Again. Remember: you're watched."

I sigh. "I warned you before."

"This time ..." The whisper deepens. "Sex or violence?"

I glance across the newsroom at Tom. He is standing behind his desk, pencil in hand — looking at me. Our ability to concentrate this morning is definitely impaired. "Sidney," I say into the phone, "let's just say ... it wasn't violence."

Pause. I can almost hear her grin. "Glory be — I'm jazzed."

"I did come home to change; you'd left."

"Was getting worried about you, girl."

"You worry too much, Sidney Harris."

"Yeah, but I never do it alone."

A pause. "Hate to interfere with afterglow," she says then. "But I got some violence for you."

"What?"

"Uh-huh, something to worry about with me. I think you need to get your ass down to the D.C. Jail. Guess who the court's appointed me to defend?"

·

THE D.C. Jail, at the end of Massachusetts Avenue, is just beyond Congressional Cemetery. The gravestones, broken, askew, look like rotting teeth in this morning's light. I remember covering an escape through that graveyard, a few years ago — someone who made it past deadline.

I park behind the barbed wire, in view of the guard tower. Sid's got it all arranged. A metal gate hums and springs open. I step through, and instantly, it clangs shut behind me. Down an outside passage, at another door, I press a bell. Another humming, electrified door springs open, then slams at my back.

Inside the jail now, I pass through the metal detector. The clip on my press ID sets it off. A female guard looks at me appraisingly as I sign in.

"Know you fixed," she says. "But babe, I gotta shake you down anyway." I remember this from another story, another case. Obediently, I lift my hands over my head and let myself be frisked.

"What's that?" The guard nudges a knot on my thigh.

"A garter."

She looks up to see if I'm joking. I'm not. She feels the knot, recognizes the shape. For an instant, our eyes meet in silent laughter.

"Crime reporter wears garters?"

"Sometimes."

"Shines my day."

She buzzes me through. I think of the people I know who are in here somewhere, people whose stories are still

in my mind. One more humming door opens before me —
and there is Sidney, grinning, in a black suit. We go into
the small room where attorneys meet with clients.

"Got you a contact visit," she says.

"Thought that's just for lawyers, clergy."

Everyone else visits through Plexiglas, on phones.

"I'm a lawyer, remember? It's cool."

"It's an exclusive — thanks, Sid."

"We'll see. Good copy — or con."

Beyond us, somewhere, another door slams.

"Here he comes."

Frederick B. Dade is brought in by a guard who eyes
us, then leaves. Dade is cuffed. Tall, lean, he wears the
jail's standard uniform: a Day-Glo orange jumpsuit.
Orange, I recall, is for those awaiting trial; blue is for
those already sentenced. I take out my notebook. Suspicious, alert, wired tight, Dade squints at me as Sidney
explains who I am.

"You said no one would listen, Mr. Dade. She will."

His eyes are a watery blue; his face angular, sallow,
with a strong chin, good mouth — probably has a quick-
flash smile, as quick as his anger. I can smell his sweat,
I feel his anger rising from him now, like steam.

"Want my wife," he begins, voice already loud. "I keep
saying it, gonna go on saying it. Just come for my wife."

"She disappeared ... when was it?"

"Month gone now. Takes the kids, the baby — leaves
them at her mother's. And she's off for these shelters —
says she don't mean to come back." His hands open and
close; an eyelid twitches. My pen is moving as he stands,
then sits again, remembering where he is. "Ain't right."
A snarl. "Bible says a wife should cleave to her husband
— "

"Do you know why she left?"

He looks at Sidney; she nods. "I hit her, I did that —
we had our bad times, some, we both drinking. Some, just
me. I go off like that, time to time, always done. Hit her,
yeah — but that's between Johnice and me. She don't
press no charges, she just walks." Suddenly he's on his
feet, almost turning over his chair. He brings his face
close to mine. "Maybe I get pissed — maybe I hit her.
But that don't make me some fucking killer, you got
that?"

"Got it." I'm writing; I'm watching. I don't pull back
— it takes effort. Sidney has moved nearer.

"You said you were angry at the shelters? People
turning you away?"

He's on his feet again, hands clenched. "Goddam rat-
traps. Hellholes, what they are — I seen. Whores, scum,
crazies — I seen who's in them, too." Sweat beads his
forehead; the veins stand out in his neck. "Been to five,
six — can't find her, they took her, they got her — and
turn me away, those goddamn bitches. 'No men here.'
Well, fuck it to hell — I see them let in other men."

Maybe he saw Dr. Heller? I keep writing. "Anyone
turn you away at Susanna House?"

"Little snip — young enough to be my kid." He
describes the schoolgirl I met before dinner.

"Other shelters? Anyone else?"

"The nun, she was okay. The bitch who talked at the
cathedral — she was hard-assed, mean, treated me like
scum.

Sue Merino, I write in the margin. Interesting.
Haven Place hasn't come up before, not even in the police
report. As I turn a fresh page, Dade suddenly lunges
toward me, his hands gripping my chair. Sidney's right
behind him. I look steadily at him, ignoring the race of
my pulse.

"You put this in the paper, Miss. I may be nobody, but I got a right to my wife. I got a right to be mad as hell. And that don't make me no killer. Shit — I hit my wife, well, I ain't the only one hits, gets mad. I seen that tall bitch, the one with the gray hair — seen her tongue-lash a girl, slap her, too."

"The tall woman, with gray hair?"

"Yeah — bitch that runs Susanna House."

"Can you describe the girl you saw with her?"

"Girl who worked at Mount Olivet. Small. Long reddish hair, pretty thing. Seen them right outside the door."

"Can you remember anything else about the girl?" "Blue raincoat."

Meredith Crane. "Do you remember when this was?"

"Two Mondays gone." A week before she was killed.

"I just want my wife back." His eyes fill now. "Someone posted bond for me, I'll be out, I'll look for her — but I won't never find her, not alone."

"I'll help you," I tell him.

"Why?" He eyes me, wary now; no tears.

"For the story, at least."

"I got a picture of her."

"Who posted your bond?" I look at him.

"Dunno." He shrugs.

"Anonymous," Sidney says. "I'm checking."

"Johnice," he's saying now. "She got this beautiful hair, she could sit on ..." He wipes his eyes. "We have our bad times but damn, they got no call to keep her from me."

The door opens, a guard appears.

"Black hair, blue eyes ..."

The door slams shut behind him.

■

<18>

BLACK HAIR, blue eyes ..."

"Uh-uh — not her." The photo passes from hand to hand. Heads shake, slowly, one by one.

I am showing the photo of Johnice Dade at the Eighth Street Shelter, about eight-thirty that night. Earlier this evening, and this afternoon, I've shown the picture at other shelters. Two women from Mount Olivet remember Johnice, two weeks back. Joan Kelly remembers her, briefly, at Mount Olivet. Zoe Heywood does not recall her. In passing, I asked Zoe about some disagreement with Meredith Crane. For an instant, on the phone, Zoe's voice grew distanced, wary. She vaguely remembered something; something small, unimportant. As to Johnice Dade — not a word.

I am still hoping for some word, some lead, tonight at this shelter. Soon I'll leave to meet Tom for a late dinner. He is still at the office. We took a rather long lunch: carryout, in a park, where we could have a few minutes' privacy. The minutes became more than a few. We are still wrapped together, no matter how we move from desk to phone, newsroom to jail to shelters. We have both found this day longer than any other. I call Tom from the shelter's kitchen. An hour more, I tell him. Not so long now.

As I hang up, Ola Harris smiles at me. Sidney's mother, she's known me for years. The mother of daughters, she recognizes the look on my face and beams. I sit with her some moments at the big round table, clean as everything else Ola touches. You could eat off this floor, and her floor at home. Tall and strong, like Sidney, Ola's hair has just started to go gray. Last year she had to get bifocals; that ruffled her feathers, she said. I can still smell the fried chicken and collard greens she made for dinner here at the shelter — her chicken batter, a secret recipe: spicy, distinctive. Ola cooked up food for the shelter tonight to fill in for a neighbor with flu.

"Easy," she says. "I'm two blocks away."

"Sidney told me to keep an eye on you."

"Uppity child. You keep an eye on her."

"No problems here? Nothing unusual?"

"Nothing." Her voice is firm. "Not here."

Not Eighth Street. A community project in a black middle-class neighborhood, this night shelter is a source of pride to everyone involved. An abandoned brownstone, the house sleeps thirty women on two floors. Its volunteers are faithful, almost all from the neighborhood. Its director, the Reverend Carrie Corwin, is a wise, gifted deacon in the A.M.E. Zion Baptist Church. The shelter has a full-time social worker and a crack alarm system. No illusions here, but a proud answer from the black community to urban ills. Good copy: I intend to feature it, next chance I can, to offset the grimness elsewhere.

"You let me wrap up some chicken for you," Ola Harris is saying now. "Only Sidney's got that recipe."

A woman wanders in from upstairs. Ola gives her a tube of hand cream from the supply shelf and tilts the woman's face up as a mother would with a daughter. "Tears — what's that about?"

The woman, weeping, leans against Ola as I slip away. When I return Ola is rocking her like a child, the two of them swaying together in the middle of the kitchen floor. Ola lifts the woman's chin again. "Gonna make it?"

The woman nods. Ola rubs some cream into her hands. The woman smiles and moves back upstairs.

"You ever see this one?" I show her Johnice's photo. Ola looks at it a long time.

"She was probably bruised, beaten," I add.

"Like half of them." Ola shakes her head.

"Her name's Johnice Dade."

"I think she was here ... two, three weeks ago."

"And since?"

Ola shakes her head. So do I, and glance at my watch. Almost nine.

"Think I'll go upstairs, ask the women on the third floor."

"Good — they turn in early here. Specially up there, our older ladies, a day on the streets whips 'em good."

As I climb the stairs, I hear the kitchen door open. I pause. Another woman's voice mingles with Ola's, and somehow the voice is familiar: Zoe's. She says something about borrowing rolls for the morning, and Ola's saying something about extra chicken, and there is more talk in the kitchen as I go up to the third floor.

Upstairs again, the photo passes hand to hand. These women remember Johnice. Their time frame fits with Ola's. Johnice was here two, three nights. Bruised cheek, black eye, cried herself to sleep, and then — up and gone. No one's seen her since, not even on the streets. I am getting an uneasy feeling now and I am trying to ignore it.

The women try to remember more about Johnice; there isn't much. Southern twang. Talked about her kids. Said she was finished with men. All men. For good.

It tallies. I spend about a half hour getting general reaction to the serial killings. Some of the reactions are pungent, unprintable. Some, sadly resigned: "How it is." I take down some quotes, but the women are sleepy; I get ready to leave. Going down the stairs, I think of Tom; my step quickens. On the first floor, before I reach the kitchen, I stop at the bathroom. I want to brush my hair, spray on cologne.

I pause, knock at the door. No answer. Pushing the door open, I find the light is on, the bathroom is empty. I stand at the sink before the mirror. Behind me is a dripping sound, steady and strong. Sounds like a leak — bad news for a house of women with only two bathrooms. I glance at the ceiling, then back at the toilet. No sign of water. The sound continues, loud, insistent. I turn toward the bathtub: old-fashioned, claw-footed, curtained in clean white vinyl.

I pull back the curtain. My hand tightens on the vinyl. Dimly, I hear my bag hit the floor.

Ola Harris is lying on her back in the tub. She is surrounded by an inch of water. Her glasses, cracked, float by her left hand. Her head is tipped back and her temple shows a welt. On the soap-dish handle I see a smear of red. Ola's eyes are wide open, the pupils fixed and dilated. Her denim dress lies flat; no breathing moves the cloth. Jutting from her mouth is an umbrella's handle: clear lucite, spattered dark with blood.

■

<19>

T HE PICTURE. The headline. "Fourth Victim ..." The story. "Ola Harris, 55, was found . . ." Front pages flash‑ing, flashing .. .

I am standing in the newspaper's pressroom, amid the unbearable clatter, amid the smells of oil and ink, and I am watching the presses run tonight. For a minute. A few minutes. Several minutes. The noise is deafening, and still I stand here watching her face flash before me — again, again, again — with the headline, the story. I cannot leave until this registers. Until I can believe this happened. Really happened. Just hours ago.

·

JUST HOURS before, flat‑calm, on automatic, I was di‑aling the rescue squad, the police. I was dialing Sidney at home, taking a breath, and saying those terrible words. I was dialing Tom at the paper and saying those words again. And then I was going upstairs to the women, to

say it all again. I was on the second floor when I heard
the sirens.

Just hours before.

Hours. I was standing there still calm, on automatic,
as chaos broke loose at Eighth Street. Paramedics.
Police. Hysterical women pouring down the stairs. Press.
Lights. Network trucks. This time I was caught right at
the center of it, not reporting from the edges. This time
I was inside from the start, answering questions from
press, police. And all the while, behind me, Ola Harris
was lying dead in that bathtub. All the while, I ached
with Sidney. All the while, I wanted Tom.

All the while, I could hear my voice, steady and even:
No, I hadn't heard anything; no one had. Yes, I'd left Ola
in the kitchen. No, she hadn't been alone.

Zoe herself confirmed that she'd been there to pick up
chicken for Susanna's, and stayed about ten minutes.
Now she took no more questions: she was needed upstairs,
in this shelter. The press was herded out. The police, all
over the kitchen and bathroom, went to work. On the
bathroom floor beside the tub's far end, they found a
wrench and a washer. Ola Harris, apparently, had been
trying to fix the leak when she'd been seized from behind.
Her temple had been slammed against the ceramic soap
dish. She had been laid in the tub. Her head had been
jerked back, the umbrella thrust down throat, windpipe,
and thorax. There were no signs of break-in or struggle.
The kitchen door was unlocked. Zoe said she thought
she'd heard it click locked behind her as she'd left.
Perhaps Ola had opened it again — to her assailant.
Nothing more could be determined then, in any case: not
till crime lab and coroner's reports, and leaks.

I called Tom. There was a long pause. And then we
were moving, by reflex. I dictated the story to a copy aide;
it would make the late city editions. Over my desk, I

knew, was a large snapshot of Ola with me and Sidney. I told Tom to have it cropped so Ola's picture could run with the piece. Tomorrow we would do follow-up, more coverage. Meanwhile, how calm my voice sounded, how fluid the dictated phrases. How terrible the words. Unspeakable. And yet — I was speaking them, in complete English sentences. Lead. Body copy. Ending. Pause.

"Nan. You okay?" Tom, back on the line.

"For now. Back soon."

"I'll be right here."

And then Jed Jackson was beside me, and the crime lab men were packing up, and outside, the networks' lights were trained on the shelter, and upstairs the women were crying. Jed and I looked at each other. A long look. For the first time, at a scene like this, we didn't say anything. We watched as Ola was laid on a gurney and covered well. We watched the gurney roll through the kitchen — the kitchen, still redolent with spicy fried chicken. We watched as the gurney rolled through the back door into the glare of all those TV lights.

Suddenly, there was Sidney, with her sister — I got Jed to slip them into the M.E.'s van, out of camera range. For a minute I climbed in with them. In five years, I'd never seen Sid cry. Her tears wet my blouse as I held her. Her tears streamed down her own blouse as she lifted the sheet from her mother's face.

In the end, I left Sid and her sister there, alone with Ola. In the end, they needed that time. I stood in the street and watched the van move slowly away. I watched the TV lights fade and the squad cars vanish. For some moments, I just stood there in the dim street. From somewhere, a bottle rolled on the cement. Newspapers blew, and scattered, and settled. My eyes filled. I closed my notebook and walked toward my car.

It was only then that I saw the man across the street. My hand was on the car door. I felt his gaze before I lifted my head. He was standing on the edge of a vacant lot, by a dark house. My hand tightened around my keys. Suddenly, recklessly angry, I stepped out into the street. The figure moved, began to dodge away. I moved after it. The man darted down the sidewalk, where he was caught in the quick spill of light from a street lamp. I saw a blue windbreaker, a tall lean form.

Starting to run, I called out. He did not turn, did not stop — only rounded a corner and was gone. I stood, breathless, on the dark street, alone again. I stood and watched torn newspapers blow past Ola's shelter.

●

NOW, AS I watch Ola's face smile up at me again, again, again, from the front page on the presses, I think of that. That last glimpse. I don't remember driving back to the paper at all. I don't remember coming up in the elevator. I do remember that Tom was with the night editor when I came in. I walked to my desk and saw the snapshot missing. A faint pale square was on the corkboard, where the photo had been. I called Sidney's sister: Their huge extended family was gathering. The pastor was there. Sid would stay the night; they'd take Mama down to Georgia next day, where her people were buried. Sidney had stopped crying. I had not begun. I still couldn't believe it.

And so I've come here. Here to the pressroom, to convince myself that this really happened. To watch page one run past over and over, until I can believe the words I wrote.

Now I feel hands on my shoulders: Tom's hands. I feel his cheek against mine. He turns me around, looks into my face.

"Long enough?"

I nod. I know he doesn't mean the story. "I'll take you home."

•

MY HOUSE seems oddly quiet as we go in. I turn on lights, as I have done a thousand times before. There doesn't seem enough lights to turn on. Without speaking, we climb the stairs, past my floor to Sidney's. She has left on a lamp; her garret is caught in an amber glow. Over her desk, the photos catch our eyes. Her sister. Her brother. Cousins. Me. And her mother. Three of us, one blown up large.

"She'd come over here and cook ..." I can see her.

"I remember." We'd had dinner, the four of us. "She took me off in the kitchen once," Tom says. "Told me not to let you get away. Wrapped up some chicken for me ..." His face is grim.

"She wrapped some up tonight. For us."

For a moment, we say nothing.

"You know, Tom ... sometimes I don't like what we do."

"I was thinking that too."

"I wanted to be with Sid. And there I was calling in the story..."

"And I wanted to be with you. And when you walked in, I was caught in editor bullshit."

"I was fielding these questions, making these calls, reporting in ... and all the while, I was hurting for Sidney. Wanting you."

Tom's arms tighten around me. "God, you were two floors above that killer. Someone who likes risks, apparently, maybe gets off on them, I don't know, Jesus. I almost said `Screw it,' and went down there, myself. In the end — I was setting up the damn story."

I decide not to mention my encounter afterwards. "Sid came down," I say instead. "The networks were ready to jump on her. I got Jed to take her into the van."

"Jed must be taking heat."

"The department's got undercover guys out."

"I guess they can't watch all the shelters."

"Not all at once."

"How was Sidney?"

"Tom, I've never seen her cry, but she looked at Ola and — " And now, finally, my own eyes fill, I am weeping against Tom's shoulder and he is holding me, rocking me against him, and after I've quieted, he holds me still. Finally, we go downstairs. We leave a light burning in Sidney's room.

There is cold chicken in the refrigerator: Sid's. It seems right, somehow, to have a meal for her, for Ola, and to talk of them, there at the kitchen table, where the four of us have sat, and talked, and laughed. Tom and I remember — good things, funny things, and we don't laugh tonight, but it's better: better together.

Until, out of habit, we turn on the eleven o'clock news. There it is: lead story. Unreeling again: the shelter, the women, the police. A close-up of Jed Jackson's face. And mine. And then, that covered body, rolling out the door.

I jab the television. The screen goes dark.

■

<20>

THE SCREEN lights up. A glowing rib cage appears.
A torso seems to hang in the dark. Down its center, a
long shaft — not bone. Underneath, in small neat letters:
Crane, M.

I am sitting in Police Headquarters on Indiana Avenue, known on my beat as "The Cop Shop"; I am sitting in
a dim room on the second floor with two detectives,
staring at a light box on the wall. One by one, X rays of
four victims are slapped up on it: X rays, courtesy of the
M.E., "authorized," Jed has told me. I don't know why,
but apparently, this is the Department's answer to my
question, "Where are you with this now?" I hadn't
expected such a detailed response.

"Clear down," Jed is saying. "Like a sword swallower."

An assistant slaps the next X ray up beside the first.
On the table before us, our white Styrofoam cups shimmer
in the eerie light.

A smaller rib cage, glowing now before us. Lesions on
some ribs, where they were broken. The long shaft here

on an angle. Beneath, precisely lettered: Sullivan, J.

"You can see the mass, center left. The heart. And the penetration," Jed is saying.

"Not as clean," Frank LaMarca comments, to my left. "Smaller woman — smaller space, that car."

He sips his coffee. To my right, Jefferson drains his. Mine remains untouched. I am wondering if they want to shock me. I spoon powdered synthetic cream into my coffee, stir, glance away; drink.

The assistant slaps up the next two X rays. Only the one marked Welch is not bisected by a shaft. Forcing myself, I look from Welch to Harris.

"Straight shot," says LaMarca.

I can hear him munching on a doughnut.

"Well — what've we got?" I ask again. We stare, transfixed by the glowing torsos.

"We've got ..." Jed says, then. "Four women. All shelter volunteers, part time. All killed the same way. All killed within a two-week period. All killed within twenty-four hours of working at shelters. Different-aged women, different types. Killed different locations, times of day."

I glance at the lit bones. "Could this last one be a copycat killing?"

"Could be," Jed says.

"Fred Dade?"

"We're watching him."

"He's got motive," I add.

"He's got to do more than tail you."

The assistant takes down the X rays.

"Other suspects?" I ask. Behind us a projector hums.

"Some old. One new." An assistant pulls a screen down before the box. "Hit it," says Jed. Faces of suspects flash on the screen. Terrence Heller. Joan Kelly of Mount Olivet. Frederick B. Dade.

"Anything new on them?"

Jed taps an unlit cigarette against the table. "Not on Kelly, we've been watching her." He glances up at the psychiatrist. "The shrink still bugs me. At two shelters right before two murders: Crane and Sullivan. Weak alibis, at home alone both times. He rotates, has access, and . . ." Jed lights the cigarette. "I got this theory the victims knew their killer. There's never been signs of struggle, there's been doors, windows open, it's gotta be someone they knew. Just can't pin anything on this shrink."

Another face comes up on the screen. A striking face. High cheekbones. Long, curling gray hair.

"Zoe Heywood?" I stare at Jed.

"Yeah — Mother Teresa." He drags on his cigarette.

"Why?" I try not to sound shocked, and fail.

"Last one with Harris. First one back on the scene."

"Only her word that the door was locked," says LaMarca.

"The women phoned her to come back," I snap back.

A pause. "No one remembers doing that, now."

"They were upset," I resist. "They forgot."

"She's not exempt, y'know." Frank LaMarca looks at me.

"But Zoe ..." I'm not being objective, I know.

"We hear she's been different lately ..." Jed says.

I study her face and sip the terrible coffee.

" ... angry, uptight."

"She knew all the victims," Frank adds.

"And she's right inside that world," says Jed.

"I don't believe this — " I break off.

Now, on the screen, slides of the weapons.

I feel an inner jolt. "Quite a show."

"We also tap-dance." Frank LaMarca whistles "Singin' in the Rain." Jed silences him with one swift look.

"You don't have to impress me," I tell them.

"Yeah we do," Jed says. "We're taking a lot of flack —
mayor, chief, community. Why haven't we cracked this?'
We need the press — we're doing all we can. Top forensic
work. Extra people on the case. Undercover cops spot-
checking shelters ..." No one mentions the gap at Eighth
Street last night.

The weapons, now in close-up, flash on the screen.
Umbrella #1, Crane: Bloody yellow nylon, steel tip.
"Woman's umbrella — but hers." Jed smokes.

Umbrella #2, Sullivan: Black nylon, blood less visible.

Umbrella #3, Welch: Burgundy — no blood visible.

Umbrella #4, Harris: Black: handle bloody, as I saw it.
I take a cigarette from Jed and inhale deep. "Again," says
LaMarca.

"Either."

"Get this about the umbrellas," Jed glances at me. I
lift my pen. "No prints; killer wore gloves. All steel tipped.
And — all expensive."

Through a haze of smoke, I see: they are. Not K-Mart
specials. Top-of-the-line articles, from good stores.
"Which means?" I look at Jed. "Killer has money?"

"Could be. Or expensive tastes."

"Rules out Dade?"

"Not for sure. He could have a bundle in cash —
stolen, buried."

Now, on the screen, the faces of the victims. The faces
caught in the bone-white flash of cameras. Dead faces.
Fixed eyes. Distorted mouths. Heads back. I see them
again, as I saw them first.

Four faces. Four women. Four captions. "And no
strong connection."

"Except the shelters." Jed crushes out his cigarette.

"And the shelters' women — they give you any ideas?"

"Naa — " Frank dismisses that. "Unreliable witnesses."

"I'm not so sure." I smoke, thinking.

•

"AIN'T SURE."

"God knows."

I am sitting with a group of homeless women, gathered around a fountain. It is hot. It is cloudless. It is about four in the afternoon, mid-June. We sit in front of the National Theater, downtown, on Pennsylvania Avenue. There is a small park here — mostly granite, with green benches wrapped around some trees. There is a huge map of the United States decorating the granite. A woman is standing in torn sneakers on the state of Florida. Someone's bags are parked on Idaho. Most of the women have their shoes off, their feet in the fountain. I take off my sandals and join them; take out my own pack of cigarettes and light up. I have definitely, seriously, started smoking again.

"Bum one?" It's Ma'am, from Susanna House.

"Sure." I slide the pack toward her.

"Hey — owe you." She grins in recognition. A blue haze soon surrounds the fountain. The water splashes, feels cool on our feet. Most of the women's feet are swollen from too much walking, too much standing, sleeping sitting up. I ask Ma'am what she thinks of all the deaths.

"Shit." She drags deep on her cigarette and thinks.

"Got everyone scared," a soft voice speaks from the folds of a blanket. It is Angel, tented in wool despite the heat, seated halfway around the fountain.

"Got everyone wired high," says Ma'am. "Even folks that don't mostly get wired."

"Like — "

"Like the folks running the shelters."

I look at her. "How's Zoe doing with it?"

"You know — ever since that Crane girl she's took it hard, I can tell," says Ma'am. "Always so even, easy — but right after that first one — she's wired too."

"Yeah," says Angel, moving her feet in the water. "That meeting, she flipped out."

"What meeting?" I wish I had my tape recorder.

"At Susanna's," says Ma'am. "Some volunteers — in the dining room after dinner one night. She gave 'em hell, yelling — "

"Zoe doesn't yell," Angel adds. "Not hardly."

"Did that night, Lordamercy."

"Who was there?" I ask, trying to sound neutral.

"Couple young girls — didn't know them. And Ola Harris — we all knew Ola, she helped out sometimes, Susanna's. There was that nun. And the congressman's wife, she was on the news, TV."

I feel my pulse pick up. "Three of the victims?"

"Yeah .. and two that wasn't."

"Did you hear what upset Zoe?"

"They did. She was hollering at them — really lost it."

I study Ma'am. "You're sure."

"Sure I'm sure."   She jerks her head toward Angel.

"I heard it too," Angel says, low.

"Things getting ugly," someone else says now.

"Where are you from?" I ask. I look at a young woman about seven months pregnant, with sores on her feet and cornrows in her hair.

"Haven Place." The woman's voice is soft and clear. "Heard someone ream out Sharon, really give her hell, last day she was there, it was in the kitchen." Her eyes fill. "Loved Sharon, mean to name this baby for her."

"Did you see who was in the kitchen with her?"

"Tall lady. Long gray hair. Looked like a movie star."

I say nothing, just sit and smoke. Around us, the traffic roars. Heat rises in ripples from the map of America. Grit blows in our faces as we squint and rest and think. Suddenly, in the fountain, my feet feel chilled. This morning's faces flash before me.

The last one is Zoe's.

■

<21>

THE HEADY scent of flowers drenches her rooms; waxy white freesia float above brass bowls and crystal vases. "Surprised?" Zoe looks at me.

Of course. I don't pretend. We are on the third floor of Susanna House, in Zoe's private quarters. I'd expected something Spartan, monastic — not this oasis of luxury and style. Here are fine English Regency pieces; family pieces, no doubt. An antique armoire. Turkish rugs. A Chippendale secretary laden with papers, journals. On a low table, in heirloom silver frames, a collection of small photographs — one of a debutante in pearls and white dress, her face unmistakably Zoe's. And everywhere the deep white aroma of freesia.

"It's a shock, sometimes, to guests," she is saying now. "Actually, though, if you can't create some island of escape, you just can't last in this work. The burnout rate's damn high..."

I study her a moment. At another time in my life, a woman like this would have made me wistful, envious.

She has style and she has mission. She has beauty and privilege, and also a ministry that shapes her life. And she has something else moving just beneath the surface of that life — something I cannot yet define, but do not envy, do not wish for myself at all.

"You really must take measures ..." she's saying. "I mean, to keep balance." She is the kind of girl I studied once: the artless grace, the courage to live exactly as she does, look exactly as she pleases. I was not that kind of girl, and I suspect she always was. I remember when, at twelve, thirteen, my hair started to turn reddish, then redder still, I bought black dye and covered it over for years. The color, I believed, was odd and had to be repressed. It took a long time before I could let my hair go natural: curly, auburn, free. Zoe, with her cloud of hair around her, couldn't have ever felt that way about herself. And yet, again, I sense something hidden about her, something held back; and again it eludes me.

"An oasis of some kind, it's necessary," she's saying now, and I bring myself back to her words.

"I remember hearing that ten years ago — from a very sensible nun," I tell her. I'd also known others, idealistic and driven, who'd lived on-site, worked constantly, and run dry fast.

"Then you understand," Zoe. says. "Most don't, and somehow you can't quite explain . . ."

I wonder why she's explaining quite this much. In fact, I wonder why she's allowed me to see this space, which could present the wrong image. She suggested it, though, when I called for another interview; another chance, too, as undercover volunteer. I am here on a Tuesday, when Susanna's doesn't close during the day. Instead, once a week the shelter becomes a center for services difficult to arrange at night: job and legal counseling, nursing and psychiatric care. This is also Dr.

Heller's day here — another reason for my presence. I think of all that activity below this perfect stillness, this cloud of fragrance. I glance at a pile of clothes over a chair: expensive silk dresses, silk shirts. For a moment I hear Jed Jackson's voice, underlining: expensive umbrellas. And my own — Meaning? The killer has money? I shut off the voices in my head so I can listen to Zoe's. She has caught my glance at the clothes.

"Next stop, for me, the cleaner's." She watches my gaze brush the designer labels. "So many speaking engagements, these days. I want to access funds from the private sector, I find it's important to look right. I'm in this rather unique position, with a foot in two worlds ..."

"Kind of like Sharon Welch." My tone is casual.

"A bit, though she was just starting ..." Zoe curls up on the couch, feet tucked under her. "A terrible loss," she adds quietly.

"And yet — you had some conflict with her."

Zoe watches me again. She does not move, but almost imperceptibly, the curl becomes a coil. "Conflict?" Her voice is even.

"A dispute, her last day at her shelter? In the kitchen?"

The coil becomes just slightly tighter; the eyes more wary. "Ah yes ... just a difference of opinion, really, over procedure. Rather mild, actually, nothing I'd call conflict. Her voice is smooth, wry. "Apparently someone else did."

A probe. I avoid it. The silence tightens.

"Wasn't there also some conflict at a meeting? Here at Susanna's, shortly after Meredith Crane's death? A heated dispute, one evening. Four, five women — "

A pause. Zoe shifts position very slowly. Her eyes remain on me. Again I smell the freesia. Over Zoe's shoulder, I glimpse the debutante photo. "There was a meeting here, yes." Zoe's voice still even. "A meeting about procedure, how to do things, train volunteers." Her tone does not change; her gaze sharpens. "But there was no dispute, heated or otherwise, just a routine discussion." She cocks an eyebrow. "Better copy, the other way."

I ask who was there. She gives two names I don't know. And three I do — the names of three murder victims.

"Of course Meredith Crane wasn't there," I comment. "You said you recalled some dispute with her, before she died. You didn't mention it was on the steps of Mount Olivet — "

This time she cuts me off and rises abruptly. "I'm not certain what you're trying to establish." Her voice has an edge now. "As I told you, sometimes you have to be tough on young, green volunteers."

"Does `tough' mean — slapping them?"

Zoe looks at me. A strong, fixed look. And then she turns toward the door. "I really have to check on the house." Pointedly, she opens the door for me.

"Thanks for your time," I say. Her locks click behind us.

"Certainly." Her tone is ironic. She hands me a volunteer's broom and goes downstairs. The scent of freesia hangs, white and heavy, in the air.

•

I STAY ON the third floor, ostensibly to sweep. Instead, I prowl. I look at Zoe's door again, noting the two locks, both deadbolts. Past her door, down the hall, is another door, this one ajar. Moving closer, I see its hand-lettered sign: Dr. Terrence Heller. A wedge of light spills into the dim hall. Through the door's small opening, I see a slice of peeling wall, then a coatrack — and a black umbrella.

Reflex: slight jolt. The smell of freesia floats into the hallway. I knock and wait.

Silence. I push the door open. The room is empty; I slip in. It's a makeshift office, in what might have been a storage room: there are a great many empty, broad shelves. Arranged before them are some canvas chairs in a jarring yellow. A metal desk is neatly arranged with notebook, datebook, and a stack of cassettes. Floating above the precise piles and pages is an unlikely, unruly cloud of white freesia, anchored in a jar. Coincidence? I doubt it. More likely a gift.

Quickly I lean over the desk and flip open the date-book, scanning four specific pages — the dates of the murders. He's scheduled for Mount Olivet the night Meredith Crane died. On the dates of the other killings — canceled appointments. Names crossed off. I make a quick note on my own page. Now I scan his entire book, fast. A recurring name tugs my gaze: Zoe Heywood. Tuesdays and Fridays, eleven o'clock, every week, at the doctor's Watergate suite. I remember Heller's regular practice is there, in an office-apartment. I flip through the book. Zoe — seeing Heller. Not on shelter business, I'd guess; not at that location. There's a code after her name: W-111. Watergate appointments are all coded that way. Shelter appointments are coded with different initials: S-316 I guess is Susanna's, MO-205 Mount Olivet. I glance at the cassettes. They are marked only with the codes, for confidentiality. I leave the office before I'm tempted to take the one marked W-111.

Outside the door, broom in hand, I stand thinking. Now there's a whole new variety of possibilities. Foot-steps sound on the stairs. I am sweeping as Dr. Heller comes into view. Tall, lanky, tweedy, he is suddenly at my side. "Well — our new volunteer." He smiles broadly; too broadly.

I nod and go on sweeping.

"I do know who you are." Conspiratorial whisper.

"Oh?" I look up at him. "Who?"

"Nan Skillen, girl reporter."

Inner recoil. Vague smile. A mistake.

He moves in close. "I found out early."

"Oh, really?" I take a step back.

"Made it my business." He steps near.

"Did you?" I watch him, thinking.

"I was hoping to see you." Fast operator. "I mean," he says, "perhaps for a drink?"

Might be useful. Just a drink. "I'd like that."

"Wait right here." He strides into his office, returns with some freesia; presents them with a practiced flourish. The flowers' smell surrounds me as I move down the hall. I pause, listening. Heller's door is closed now; still, it's thin plywood. Through it I hear voices. No one has come up the stairs. I slip down the hall again and listen abashedly, outside his door. He's playing tapes, I realize, probably reviewing cases before he sees patients today. As I turn away I'm arrested by a voice: a voice ragged with tears. A familiar voice nonetheless. It speaks one broken sentence, played back over and over. In the dim hall I stand transfixed, listening. "Used me, hurt me . . . rammed it in my mouth ... again, again ..." The voice shreds away into sobs. There is a click. The whir of Rewind. The voice repeats. The tape rewinds. Quickly, quietly, I go downstairs.

.

DOWNSTAIRS, CLUSTERS of women waiting at well-marked doors. On the second floor is the nurse, the lawyer, and prenatal care. On the first, social services, job counseling, Housing Opportunities for Women. A low murmur drifts from the rooms, along with a pervasive scent. As I glance through doorways, I see sprays of freesia, in jelly jars, in juice bottles, in cans that read Blue Lake Green Beans. Like white lace, the flowers float in the rooms, over battered chairs, over bent heads. The freesia change the shelter in some indefinable way — their fragility, their perfume, their extravagant beauty. The way they shimmer, enchanted, whiter in the morning light.

I watch a woman carry a flower from the dining room into the front hall. She sits in the window seat, cupping the petals in her hand. I sit beside her and glance out. No vague male figure across the street, half hidden, today. Only one man in sight, hunched on the curb: at first glance a wino, in a torn T-shirt, with a bottle in a paper bag. At second glance I realize it's Frank LaMarca undercover, watching the shelter. His shoes are too shiny. I hide a smile.

The woman beside me is speaking of gardens; she had one, long ago. A squabble down the hall makes her pause. It subsides; it is easy, then, to turn the talk to other squabbles — a meeting, here, where voices were raised. The woman remembers it and remembers the raised voice as Zoe's. She is about to add something, when, looking out the window, she stiffens. In an instant the flower is left on the sill and she is wrenching the front door open.

Two women stagger in; between them, a third — a girl, maybe twelve, her face bruised and her arms limp, slung over their shoulders. Abruptly the front hall recedes; everything seems to narrow in around her. For a moment, the girl lifts her head. One eye is swollen shut; the right side of her face is beaten pulpy, purple-blue. Blood mats her hair and streams from her nose; a shard of bone spears through its bridge. Her head looks mashed in, lumpy, as the open eye roves, trying to focus; for an instant, as it meets mine, I feel an inner lurch. The white of her eye is brilliant red.

Without warning, the girl collapses on the floor. Her short, thin dress is torn at the shoulder. More bruises show there, and then her legs spread wide. I can see caked white streaks on them, and caked dirt — then blood pouring down between her thighs.

"Jesus God." The woman beside me is running for Zoe, and I am running for the phone, then outside for LaMarca. By the time I've returned, Zoe is holding the girl and the nurse is there, with LaMarca, his badge showing now. Blood keeps pouring from between the girl's legs, and nothing, no dishcloth, no towel, can stop it. LaMarca tries to ask questions. No one has many answers. Even the women who brought the girl know little.

"Found her — crawling up a street."

"Thought she was drunk."

"Runaway, been here two nights."

The girl on the floor starts to go into convulsions. Her back arches, her eye rolls back. Her body jerks, arches again. Urine spatters the floor now; more blood. Foam appears at her mouth, and then blood there, too. Her breathing comes rough, ragged, halting. All at once, in Zoe's arms, the girl goes limp; her breathing rasps, rattles — stops.

"Holy Christ." LaMarca grabs the girl, pushing on her chest, while the nurse tries to clear the windpipe. Sirens, now, outside. The nurse cannot clear the girl's throat; LaMarca's pressure only forces up blood. He pushes harder, as Zoe kneels beside him, holding the girl's head.

Boots are thudding through the door; paramedics crowd in. They lean to the girl as LaMarca steps back. I hear him say, "No vitals." Before the rescue squad can lift

her, Zoe is cradling the girl again — Zoe, on the floor,
freesia in her hair — that dead girl in her arms. Petals
falling on her shoulders; dark blood on her arms. Zoe
rocking, rocking with the girl. "It's all right," she's
crooning, she's keening. "It's all right, all right. You
won't remember in the morning."

.

ALL THE way back to the paper, I hear it. All right, all
right ... won't remember ... All the way through traffic,
it echoes. Used me ... hurt me ... again, again . . .

All through the day I hear that voice; that one voice,
I know now. I hear it as I sit by Tom's desk and tell him
the story — and later, as we argue, together and
separately, with the city editor, then with Gelson, Metro
chief. They want to bury the story someplace inside the
section — after all, it's some anonymous girl, routine
inner-city assault, news but not big news. Key point: no
relation to the serial killings.

"Doesn't that kid's story deserve to be read?"

"Hey — how it is." Gelson, thin, intense, raps it out.

"Which means? Welch sells papers, this kid doesn't?"

"That's right, and you know it, Nan — chill out."

I turn sharply, move back toward my desk. Behind me
I hear Tom starting to argue the case. His voice is
controlled, but very sharp and very dry and very New
England, and at first he seems to be winning. Then
Gelson hits low. "Tom, you got some needs here?"

"To get the right play, yes."

"To get your reporters on page one."

"That's not the point."

"Isn't it?" Gelson squints. "You'd do anything to start
winning prizes again, Tom."

"What are you saying?"

"Anything to be the star again. Know what I mean?"

Tom leans forward. "Do you?" His voice could slice wax.

I rise from my chair, turn, smoke, pace. A few minutes later I glance across the newsroom, toward the city desk. Tom, pacing and smoking, glances over at me. Suddenly, the mirror image makes us smile. We both know there is nothing we can do about this — except keep one promise we've made each other:

Once we leave tonight, we won't discuss it. At all.

■

<22>

Straight from the paper, I drive to Tom's. Waiting outside his apartment, I feel sticky, grubby, stained — as if I reeked of freesia and dried blood. The door opens and inside there is music and green rugs and Tom, in a clean shirt, lifting me into his arms. I feel dirtier still. I let him arrange the food while I take a quick shower — and try to let the whole damn day rinse off me.

My hair wet, my skin damp, I leave my clothes on a towel rack. Tom's blue windbreaker and shirt hang on the back of the bathroom door. I put on the shirt, button it minimally, and step back into the living room.

Tom is leaning over the long pine coffee table, lighting three candles all stuck in jelly jars. He turns, a candle in one hand. The light stays suspended there as he looks at me. I approach the table, where he has set out fast food burgers and fries on paper plates; Pepsi in paper cups. But the oat grass, in a vase on the table, does not in any way resemble freesia. "Beautiful," I murmur. I take a sip of my drink. Tom's eyes have not left me.

"Well," I joke, "and how was your day?"

"Relaxing ... peaceful."

I stare at him. He sounds serious. "Yeah, slow news day, here in New England," he continues. "Very small, manageable paper — got everything wrapped up by three. Came home, walked along the dunes, picked this grass for our table. Did a little writing, the poetry collection. Got some fresh crabs from the market and came back, waited for you. Out back. In the hammock."

"Oh God ... wish I'd been there ..."

"You were. You are."

"Ah." I connect. "Yes, well, I wrapped my profile on the lighthousekeeper. Left the paper at two. I picked up some berries for dinner. Took a swim in the lake — then I found you out here. In the hammock."

His fingers are in my wet hair. Our mouths touch and press, and he eases the shirt off me, I feel the cloth fall away. His hands move slowly down the length of my body; my skin is still damp. Lying on the deep rug, I undress him as he bends over me, his lips lingering on my breasts. We twine together, then, so lost in each other the rug might be a hammock, is a hammock, where we sway and rock and move — swept, tonight, in a feeling even more powerful than before, and we flow and turn, as if there is no closeness that is close enough. Tom leans back, the couch behind him, and draws me against his chest; I bury my face there, and brush with my mouth a line of soft hair. His hands cup me, lifting me down onto him, and we are caught up now in sweet fire, hot and deep and taking us deeper, past all we have known.

A breeze from the open window touches my back as his fingers trace my spine, and I rest against him; he against me. We breathe together, and stir together, and sense, still, that depth we reach only together — there are no

words for the strength of what we feel for each other
tonight.

Much later we take the dinner to bed with us, and
after a while, drift toward sleep in each other's arms.
Tom rests, his head against my breasts, and I hold him,
unable to sleep myself. I have never loved a man like
this; never let go with a man like this — never could,
never cared. Only Tom and his love have drawn me forth,
at last, from some far place — and with him it is right, it
is life; I feel peace. And still I cannot sleep. I hear the
sounds from the street and watch the play of headlights
on the wall. In these lights, suddenly, I see faces, flashing
in quick succession:

The bruised face framed by the door. The debutante's
face framed by silver. All the faces framed by the camera.
All the glowing torsos.

Shaking, I ease myself from Tom, from bed. I put on
his shirt again and stand, smoking, at the living-room
window. The shaking stops. But still the images flash, a
nightmare jumble now:

Meredith's young face on the old nun's body.

Ola's dark face on the congressman's wife.

The debutante in pearls convulsing in a shelter.

Zoe's elegant face on the bruised, raped runaway.

It's all right ... you won't remember ...

I press my fingers against my eyelids and put out my
cigarette. Behind me I hear some movement in the room.
Tom is with me at the window, now. "What is it?" He
draws me into his arms.

"I don't know ... faces, flashing."

He nods. "I remember. Happened to me sometimes,
when I first stopped drinking. Not pretty."

"Whose faces?"

"Everyone I was trying to forget."

"Did they go away?"

"Once I let them stay."

"God. Now that's a nightmare."

"Yes." His dark chuckle. He takes me back to bed and holds me till, at last, I sleep.

I dream of white flowers.

■

<23>

WHITE FREESIA fill yet another bowl — this time in Terrence Heller's Watergate apartment.

He has just shown me through his office-home complex, and we have circled back to the living room. The carpet is plush; the decor throughout, red and black. Over the couch hangs a giant clay wall sculpture. I realize it is a series of breasts of varying shapes and sizes. To one side, on a chrome shelf, is a large African doll: leering, it squats, phallus thrust forward. I turn, sensing a face to my left: an ebony mask, crimson tongue protruding. Beside it is a photograph that appears incongruous. It is an artistic shot of young women in white dresses; debutantes, it seems. They are shoeless, lifting their skirts to step into a fountain. The shot focuses on bare legs, bare feet — this, I suppose, is what ties it to the room's motif.

Terrence Heller appears beside me now, a tray in his hand. Ice clinks in tall glasses. "Shall we have these on the balcony?"

Glass doors slide open. Before us now, there is a sweep of sky and river and fading sun.

"Stunning view." I try for polite middle distance.

"Expensive view," he says. "But worth it."

He moves closer; casually, I sidestep.

"I need this," he adds, "after the shelters."

"I admire your commitment there." I sound stiff, but I do mean that.

"Thank you," he says quietly, simply. A pause. "Look, I'll admit this. I've admired you for quite some time."

Moves fast. I sip my drink, a wine spritzer: something that won't cloud my wits. I study the river, Heller studies me. "I just assumed you were taken," he goes on.

"I assumed you were." I pause. "You — Zoe."

"Zoe." He looks suddenly flustered.

"I just thought ..."

"Well ... for a while. Not now."

"No?" I drift down the balcony.

"Now, just a colleague, just — " He looks at me, questioning. "We are off the record, aren't we?"

"Of course." I take another sip.

"She's also a patient," he says then.

A pause.

"Her work must be very stressful," I say.

He is beside me again, his hand on the small of my back. "Well, between you and me ... it's not only that. She's got some sexual stuff ... actually, I find it intriguing."

"You listen to a lot of secrets. Intimate secrets."

"As crime reporters do, I'd think ..." His face is near mine. "Intriguing?" he asks, lower, "for you?"

His sandy hair looks freshly combed. There is something earnest about his eyes; they seem to contradict the long, sober shape of his face. He smiles, watching me.

I'm wondering what he wants in return for professional secrets.

"The secrets," I say. "No, not really."

"What then?" The smile moves closer.

"The story."

"Ah, the story." His arm slips around my waist. I drain my drink. Time to leave.

"A refill?"

"No thanks ..." Used me ... hurt me ... Zoe's voice; Zoe as a patient. "I really have to get going ..." I say.

"Is that what you really want?"

He rammed it in ... I think of that tape, rewinding, replaying. I think of umbrellas in women.

"You're breathless," he says.

"Am I?"

"I can feel you wanting this ..." He runs his finger down my throat.

I grab his hand. "I'm kind of curious." I look at him directly. "Speaking of secrets. Did Sharon and Meredith want it ... this fast?" One final gamble. It pays: quick flash of fear in his eyes.

"I don't know what you mean." He looks away.

"I think you do."

He looks at me: fear again. I drop his hand. "I think you got about this far with them." I turn to go. Suddenly, his fingers close hard around my wrist. He twists me toward him, at the balcony's edge. I keep my balance and look straight into his eyes. "Not smart," I say evenly. He lets go.

I am off that balcony and through the apartment in seconds — and out the door. I don't wait for the elevator. Only on the stairs, I realize that my knees are trembling and something hurts.

•

TOM WRAPS an ice-filled cloth around my wrist. I wince. He swears.

"It's okay," I say.

"It's not." He adds more ice.

Sitting in my kitchen, I wince again.

"Son of a bitch," he mutters.

"It was a good interview."

"It was a goddamn risk." His voice is rough, pained, tender, angry.

I glance up at him. Rough voice — soft gray eyes, shifting hues. He is looking at me as he did last night and as he has throughout this day, across the newsroom. I touch his face and say a hard thing. "There's always a risk."

"That's the trouble."

"This beat — "

"I hate it."

"I know it."

"Nan. Love you so damn much."

I draw his mouth down on mine till we are breathless — till we hear ice cubes scattering all over the kitchen floor. We have to stop; we have to smile.

"The pain — ?" He asks, finally.

"What pain?"

"Hope I never see that bastard."

"He did come through with some stuff." I tell Tom the rest. He listens, smoking.

"I keep hearing that tape ..." I finish.

"You think Zoe was raped? Molested?"

"Sounds like it. I'm just wondering ..."

"If she's acting it out? In reverse?"

"Avenging it ... with a symbol, a shaft — "

"An umbrella." Tom looks at me.

"Jed Jackson's going to hear about it."

"Then again — Heller."

"Violent, erotic. Breaks confidentiality."

"Puts moves on two of the victims ..."

"Two that we know about," I remind Tom.

"You don't think that Heller ... and Zoe ..."

"Of course I do."

"No, I mean ... Could they be conspirators?"

I pause. "Interesting idea."

"To cover their own secrets?"

I look at Tom. "Those women could know ..." I can't quite grasp it. Suddenly, I see Heller's erotica again, and that photo of girls in white dresses. Debutantes ... Zoe. "I'm not sure yet. Even that art collection — "

"What art collection?"

I'd forgotten that part. I describe it. In living color. And before I can get to the debutantes, we are laughing, we can't stop. "Oh God," I gasp.

"It really ... isn't ... funny." Tom laughs harder.

"I know." I wipe my eyes; something stills me.

Used me ... hurt me ... over and over.

"What is it?" Tom lifts my chin.

It's all right ... you won't remember.

I hear it again.

■

<24>

THE CALL comes in, late morning. Comes amid out-
going calls, and short-circuits them and everything else.
I have been looking at my list:

    • Sidney — check fit.

That one's just been done. She comes home tonight; I
will pick her up at National.

    • Follow-up: 8th St — Susanna's.

    • Check further: Dr. H., Zoe.

The call comes in from the guard downstairs at the
main desk. He says a gentleman's here to see me. Damn,
I think. Heller. The guard goes on: the gentleman will
leave a note if this is inconvenient, or if I prefer. And
then he gives the man's name.

Dr. Karl Gordon.

I sit there, the phone in my hand. The guard repeats
the message. "Want me to send him up?"

"Ask him just to ..." I break off. In an instant's time,
I see my young father leaping on a table — my aging
father, through a fountain. Prominent man ... lonely ...

wants to catch a glimpse ... I see a graying man buying a paper ... wants to talk to her, loses nerve ... I see Sidney lifting the sheet from her mother's face ... after all, she's his kid . . .

"Ask him to come up," I tell the guard. I close my notebook. I sit; I wait. And then I see him walking across the newsroom, pausing once for directions. Heads turn. Tom looks up. My father's eyes search the desks till at last he sees me and slows his pace. I stand up, feeling the tick of my pulse. Absurdly, I feel like a child, awed by the force of him, the sheer power of him simply walking through the front door at home.

We murmur polite greetings. He stands there shifting his briefcase from one hand to the other. We are awkward, stiff. I shouldn't have let him come up. Under the fluorescent light, his hair looks so gray. No: I should have done this. It's awkward, it's hard. But somehow — it's time.

I suggest lunch upstairs. The cafeteria at this hour is fairly quiet, before the major rush between noon and one. Everything blurs before me as we walk toward the elevator: desks, faces. Except Tom's. His eyes seem to send some strength. My father follows me; and then we are on line, we are juggling trays, we are gazing together at green jello, white bread. I apologize for the food. He apologizes for "just coming.

"It was the only way I could manage," he says, then. Picks up his fork, lays it down again. "I've tried other times, and somehow, after all these years ... I'd have a failure of nerve.

A failure of nerve. One of his phrases: I remember. "I know," I say quietly.

"I frightened you."

"Yes."

"I'm sorry." He studies his fork. "I'm sorry about a lot of things."

There is a terrible silence. I don't know what to say. I want to forgive him. I want to accuse him. I want to tell him how damn hard he made it for me — I want to tell him it's okay, it's okay. Let's start over; make the best of what's left. So much hangs between us, memories layered like veils. We eat, caged in that silence. This is not why I asked him to come up; this, somehow, is not right. After all ... she's his kid. After all — he's my father. I try to think: think of something, anything, to say ... Think back on all the tales that you remember ... of Camelot ...

"I remember the evening you launched the clinic," I say, finally. "Thought of it the other day — all the lyrics of Camelot came back to me."

He smiles, tentatively. I realize with a shock that he's afraid of me: afraid of all the ways I can hurt him with memories. Afraid of me — who lived in fear of him.

"And you know what?" My voice is a little too bright; best I can do. "I remember you taking me to that show. My first Broadway play, you got matinee tickets. I was so thrilled. Kept the Playbill, all this time."

For a moment, I think his eyes glint, wet. "I remember," he says. "Richard Burton was still starring, and he had that gravelly voice, talking those lyrics ... `Ask everyone if he has heard the story ...' "

" 'And tell him loud and clear if he has not ...' "

" 'That once there was a fleeting wisp of glory ...' "

"'Called Camelot.' "

We look at each other.

"King Arthur ..." he says, at last. "Great. Glorious. Flawed. I've thought about that more, lately. Maybe that comes, getting older." He looks at me. "I know you've kept away for good reasons. I know ..." It is hard for him.

"There were bad times. I was always working, away too much."

Suddenly the old anger rises within me. It startles me — its strength, its pungency, as if I've uncorked some old bottle of poison. No: he has. I try to keep my voice even. "Do you really think that's all? Enough to keep me away — fourteen years?"

He looks at me; again, I think, in fear.

"It was the anger, Daddy," I say, my voice quiet. "It was the rages — exploding, no reason. The terror in me; the guilt — "

He waits, eyes on my face. I have never seen him look vulnerable before. And so gray. He seems to expect something more. He bows his head.

I've been waiting twenty, twenty-five years to say that. And I have. It's enough; enough. "There were good times, too," I say, then.

He lifts his head.

"I remember you taking me for walks in Central Park, around the bridle path ..."

He watches me closely; again I sense fear. I wish my mother were here, with her social grace — her ability to converse in the most difficult situations, with the most difficult people. She would know what to say now; what to do. My beautiful chilly mother — a warm hostess. A woman I never knew. Her memory does not help me. I grope for one that does. Nora Callahan's face rises to mind. Nora: more mother than Mother. I think of her ... and now know what to say. "And," I go on, "I remember going to your office on the way home from school. I'd sit in the waiting room. And your secretary would smile at me. Special smile, I liked that. She had more teeth, I thought, than any human being I'd ever seen.

A flicker of a smile on his face now. "Mrs. Sacher."

"Yes. And she'd sort of half-whisper to people, I was your daughter. I'd feel so important. And then — you'd take me into your consultation room, just for a minute, between patients. You'd give me one of those terrible lollipops for the little kids ..."

"Turned their tongues purple. Every flavor did that, I never understood ..."

"That's right. But they didn't know that. I'd walk out with a handful. And Mrs. Sacher would be whispering. Everyone would look at me. I'd leave feeling — royal."

It's true and he hears that truth and now he's smiling; really smiling. And for an instant we are there again, together in the old office. In a good time. In a brief circle of light. In a light we both see. And that changes everything. Something between us eases, and he is talking about his practice, the clinic — he is animated, up, alive. The strain is gone, the awkwardness past. He shows me pictures of new buildings, newly planted trees, bright brochures for lectures, workshops, outreach programs. And suddenly I don't hate this place anymore, this place that always seemed a rival. That old tightness lets go, at last.

He is asking me about my work now. He is saying he has followed it — he's been proud. How those words would sail me through days, weeks, once. I would treasure them secretly, like the mints I took home from the Plaza. Like the Playbill, the rosary beads, in the hatbox. And now? Not quite the same. Not quite the power. But still treasure.

" `Ask every person if he's heard the story ... tell it loud and clear ...' " He comes back, again, to Camelot. But in a different way. "You always do that, it's been my observation." He looks at me. "You're the storyteller now."

"Didn't the king pass a candle to the storyteller?"

"Yes. At the end. I'll try to remember that."

Around us the cafeteria is starting to fill up with voices, laughter, shuffling feet. For a moment, amid it, our table is quiet. Not the quiet of strain; the sacred quiet of hard-earned peace.

We stand. I've forgotten how tall he is, how broad-shouldered and hard through the body. Always an athlete. But then the light catches him again. I see the sag at the jaw I'd not noticed before, new lines at the eyes. So much gray in his hair. For an instant his face looks fragile and old.

I walk him to the door of the building, downstairs. I watch him step into the street. His stride is strong. He turns, raises a hand to me. I raise mine to him. His face is sad.

.

TOM IS on his feet the minute I get off the elevator. We get back on, go back upstairs. Find a table in the back. I smoke. And tell him this story, which will never make any page in any paper. "It was okay," I conclude, amazed.

"It was time?"

"I was thinking that ..."

Under the table, I reach for his hand.

"I know," he says. "God. How hard."

"It was, till the end."

"I remember."

"You had a talk ... before — "

Tom nods. My hand tightens on his. I'm quiet then, thinking. There is a long pause. "You happen to own a tuxedo?" I ask, finally.

Tom looks at me.

"We happen to have this invitation ..."

■

<25>

THE FIRST bomb threat comes at 4:00 P.M. At the paper, I watch the report tick over the wire. Awards ceremony jeopardized ... bomb squad on site ...

The second threat comes at 7:13 P.M.. We hear it on the car radio, as we drive home. Anonymous tip ... JFK Center security tightened ...

Reports keep coming in till 8:30 P.M. We hear them as we dress, go out the front door. Ceremony will proceed ... no explosives found ...

I am grateful to God I'm not covering this story.

•

A LIMOUSINE HAS been sent for us. We emerge from it into the blinding glare of TV lights and squad-car lights, and above, a helicopter's searchlight, and before us, the Kennedy Center's own lighting. The building's marble walls shimmer, unearthly white in the dark. We blink.

Tom takes my hand and we walk forward. This doesn't look exactly like Camelot.

There are bomb-squad trucks. There are bomb-squad cops. There are bomb-squad dogs. One of the dogs is urinating on the metal detector at the Opera House entrance as we go in. Behind us I hear Sidney comment to her date. I'd hoped this event might cheer her, distract her. Now I wonder.

We all wonder, as we have since 4:00 P.M. this afternoon, why someone would want to blow up the Humanitarian Awards ceremony. These awards are new, designed by the presidential staff, with congressional leaders. This is an event to showcase "what's right with us," as the program reads; to showcase Americans who help others — "who serve the country and the world."

The standards for recipients have been high: three chosen from a group of fifty, then twenty, then ten. The presenter, Mother Maria Chartree, is saintly; perhaps that in itself makes her a target. Or perhaps someone has a vendetta with the awards committee led by Representative Welch. Then again, someone might simply wish to shake up the Washington glitterati: much in evidence just now, in the Hall of Nations. A swirl of them — glint of diamonds, sweep of satin, a gown made entirely of ostrich feathers. All interspersed with plainclothes cops in ill-fitting tuxedos, with uniformed police and security guards.

Discreet murmur of greetings. Crackle of police radios. I wonder how many bullet-proof vests lie beneath the cummerbunds and gleaming shirt studs on the men. There are senators and social types; there is the mayor and staff. I see White House brass and congressional brass and embassy brass; top names from the scientific community, the religious community, the social services community.

And the shelter community.

That last one is what makes me nervous. But the field is so wide — the threat could be against anyone.

We pick our way to the box reserved for my father's guests — pick our way through jewels and badges, detectives and doyens. I recognize some of the cops — too many. I even recognize some of the dogs. I try to focus instead on the plush box, on the stage below. The heavy curtains are closed. Presenter and recipients are hidden away in dressing rooms with the entertainers who will contribute to the evening.

Think back on all the tales that you remember ... of Camelot ... I think back on that evening so long ago, when my young father jumped on the table, his face alight with a dream. I hope nothing will mar this evening, nearly thirty years later. The poor kid in him, the kid who grew up in slums, who was beaten in the streets — that kid wants this award, this culminating honor, with every strand of being. And he should have it.

My hand tightens on Tom's. "It'll be fine," he whispers.

We stand at the rail of the box and look down. Now I can see all the press — circling, circling. Major networks, cable — and, of course, print journalists. We spot Sam Wile with his camera. I glimpse my friend Gina, from Trends, jotting in her notebook. This is her baby, her story — thank God. And she's promised to keep my name out of the coverage.

"Relax," Sidney tells me. "We're at the ball."

And for a few minutes, we are. Despite the chaos, the Kennedy Center looks festive. The carpeting glows crimson. The great chandeliers glint like exotic stars, showering light. Below, there is a swirl of color: women's evening dresses, flowing, shifting, bending, in the hues of a summer garden. For a moment I recall my parents' parties, and how the women looked, to me, like long-stemmed flowers, petaled in silk. Now I look down over another railing, this time in silk myself. Behind me, I feel Tom's hands on my waist. An hour before, his fingers were fastening all those tiny buttons up to the middle of my back, where the dress stops. Cold. A new dress, out of my standard basic-black pattern. This gown is strap-less and low, with a fitted bodice; a long, clinging, slit skirt — all in aquamarine. The saleswoman said it set off my hair. I've never looked like this before. I hope to God the thing stays up.

"This is incredibly difficult," Tom murmurs.

"Why?" I lean back against him.

"Because ..." His lips skim my shoulders. "You are very beautiful and very bare and ..." He whispers now. "I know you are even more bare and beautiful ... under-neath."

I lean back against him. "And you're very unbare. Very knockout, all the same, in black tie. Even rented black tie."

"Do you remember coming here this spring?" he asks.

I do. After months of going out for lunch, for coffee, we finally went to a concert here, and came back other times, just to walk on the veranda by the river, Tom in his old windbreaker, me in my jeans. "I never thought we'd come back — quite like this," I tell him.

His hands slide down my arms. "Another New Eng-land saying: true dreams abide."

And maybe, I think, that's right. Maybe sometimes, despite old nightmares, old pain, police lines and police lights — maybe sometimes Camelot can still break through, that placeless place, with its fleeting wisps of glory. Tonight, it will for my father. And I will see it. A true dream, abiding.

A cop I know knocks, puts his head in. "Things look clear," he tells me.

Sam Wile knocks, then enters the box. "Had a good talk with your dad, backstage."

"Everything okay?"

"Looks it. He'd like a picture. Me too." He takes a couple, then he's on the run again.

I lean over the rail watching him, watching things settle. And then I see two figures:

An elegant black dress, long gray mane of hair. Zoe slipping into an orchestra seat, third row, aisle. Terrence Heller's sandy hair and rangy frame beside her.

Reflexively, I start scanning the Opera House. My eye, trained, practiced, picks out faces. More shelter people than I thought. I glimpse Joan Kelly, other directors. Zoe is not sitting with them — she seems set apart, somehow. Feeling abruptly uneasy, I scan the box tier. Glitterati up here. In another box, nearest the stage, I see Representative Pete Welch, Sharon's husband. My eyes have just begun to skim the first tier, above us, when Sidney grabs my arm. She says nothing, only gestures.

Up in the top tier, back corner, standing room: Frederick B. Dade.

The last face I see as the house lights dim is Jed Jackson's, at an exit door below, near the stage. His eyes move from Zoe to Heller — then up to me. He hasn't seen Dade yet.

The great hall fades out.

·

I DON'T HEAR much of the introduction, made by a famed actress, long a supporter of social causes. Leaning over, I keep watching certain heads; watching the house. Along the side aisles, dark forms move: press, police.

Joan Baez is presented, to set the evening's tone with
music. Her angel voice is lifting: May God bless and keep
you always ... May your wishes all come true ... May you
always do for others ... And let others do for you ... A
sharp knock hits the door of the box. Light slices in from
the hall. A cop enters; I see the flash of his badge. He
leans over me. "Jackson wants you."

"What's wrong?" Tom sighs.

"He's at the first exit by the stage."

The cop jerks his head toward the orchestra level. Moments later, lifting my hem above my ankles, I am
following him down the carpeted stairs. Finally, I am
standing by Jed, just inside the side doorway of the Opera
House. I know we must be faintly visible in the light from
the stage — at least to Tom and whoever else is watching;
perhaps to Zoe and Heller, who are not far away. Maybe
that's the idea. I look at Jed.

"See those two?" He nods at them.

"Just before the lights went down."

"Watching them. Since your tips."

"I wondered why Homicide was here."

"Wonder why Dade's in the balcony."

"Thought you'd seen him." I glance at Jed.

"Full house." Jed pauses.

"What?" I know those pauses.

"Your dad ... he have any enemies?"

My stomach tightens. "Why?"

"Routine."

"Do the others?"

"We're checking." Another pause.

"What is it?" I prod.

"Off the record — "

"Of course."

"Someone called us, another threat."

"When?" My stomach tightens again.

"About four. Anonymous."

"Against anyone particular?"

" 'A plaster saint.' "

"That could be any of them."

"Yep." Jed sighs.

"Tie-in with the bomb scare?"

"Can't tell. Garbled voices."

"Shit," I say quietly.

"Don't worry." Jed looks at me.

"Oh sure."

"Mean it. We even got FBI, since Welch."

"You know where I am." I nod upwards.

"You're off-duty. As of now."

"Gina Maxon's covering this — "

"A party reporter?" I see his spit in the air.

"A good reporter." I pause. "Don't worry."

"My fair lady."

I glance at the stage. A tribute is being made to the first recipient. Dimly, I hear the words ... Frances Bailey, elder in the Society of Friends ... founder and director of centers throughout South America and this country ... a blend of spirituality and counseling ... nourishes soul as well as mind ...

I turn and go through the door. And trudge back up the stairs. Tom is waiting for me outside the box. Briefly, I tell him.

"It'll be okay," he says.

"Probably nothing."

"With a cop surplus."

"We're missing the Quaker."

He takes my hands. "All right?"

I nod. We slip back into the box. The Quaker, head bowed, stands before the applauding crowd. A medal gleams from a ribbon around her neck. The audience rises for her. She opens her hands; bows her head again.

As she is led off, stage left, the small nun, Mother Maria, returns to the microphone. She has an ancient, creased face, with wise, peppery eyes. Her dark veil falls over a habit fashioned as an African dashiki. Tiny, wiry, unworldly, she looks a bit overwhelmed by all the pomp and flurry around her. Her voice still has the flavor of her native France. She begins to speak again, as the National Symphony Orchestra slides into place behind her.

"I grew up in the Paris slums," she is saying. "As a child I nearly died. It was a doctor working among the poor who gave me my life back. A doctor, a common man himself ..." And I know it is my father, next. I don't have to look at the program. Mother Maria steps off to one side.

The lights come up brighter on the stage.

Mstislav Rostropovich, in tails, moves to the conductor's platform. The audience rises to its feet. He bows; turns to the orchestra. His baton lifts. There is a hush. And then, arching through that vast space, the fullness of visionary music: Copland's Fanfare for the Common Man. The powerful sounds fill the hall, and at last, into the final fanfare, he walks. My father.

For a moment, the whole scene swims before my eyes: the lit stage, the radiant nun, the music's echo — and my father, no matter what he's done and left undone, Karl Gordon, common man, stands in the center of Camelot.

Mother Maria is speaking again: "... with his dedication, and compassion, he has revolutionized outreach medical care for the very poor ... not only in America, but in clinics throughout the world ..." A montage of huge slides flashes behind them, slides of the Appalachian clinic and then all the other clinics modeled on this first one — and faces, faces, children's faces, hungry faces, poor faces, smiling faces.

Mother Maria's voice continues. The TV cameras move in closer. There is more applause. And as the applause dies away, as my father steps forward to receive the medal — there is another voice. Not Mother Maria's. Not Karl Gordon's. Not presentation — or acceptance.

It is protest. It rises from the third row, aisle. Zoe steps forward. She stands just below the stage, just within camera range, and faces the audience. The lights catch her there; her hair seems to float, radiant, unreal.

"This man is not worthy," she says in a clear voice, a voice that can hit the back wall. "This award is a travesty. This man, this `doctor' — is a pervert. This `common man' you applaud is — a sham." She strides up the aisle.

And walks out.

∎

PART THREE

<26>

FANFARE FOR a common man.

I fast-forward through the orchestral sequence. The protest. The award. The acceptance. The audience rising to its feet. I speed the videotape ahead, to news coverage outside the Kennedy Center afterward; after ceremony, protest, finale.

Aftermath for a common man.

We stand in my dim workroom, Tom and Sidney and I. We stand there later that night, watching three lit screens. On one, in freeze-frame, the face of Zoe Heywood. On another, the face of Jed Jackson. On a third, the face of my father. Their features waver slightly within the frames. They seem to gaze out at us through the haze of our cigarette smoke. I slow down the tape on the third screen. The sound track comes back on. The scene unreels again:

Karl Gordon leaving the Kennedy Center: striding, tall and vigorous, through the great doors toward the waiting press. Glow of marble behind him. On a red ribbon his medal, throwing sparks of light. The invisible reporters throwing audible questions. He listens, composed, head bent slightly. He lets the questions come, lets them subside.

"I feel saddened for Ms. Heywood," he says slowly. "I've known her family for years. There's been ... a long struggle with psychological problems. I know this must be a difficult evening for her — as one of the nominees for this award."

Startled, the press reacts: a rush of new questions. Where was she in the running? Short list? Long list? When did she know? When did he know? Does he see any connection between this and the bomb scare

He holds up a hand; shakes his head.

Did she ever accuse him before?

He hesitates. Then answers. "When I first arrived in Washington, Ms. Heywood did visit me. I believe it's appropriate, now, to say ... a threat was made at that time. I felt concerned for her then and I feel concerned tonight." His voice is earnest. "My hope for Ms. Heywood is the finest help. .

Freeze-frame. Beside me now, Sidney squints professionally: the gaze of a litigator selecting a jury, appraising a witness. "Non-defensive. Non-aggressive. Objective. In character as a physician ..." She nods. "Good witness."

"That checks out?" Tom asks. "Zoe was a nominee?"

I nod. I've just been on the phone to Gina, at the paper: she's writing it up in brief for the late city editions.

"On the long list? Short list?"

"Short list. Kept confidential."

Tom smokes, thinking. "That'll backfire like hell."

"Talking backfire — " Sidney half-smiles. "Gina get more on the bomb scare?"

"Nothing." I light a cigarette. "But Jed says — off the record, in confidence — any suspect could have made threats, then shown up to throw suspicion on someone else. Or there really was a bomb. Someplace. That never went off."

"I prefer the first scenario," Tom says, dryly.

I press the remote control. The face on the second screen flickers to life: Jed Jackson sweating under the lights, speaking as if to answer Sid's question.

"Nothing definitive, no."

Link between bomb threats and protest?

"No evidence at this time."

Why homicide detectives on scene?

"We like to be careful." He does not mention the tip. He does not mention serial killings. "We continue to monitor various situations." Jed knows when to shut up.

"Cagey, smart, good cop." Sidney's attorney voice again. "That sucker ain't gonna tell nobody nothin'," she adds, in her street voice this time.

The tape runs. The coverage cuts to the post-awards reception. The three guests of honor are posed before a floral arrangement. All three faces look pleased, lit, as if no disturbance ever occurred. I remember stepping quickly out of camera range there. Looking closer now, I see a slice of my gown in the frame. I was still angry then, upset, keeping it in. But after the reception we'd taken my father out for champagne — a private half hour, a good half hour. The evening hadn't been ruined after all. The press hadn't followed us. I think they'd found Zoe more interesting.

Now, on the videotape, her face jumps from stillness to motion. She too stands against the cold shine of marble. The cameras catch her as she stalks from the Kennedy Center — she, the first to be interviewed. In close-up, she appears to be shaking: not with fear, but contained rage. The skin across her high cheekbones is taut. Her cloud of hair drifts on the breeze. "This is an outrage." Her voice is very distinct; her patrician accent discernible. "I stand on that." She glances about, eyes narrowed. "You don't believe me."

A jumble of questions.

"You think I'm some — " Her voice tears suddenly, like silk on a nail. She looks about again. "I see how you're staring — you reporters." She spits the word at them and turns sharply, refusing more questions. Terrence Heller appears behind her just as the shot ends. The camera cuts back to the correspondent doing a stand-up by the Kennedy Center fountain. "A disturbing incident, marring a spectacular evening ..."

Freeze-frame. For a moment, no one speaks.

"Angry lady," Sidney observes. "On the edge, barely in control." She shakes her head. "Uh-uh. Not on my jury."

For a moment, I close my eyes. I don't want to see Zoe this way, don't want to think of her this way. I try to focus again.

"I wish I could remember how her family connects." I sigh. "Dad must have known them professionally — maybe as patients. He was very serious about confidentiality." I've just said the same thing to Gina, giving her some "deep background"; still keeping myself out of it, remaining anonymous.

I bring my father's face back up on one screen. We flash through the coverage again — quickly, one last time. The only face we spot and stop for is Sam Wile's, his camera on his shoulder, a tripod in his hand. He seems to wink at someone off to the side. I remember — it's me, on the periphery again.

Sidney takes the remote control from me. She speeds the tape, slows it down, fast-forwards again, scanning for the face of Fred B. Dade. It does not appear. He's keeping low, he's keeping quiet, he knows he's under surveillance. Living at the YMCA, he's still looking for his wife. Still no news — anywhere — on Johnice.

"Fred Dade, another fucking loose end," says Sidney. And abruptly bursts into tears. "Mama never wanted us to talk like that. Mama — "

For a moment, Ola's smile comes before us all again. Sidney leans against us and we sway with her weeping: the three of us, before those three faces suspended in the dark.

Finally, Sid snaps Zoe's off, and turns to me. "Whoever it is — Dade, her, that shrink — you call me first."

"I promise."

Sidney wipes her face. "You better promise not to see any of them alone, too."

"Yes," Tom adds, firmly. He looks at me. I click off the other VCRs. We stand there one more instant, facing those three squares of darkness. And then Sidney is turning on lamps, emptying ashtrays. Her gestures so like Ola's, her brisk hands telling us now: she's all right. All right, I know — till something else brings it back. After she's gone up the stairs to bed, Tom looks around the room.

"Somehow," he says, "this wasn't quite the way I imagined tonight ending."

"It could have been in the newsroom."

"Perish the thought."

Tom looks at me and turns out a lamp.

"You're going to see Zoe tomorrow. Alone. Aren't you."

"What makes you think that?" I keep my voice light.

"We asked you not to."

"And I won't." I turn out another lamp.

"I know you — you will."

I turn the lamp back on and look at him. "Tom. You don't do this."

His face is tight now. "You'll take these risks — no matter what I ask."

"Didn't we have this conversation before? That night in the kitchen, after the shelter? I think you reminded me I wasn't a cop." My voice has an edge.

"That was a while ago. Now it's different."

"Because of us?"

"Because of the danger." Each word is sharp. "We talked about risk. After Heller."

"And you understood. I thought. Maybe I was wrong. Maybe it's just the stories, after all, for you — above the fold."

"That's cheap, Tom." I turn. "And you know it's not true. God, my father's been attacked, Sid's mother's dead and you demand I hold back."

"I'm not demanding anything." His voice is cool and hard now; the editor's voice I first knew. "I'm just asking you not to see that woman alone."

"That's not all you're asking." My voice is not cool; I can't help it. "You're making professional calls for me — I thought that stuff went out in the seventies. The early seventies."

"I don't think caring for someone ever went out. It's not what I'd call a trend."

There is a brittle silence.

"Is this about caring? Really?" I snap off one more lamp. "I think it's about control. And I'm tired of it."

Another silence. The room seems to lengthen between us.

"I'm tired too." Tom's voice, pared, swift, cutting. "Find someone else to rebel against, Nan. I'm tired of the whole struggle."

We stand in the half-light, looking at each other. Tom turns. For a moment he seems to hesitate. Then he walks out of the study. I hear his steps going down the stairs. I close my eyes. Below, the front door slams.

■

<27>

SOMETHING ABOUT last night; it got to her."

Something about last night. They don't know what it is. They don't know if they should tell. Their worried faces draw close to mine — the dark face of Ma'am, the hooded face of Angel, down the street from Susanna House. They didn't know how to find me. They thought maybe I could help. They thought maybe I would come. They thought maybe someone from outside . .

We sit in a doorway in sunlight and smoke. I'm on my way to see Zoe, but I wait. I wait and watch them and smoke; watch them find what to say, how to say it. At first I think it's about Zoe — something they're afraid to spill. Something they're not supposed to tell. Something they just can't keep back. Our cigarettes are half gone when I find I'm half right. And half wrong.

It's about the missing wife. Johnice Dade has surfaced. "In the park, this morning ... just like that."

"Scared ... doesn't want anyone to know." Angel hesitates.

"It's okay," I tell them.

"Something about last night; it got to her."

"All she'd say." Ma'am smokes.

"Husband find her?"

They shake their heads. They don't know where she is now. They think she'll turn up again. They think she should talk to someone. Someone "safe." Someone "outside."

I offer — if she'd want that. I'll meet her anytime, anywhere she says, in complete confidence. They look relieved. I feel mystified, then uneasy. Last thing they say: Don't tell nobody. Don't tell Zoe.

Minutes later, Zoe unlocks the shelter door for me. I go in. The lock clicks shut behind us. Susanna House is quiet, empty, dim. I walk over the place on the floor where the runaway died. There is a faint stain. I glance through the dining room where a fly drones over the tables. The sound is oddly, disturbingly loud. The silence is deep. Now I realize why: no one, at all, is here. I glance about. All the shades are drawn; the shelter sits in its own twilight. Suddenly I wish Jed knew I'd be here. I wish Tom knew. There is pain, thinking of Tom — pain I woke with, pain now, as I follow Zoe up the stairs to the third floor.

Her phone is ringing as we enter her apartment. She ignores it. The shades are down. She turns on a lamp. On the desk and low table there are fresh white flowers. Today their fragrance is oppressive.

"Thanks for coming." She curls on the couch.

"Glad I could."

She'd called me at the paper first thing this morning, before I could get to her. Tom was just going into a meeting as I left; explanations were avoided. Now I take a chair within reach of the door. I place the location of the phone. I realize I no longer understand what I'm dealing with here, with Zoe.

The phone rings again. She sighs. "I just can't stand it, all these calls, the press. This morning there were people, cameras, at the door. They'd be here right now, if they didn't think I had a meeting uptown." She leans just slightly forward. "I wanted to talk to one reporter, just one, I wanted to correct an impression ..."

"Which is?"

I sound abrupt, I know. Anger returning — for last night. I look down at my notebook and lift my pen. Zoe begins.

"The impression that my statement last night had something to do with the awards. It had nothing to do with them, with my loss of that final prize. A lot of things drive me, but laurels don't happen to be among them. The whole thing's been so distorted, so misinterpreted, I mean it's incredible. It clouds what I meant to do last night— "

"Which was?"

"Tell the truth." Her voice shakes. "Tell the damn truth, put the record right. Someone has to understand that."

"Why is this so important?"

She takes a flower from the bowl before her. The freesia trembles in her hands. Slowly she turns the flower; then, even more slowly, she pulls a petal from it. A moment passes; I can see she's fighting to control her voice.

"Important ..." The words come more evenly now. "Important because I know this man, and what he is, and I have since I was a child." She turns the flower as if to study it. "I was brought to him as a patient, he became friends with my father, close friends ..." She stops again; again her voice is shaking. "Karl Gordon brought out a ... darkness in my father, changed him, marked him, and

through him, me. My father molested me repeatedly.
And it was the great Dr. Gordon who brought that sickness out." From her hand, petals shower.

I watch her. I wait till the shredded flower settles to
the rug. "And why would you want to tell me?" I ask, my
voice even. "Why, specifically — me? Why would you
send for one reporter, just one: the one who is Karl
Gordon's daughter?"

There is a stunned silence. Zoe looks at me. For a
moment, it seems she doesn't believe it. She searches my
face for a resemblance. There is none — as it happens, I
take after my father's mother and grandmother. Still, I
thought somehow Zoe had found out.

"You have a different name," she says, finally.

"I was married."

"I didn't know."

"Didn't you?" I watch.

"Honestly, no."

"I think you did."

"Oh — and this is part of my revenge?"

I say nothing. The silence deepens. On the couch,
Zoe's coil tightens. I make a few notes. She watches my
eyes move from her to the petals scattered on the rug.
She can hear the faint scratch of my pen. The air seems
to tighten. She watches my notebook.

And suddenly she is on her feet. The vase of flowers
overturns. Water runs over the table, cascades to the
floor. "You're making a mistake, a bad one." Her voice is
low, disturbing, rough. "You're writing up some damned
wrong impression. And you don't even know — "

"Just what is it I don't know?" I look directly at her.

"You don't know about them, do you? No, I can see
you don't, or you don't remember. My father, your father,
what they did — "

"Look Zoe," I cut her off. "If you can't come up with facts, specifics — I'll be frank with you: you'll be written off. Have more outbursts at reporters — the press can fry you. And who'll suffer? The women here. The shelters. You want that?"

Slowly, carefully, she picks up the vase. She reaches for petals that fall, again, through her fingers. I make another note. Abruptly she stands, the vase in her hand. "And who else?" Her voice rises. "All those kids in that damn clinic of his."

"You have evidence to support that?"

She says nothing.

"You have facts?" I push. "Outside confirmation?"

Silence. Inwardly, I take a breath. She doesn't.

"Your accusation's been checked," I say evenly, "with a range of reliable sources. Nothing supports what you say. To the contrary ..."

"Oh, of course."

"All you've got is an impression." I look at her. "Biased. Personal. Emotional. Based on memories decades old. And, I'd guess, based on your own father."

Zoe sits on the couch again; her eyes narrow. Green eyes. Hypnotic eyes. The eyes in the debutante photo. "There are four dead shelter volunteers, as you know." Her voice shifts: controlled now, sarcastic. "And you're such a fine reporter, you've already noted, of course, they all died since Karl Gordon came to town."

"You'll have to do better than that." I hold her gaze.

"I will." Again, her body seems to coil. "You knew Sharon Welch was at his clinic workshop last month, everyone knows, it was in her eulogy." Zoe leans back just slightly. The green eyes narrow again. "It seems you reporters, you press — " she bites the word. "Seems you've missed an interesting thread. Sharon discovered the workshop, got excited — got other volunteers to go with her. Three, to be precise. Their names were Meredith Crane, Sister Jo Sullivan, and Ola Harris." She lets that information drop like stones in a pool, and listens for ripples. I am careful to shown one.

"Those were the women in your meeting." I look at Zoe. "That angry meeting — conflict, raised voices."

"Those women." Zoe's voice is sharp. "Those women were quite taken with your father. They wanted to change things, our volunteer set-up, they wanted to model it on his." Her words come faster. "Yes, I raised my voice in that meeting, I told them, tried to tell them, I — "

"You weren't straight with me." I stop her again.

"What difference — don't you hear — "

"How can I trust what I hear? How can I know if you're being straight with me now?"

"You can look it up." Her voice snaps, whiplike in the fragrant room. "Don't believe me, check the workshop."

"I have. That workshop was for fifty. Not four. The other forty-six participants are alive. Sorry, Zoe." I close my notebook. "It doesn't quite play. Except from another angle, perhaps. Your hatred of this man could be seen as jealous, irrational. Irrational enough to provoke hatred. Hatred of anyone who admires him instead of you — perhaps murderous hatred."

She uncoils; she stands. "Let me tell you something," she says, her eyes suddenly so sharp, so green, they seem to throw sparks. "I did visit your father when he got to town. I did threaten his reputation. I told him I thought those four women probably knew about him, and if they didn't I'd make sure they did. I told him he'd be exposed, disgraced — he'd never get that damn prize he lived for, yes, I told him that. I stood in his hotel room his first day here and told him, and within two weeks those women were dead."

I look at her steadily. "What exactly are you implying?"

She looks away from me; can't quite say it. Suddenly
she seems to back off, losing nerve.

"Are you implying something more than child molest-
ing?" I press harder. "Something more than sexual
perversion?"

She glances at my notebook, my pen. She says
nothing. She may hate Karl Gordon but she isn't stupid
and she isn't naive about press. It's hitting her now, I can
see it: the bind she's in. Karl Gordon's daughter — is
press.

"If you're implying what I think, Zoe — why didn't he
just kill you? That first day?"

She looks at me. Abruptly, her eyes fill. "He can't,
there's a bond, it's too strong ..." Her eyes shift again,
angry now, a quick-flash change. "You don't understand.
I didn't understand myself, completely, till I saw him
again, but you — you refuse to try — "

"I think I understand quite enough." I close my notebook and stand up. "I understand something about psy-
chology. About projection. About mixing fathers up —
and changing stories." I look at her an instant longer.

"You're going to write it up that way?"

I say nothing.

"You're going to cover for him?" She takes a step forward. I let myself out. As I shut the door behind me, I
hear something heavy shatter against it. The door shud-
ders. There is the splinter of very good crystal falling just
beyond the rug.

Again I am running down flights of stairs; again I am
aware, afterward, that I am shaking. I hear my heels
click; and then, as I near the shelter's front door, I hear
heels click behind me, down the stairs. I wrench the door
open, dart out into the street. It's empty. I keep moving,

walk fast — and then I am running once more. Behind me, the shelter's door slams and Zoe's quick steps are behind me again; I am skidding in high heels, I know I can't outrun her — long-legged Zoe, long-striding Zoe, in low heels and trousers. Cars flash by, and doorways — my breathing rasps, my side hurts. I look for a store, a bar — anyplace public, anywhere I can dodge. She is gaining on me, I can hear her, and the sun is in my eyes turning everything black around the edges.

I round a corner, my heel catching in the cracked pavement, and then I am moving forward once more, past boarded-up storefronts, doorways where women sleep. I think of dodging into one of those doorways, taking refuge behind those women — can't use them, can't risk it; can't run much longer.

Suddenly, just ahead, I see a diner, a luncheonette — I don't know what it is, but it's open. I plunge in. A couple of people look up from the counter. A couple more look up from the Leatherette booths. There is a smell of eggs and bacon and coffee. I take it all in as a blur, try to focus — to spot a pay phone. No phone. I sink into a booth and watch the door. Everyone else watches me. I try to get enough breath to ask if there is a phone in the back.

And then Zoe is at the door. I see her as if in slow motion — the door seems to open very gradually, in a sweep, and she seems to flow into the restaurant as if wading hip-deep in water, wading toward my booth; coming, coming relentlessly, steadily, her hair floating out behind her.

The proprietor, a small, wiry black man, darts out from behind the counter. He's seen trouble before, knows how it looks, spots it now.

Zoe is standing over me now. "You ruin me," she gasps, "you ruin me, and you ruin Susanna's, the women, you know that."

I watch her; say nothing.

"Damn it — " She brings her face close to mine. "You have to listen."

I remain silent.

"For God's sake, they made films — " She reaches out as if to touch me, shake me, grab me — catches herself, pulls back.

"And where are these films?" I ask, evenly.

She looks away. I'm out of the booth. I stand facing her. "Where's the evidence, Zoe?" I say.

She looks at me. "I'm the evidence," she says, finally.

She walks slowly toward the door.

•

AFTER SHE leaves, it seems I sit there a long time — there in the peeling vinyl booth, at the chipped, stained table. I note down everything she said; everything I can remember. I smell smoke and ketchup and lard and, under all, Zoe's perfume. Her words, on my notebook's page, look spiky, brittle, bizarre. I study them some moments longer: quotes, more quotes, increasingly fantastic, theatrical. I close my notebook. I am steady now, ready to leave; prepared to write.

I am not prepared, yards from the diner, for the sound of footsteps behind me again.

I wheel around. All I catch is a flash of a blue windbreaker as it slips around a corner. Standing there in the sunlight, I feel abruptly chilled.

■

<28>

EVIDENCE. MISSING evidence. Confusing evidence.

At the paper the next day, I am on the phone with Sidney, and we are in what she calls "an evidence mode." The mode, this morning, has sizable gaps. I've relayed the conversation with Ma'am and Angel. I've relayed Fred Dade's latest appearance.

"Missing — the key piece: the wife, Johnice." Sid's heels as she paces. She listens to some of my interview with Zoe. "Missing — too damn many pieces."

Across the newsroom, I notice a sudden gathering around the city desk. A quiet flurry. Unusually hushed. Something's on; something's wrong.

"Zoe is not tightly wrapped," Sidney's saying. "Maybe your dad told those volunteers about her — so she has to discredit him and

The managing editor is leaning toward the Metro chief. I watch them, in a tight huddle now with the city editor and Tom. Something strange about it. Those

whispers, that hush. And then, grim-faced, they all turn
— toward me.

"Call you back, Sid."

For the phone, I've taken off an earring. I put it on,
stand up — just as the managing editor beckons. His eyes
are somber. He definitely means: me. As I leave my
desk, my phone starts ringing, ringing. It rings as I join
the hushed conference, as I go back for my notebook —
and run for the stairs. Only there, alone on the steps, do
I let tears fill my eyes.

It's Sam.

.

I HAVE BEEN in Sam Wile's house for many occasions
over the years. Birthdays. Parties. Sunday supper, just
the two of us. Big New Year's open houses; a tradition.
Now, I cannot quite grasp that I am in this familiar home,
this familiar room — for this occasion.

There is a crowd. The white floor is smudged by black
shoes: shiny police shoes. The air jolts with the crackle
of walkie-talkies. And in the center of the room, as
always, but not quite as always, is Sam Wile. Sam —
friend, photographer, sprawled on the white floor, caught,
himself, in the bone-white flash of crime lab photographers.

I look away. To steady myself, I look at the room —
his workroom, his room for relaxation. I see the long
white counter, a central island — I've seen it covered with
photos to be cropped, negatives in strips, and also with
platters of deli meat and potato salad. There are the
stools that seated friends; that got moved around the
room. There, at one end, is Sam's easy chair and lamp.
At the other, his wall of file drawers, going back to the
late fifties. And across the longest wall, between the

windows, a montage of his photos, built up over the years. I remember studying this wall many times. I study it now; and swallow.

I haven't felt sick on a crime scene for years. My eyes catch a favorite picture: an artistic shot. Along the bottom, Sam's five kids when they were small — the kids in a row, each face with a different expression. And above them, filling most of the frame, sky — just clear, lit sky. Blue-white sky in this white room. A white room full of cops: three detective teams, three crime lab people, two uniformed police and two more outside — and some top-level "brass," noticeable in their white shirts: I recognize the head of Homicide and the head of the district. Frank LaMarca's on the phone; Jed Jackson appears at my elbow.

He shakes his head. "Tried to call you," he says.

"Heard it. On my way out."

"My honchos called your honchos."

"Yeah." My mouth is dry.

Get a grip. Do a good job for Sam.

I open my notebook. "When was he found?"

"About forty-five minutes ago."

"Who — "

Jed jerks his head toward a woman crying in the corner. Dorothy: plump, plain, gray-brown hair — Sam's longtime housekeeper. She'd moved with the family from Manhattan; there were still three kids at home, then. I remember, I was in high school. Sam had switched from a New York tabloid to this respected Washington paper — only to get divorced a year later. He'd stayed in his big suburban-type house in northwest D.C. so all the kids could visit, all at once; they often did. He had a studio and darkroom here, too — did his own work at home. Still, Sam was often lonely here, I knew; a man uncomfortable with solitude, always having people over. Now,

I see two coffee mugs on the counter — one green plastic, one red.

"This morning?" Not touching them, I look at the mugs.

"Instant coffee, a trace, congealing. Last night."

I turn toward the counter's far end. The photographers are finished. The medics are gone. "Any idea when he — ?"

"Medics' guess, last night, late."

"Break-in — theft?"

"No sign." Jed is sweating.

"Unusual visitors, cars?"

"We're still ringing doorbells. So far — nothing."

The mugs are bagged by the crime lab guys. The place is still being dusted for prints. I delay one more moment, then force myself to move. By the counter's far end, there is a streak of blood on the white tile floor. I see another bloody smear on the counter's sharp edge. And lying by the blood, on the floor — Sam. He is sprawled on his back. He wears an open-necked sport shirt, blue-checked, and khaki pants. His arms are flung wide. On his right hand I see his class ring from college — NYU. He'd always worn that ring; I remember he used to get our attention, as kids, by rapping tabletops with it at birthday parties. My hand pauses over my notebook.

I look up. Take a breath. And start jotting notes again. Sam's clothes look untouched, unrumpled. The gray hair, slightly disarrayed. A bloody welt on the side of his head. I glance from the welt to the counter's edge and back. Sam's eyes are half open, showing the whites. His neck is distended, head flung far back. His lower jaw looks dislocated, out of line. His lips are stretched, torn at the corners; a thread of blood runs from each. And, jutting from his mouth, is the top of his portable tripod with his Minox camera firmly attached. I can see the aluminum gleam from the tripod's top, its safety latch intact, compressing its triple legs. I can see the camera, its lens like a third eye staring from his mouth. The camera is turned, with his head, toward the wall of photographs — away from the door.

My notebook trembles in my hand. My writing is be-coming illegible. I stop for a moment and lift my eyes to the photos again — my gaze is held by the picture of kids and sky. Silently, I return to Jed. "Looks like the umbrella M.O. — " I begin.

"Without the fucking umbrella," Jed finishes.

"Blow to the head, all of it, right down the line."

Jed glares at the floor. I keep writing.

"With one hell of a twist," he adds.

I glance up. I don't have much to say.

"There's film in the camera," Jed says, low.

I stare at him.

"It can take three shots at a time on auto."

"There — " I gesture toward the body.

Jed nods. I swallow; force out more notes. A pair of cops come in from the street; report that no neighbors saw or heard anything unusual, last night or this morning.

"Go ask again," the Homicide chief growls.

A crime lab cop comes over. "Two things," he begins.

One is a bill for a photo purchased at Sam's most recent exhibit, a month ago: a bill for a picture titled Debutantes at Fountain. The bill, found on Sam's desk, was half hidden under a thermos of Kool-Aid. Payment on the bill was due last week. The purchaser's name is partly smeared by the thermos, accidentally or on purpose; possibly by the intruder. The last letters look like ler.

The photo on Heller's wall flashes in my mind: the debutantes in white dresses stepping barefoot into a fountain. They made films ... Sam couldn't be tied into that. Could he? That was Zoe's imagination, or fantasy, or projection, anyway. And Heller — perhaps he had only purchased a photo; nothing more. Still, I tell Jed; he scribbles rapidly in his small pad.

Any more on him?" I ask.

"We're on it." Jed sounds grim.

"Second thing," the crime lab guy is saying.

A file is missing, though perhaps unrelated; just dd that the drawer marked 1962 is empty of photos. The house is checked, the housekeeper is interrogated — Sam was not at work on anything in that drawer for any reason, as far as she knew. The drawer is also not quite shut; like Sister Jo's car door, the catch is not quite engaged. Immediately, the drawer is dusted. Prints show, but they could be Sam's, they could be the housekeeper's. The lab people will have to check. Jed glances in the drawer — calls the team back. Stuck against the side of the metal drawer, caught in the groove, is one snapshot: overlooked. It is a photo of a little girl, grave-eyed and delicate, wearing a coat with a velvet collar. Behind her is a path and trees.

"One of his kids?" Jed asks.

I stare at the picture. "No."

"You sure?"

I take a breath. "That's me."

Startled, Jed looks up.

"Sam was always taking pictures of us — his kids, their friends. I was in school with his daughter, I remember ..." I break off.

The photo is bagged. I close my notebook. Jed is watching me. "You all right?"

"Just fine," I snap, rather than cry.

"Call me," he says, still watching.

"Likewise," I snap again.

Jed presses my hand; unusual. "My fair lady."

•

IT IS very quiet, this afternoon at the paper. I am writing the story on deadline, but deadline is not building the way it always does. Everything is muted. Faces are shocked. There is talk of a memorial service. There is still silence between me and Tom; there is still pain. It is the city editor who tells me how many inches to write. I keep working, for Sam, for Sam. Everything seems to hurt: my bones, my back, the fillings in my teeth, the roots of my hair. Reports come in over the hours: an exceptionally quick report, through Jed, from the M.E., from the crime lab. The tripod has been extracted. It was bound so tightly, it acted as a shaft. The film in the Minox has been developed. For now, it seems to show only shots of the photo montage on Sam's wall. The police are unwilling to make a definitive link between this murder and the others, nor will they rule it out. I get one of those waffling statements; without attribution, as always.

And then there are the calls I must make to Sam's kids; kids who are grown now, no longer kids at all. Their voices waver through the line — voices I've not heard for a long time. Voices cracking in offices and kitchens, in Vermont and Iowa, cracking on the word Dad.

After the last call, I lean back in my chair and, just for a moment, close my eyes. As I open them I see Tom by his desk, standing there, watching me. I lean forward again, light a cigarette, put it out. The words on the screen run together. I get up, walk, refusing to look anywhere but straight ahead. In the hall, just beyond the newsroom, is a water fountain. I reach it, grip its cool metal base, try to breathe slow. As I lean over, tears spatter its aluminum drain. I take another breath, trying to stop; I cannot. Someone is behind me now. Head turned, I step aside — and feel a hand on my arm. Without a word, Tom turns me around and looks into my face. I see the pain in his eyes; I feel his hand tighten.

"God, Tom, it wasn't — " My words come out in a tangle. "You were right, not worth it, I — "

"No." He touches my face. "I was wrong."

He draws me to him, and we say the things we wish we'd said after he slammed the door, and then he cannot find a handkerchief; he wipes my face with his finger and then with his mouth, and afterward, back at my desk, I can still taste the salt from my tears, from his lips.

Tom stands by my chair off and on throughout this long afternoon. He could edit the story at his desk, on his screen, but he does most of it here with me. We both need the closeness, the presence. I confer with the guy in Obits, who is writing an Appreciation. I take the last of my call-backs. I redraft. Tom sits down at my screen and edits. We smoke. We take out an inch. It's done. It's deadline.

The story goes to copy desk and clears. I sign off on the computer. For a few minutes I sit there alone, looking at the blank screen. I still see what I have seen all afternoon, flickering through the glowing green letters.

I do not see Sam, or the murder scene, or the story.

I see the face of a child in a velvet-collared coat. A grave-eyed girl standing in Central Park. I see her face all the way home.

■

<29>

IREMEMBER THAT coat. And walking with my father around the the bridle path in Central Park ..."

In Tom's kitchen that evening, my hands pause over boxes of take-out Chinese food. I've been home to get clothes for tomorrow, and I've been to pick up our dinner, and that photo's still in my mind — after everything that's happened. I shake my head. "Can't get past it."

Tom spoons cashew chicken onto plates. "It's a shock, the whole thing is — bizarre as hell."

We look at the food. We aren't hungry. We set it all out on the coffee table anyway. We light the candles. We sit on the rug and unfold our napkins. We are determined to have dinner; to keep our nights separate from our days. Especially days like this one.

"Sam had me to dinner my first week at the paper," Tom says, as we start. "New job, new city. New apartment, the place was a mess; I felt lost. Didn't think I should, didn't want to, thought it didn't show. Sam knew, somehow. Lonely himself, I guess he recognized it. We sat in that room, at that counter ..."

"Where they found him." My fork pauses.

"He'd made some terrible casserole and burned the rolls." Tom half-smiles. "Nothing ever tasted so good."

"Sam's standard Sunday evening suppers. I remember — even when we were little. His kids were my dad's patients. Sam would call late at night, when one of them was sick." I sip wine, thinking. "He knew, somehow — trouble in my family. Drew me right into his. He knew there was this long estrangement, too, from my father. Sam never let me forget he was there — " My eyes sting. I put down my fork. Tom touches my face.

"You wrote him a fine story."

My eyes fill now. "Sick inside, all the way."

"Never showed."

"The editor helped."

We smile; smile thin, the way Jed and I do. I pick up my fork again. A bite of chicken; another sip of wine.

I tell Tom about the interview with Zoe — omitting certain details. Like the chase down the stairs, down the street.

"She seemed pretty unraveled." I finish.

He looks at me. "And then another victim turns up."

"Yes." I. say, quietly.

"Just a slight variation on the other killings."

"Tom. God, I don't want it to be Zoe."

"Who was Sam, for her?"

"He photographed her ... Ill find out."

The cashew chicken is almost gone. The candles are lower. The rug is soft and the wine is good. A light rain outside makes our table seem even more an island — peaceful, safe. And still all the bad images keep flashing up before me. White room, red blood. Dim room, green eyes ...

"Maybe the awards did flip her out, denial or not."

"Kind of extreme reaction," Tom says dryly.

"Like her anger at those four volunteers, just for being at the clinic. Just for admiring my father — just as Sam did. It's as if she's got some kind of pathological jealousy — "

"Did Ola or Sidney ever mention that workshop?" Tom asks.

"No ... but they wouldn't, they knew about the estrangement."

I put out the candles. "You know what we're doing? We're talking shop — "

"Nonstop," He shakes his head.

"And we swore ..."

He pulls me to my feet. "You're right. Finis." He kisses my forehead; we clear the table.

In the kitchen, we talk about taking my dad out to dinner — tomorrow night's his last in Washington. He's delayed his departure for Sam's memorial service, day after tomorrow. Suddenly, tears fill my eyes again. I stand, head bent, hands in the sink. Tom turns me around.

"Leave them." He leads me from the kitchen.

In the living room, he turns out all but one lamp and finds some quiet, reflective music — Ralph Vaughan Williams, music that makes me see moors and lakes. Then, on the couch, Tom gathers me into his arms and we lie there listening to the music and the rain. Gradually I drift into a half sleep. The moors and lakes fade away. And gradually, relentlessly, other images start flashing behind my eyes again.

Sam's face. Dead, distorted. The runaway's face: bruised, beaten. Zoe's face, green eyes narrowed. If you don't listen ... The debutante's face, above her pearls. I'm the evidence.

The face of a child in a velvet-collared coat ...

•

CENTRAL PARK. Almost thirty years ago. I am walking
on the bridle path with my father, my hand in his. It is
autumn, just cold enough for my new coat, and I am very
proud of it and very proud to be out walking with my tall
father. This is rare time with him; my time with him.
This is Sunday morning, early, and the park is quiet, the
park is ours, and the air tastes like apples. We pass a
man walking a large golden dog; the man waves and we
wave back and pass on. Suddenly a horse thunders down
the path, its rider a dark shape — the hooves fly too close,
the horse seems about to trample us and the ground
seems to shake. Frightened, I press back against my
father. He laughs, pulling me off the path and toward the
safe trees. His hands stroke the collar of my coat, the
velvet collar, and then the buttons; he opens them, one by
one. He is asking me if I am hurt, he lifts my dress, he
says, to see; we are back in the trees and now I feel afraid.
He pulls my panties down and looks at me there a long
time, and then he is forcing my hands into his own pants,
open now. He is hurt there, he says, working my hands
against him. Working them harder, harder, and my
fingers ache, a sick feeling builds in me, and fear — and
then hot white liquid is exploding from him, spattering
my face and my new coat and I start to cry. Stop it, stop
it, he is angry, I've seen him like this before and I am very
afraid now. I am pulling away and he slaps me, twice,
across the face. I reel backward, feeling my breath come
in jabs; I taste tears on my tongue. Stop it I said, stop
damn it — he hurls me down, hard, on the stony ground,
and I feel my knees tear open and my palms sting and I
am crying harder now; head bent, I cannot move. And

then he is lifting me, he is pressing me against the cold tweed of his coat. It's all right ... you're my girl ... our secret ... you won't remember ...

.

"NAN, N A N — " Tom is holding me, rocking me, waking me, and as I wake I am crying; crying so hard it hurts deep inside.

"Darlin' ..." Tom takes my face in his hands and still my eyes fill, I remember the dream, I remember it all; everything within me churns, and then I am struggling to stand, to run.

In the bathroom I lean over the toilet; I am sick, sicker than I have ever been, and something deep inside seems to wrench loose, come up. Tom is there now, kneeling beside me, holding my head, and still the waves of sickness come, wracking my whole body; under Tom's hand, my forehead is damp, my back wet. And then it is over. For an instant, exhausted, I lean against him — then, suddenly mortified, I flush the toilet, stand quickly: too quickly. I sway on my feet and the tile wall starts to fade; small pinpoints of light explode before my eyes. I feel Tom's arms around me, steadying me, until the pinpoints fade and past his shoulder the wall looks solid once more. I lean over the sink, rinse my mouth; my knees sag again. This time I let him lift me into his arms, carry me to the couch; I close my eyes. When I open them again, Tom is beside me and there is a cool wet cloth on my head; there is a fizzing glass in his hand. He is watching me, his eyes shifting grays: alert, tender, scared, pained. I think of the bathroom; abruptly I feel hot, shamed.

"Never — " My words crack. "Never wanted you to see me like that. No one has."

"Darlin'," Tom's voice is wry. "When I was drinking, I can't count the times my head was in the toilet. Sometimes a wastebasket, a sink." He smooths the damp hair off my forehead, offers the glass. "Can you get this down?"

I can, about halfway. And then I remember again; I feel new tears behind my eyes.

"You were dreaming ..." he says.

"Tom." I look at him. "It wasn't a dream."

"You were drifting ..."

"It happened." Slowly, I sit up. "I remembered. The little girl in the coat with the velvet collar. With her father. In the park. I was in that ... twilight state and ... it all came back. God, Tom. It's true."

And halting, stopping, starting — I tell him. That time. Other times. A basement room, dimly recalled. The maid's room, Sunday afternoons, while my mother napped. Long periods of safe time; then it would happen again — till I was nine, and Nora left, and suddenly it stopped. Did she catch him? Confront him? I couldn't know. I could only see those times flashing up before me now, called back by those flashing faces — the bruised, the battered, the beautiful; the dead.

"He told me I wouldn't remember. I obeyed him. Tom, I forgot it for years. But then all this started to happen. And today, after I saw that picture, something broke through, I couldn't hold it back."

Watching me, Tom's eyes fill. "Nan ... I wanted to believe, as much as you did, that you always got away ..." He holds me a long while.

"You're the only one who could understand like this," I say, finally. Then, ironically, "You — and — "

"Zoe?"

I nod. "She was right. About this. God, Tom — that could mean so many things. Maybe — "

Tom lays a finger against my lips. "Maybe your father was a sick man who got well. Who's made other people well. I'm betting on that. Look at the good he's done, his record, the healing. Maybe he chose to heal because he knew sickness — up close. That doesn't fit with killing."

I take his hand. "Yes." I know he's right.

He sighs. "Wish I could just — fix it. Change the damn slide, change those pictures in your mind. I hate looking into that darkness. Even my own. I don't know how you do it, day after day, I had to stop."

"With strangers, it's not exactly the same. With someone like Zoe, like my dad — it's worse than any dark story."

Tom nods. "The idols, the icons. The worst, for me. All those years I tried not to see — in my father, in this English teacher I worshiped: both of them, the shaking hands, the burns on the ties. The terrible things they could say. All those years, fearing I might turn into one of them. An idol's darkness — it's almost worse than your own."

"I never wanted to put you through it again."

"I didn't quite finish it the first time." His voice is dry. "My father, all that stuff. I shut it off, wouldn't let myself. Too dark to look at — alone."

I touch his hand. His fingers press mine.

For a moment, we're silent.

"I'll look at it with you, Nan."

"I'm afraid to look ... too hard."

•

BUT I DO look. The next night, at home, I find myself looking at a box on the top shelf of my closet. I lift down the hatbox of mementoes; I find the program from Camelot. I find the letter on the prescription pad, the

photo, a bracelet, a scarf — everything from him.
Quickly, I tie them together and quickly, I drive to the
canal that runs through Georgetown. For an instant, I
stand by the water. The canal is high, stagnant, littered.
I let the package go. My eyes burn as I watch it float,
then slip beneath the dark water.

I'll look at it with you.

Tonight, I'll look alone.

■

<30>

IAM LOOKING, and looking hard today, because I have to. I am looking at Terrence Heller across his living room, and I am looking hard at the photograph behind him: the girls in white dresses. Debutantes at Fountain. I still cannot make out their faces, which are in shadow.

"All I did was buy a picture," he is saying.

"Why

"Why that one?"

"Why does it matter?"

"One of those debutantes is Zoe," I say, flatly.

"What's your obsession with this?" He lights his pipe.

"I might ask you that."

Heller looks at me through the smoke. "The enjoy-ment of women, of sexuality — surely that's not, in your view, an obsession. If so ...

"I'm not here for therapy." My voice is level. "Did you know Sam Wile?"

"The police have already questioned me."

"Then you have nothing to hide?"

Heller gets up, walks to the balcony. "Nothing."

"You told the cops about you and Zoe?"

"It didn't come up." He turns.

"Did Sam ever talk to you about making pornographic films? A long time ago? With young girls?"

Heller's eyes snap. "Never. Nothing like that."

I pause again. "So you did know Sam. Well enough to talk with."

Heller's face tightens. "How clever of you."

" `Nothing like that' — means?"

Terrence Heller takes a step toward me. "Loneliness," he says slowly, deliberately; each syllable seems to hang in the air. "Sam was a drinking pal. We talked a lot about loneliness. His, mine. Does that surprise you?" He stands before me now.

"It does. It surprises you and you don't believe it. You don't choose to believe it. You wouldn't believe a great many things about me, would you? Because of this — " He waves a hand toward his wall sculpture. "And this —" A nod toward the photo. "You wouldn't believe I work with the homeless because of my conscience. You probably wouldn't believe I paid Fred Dade's bail."

"I don't."

"Of course."

"Why would you?"

"Because he didn't have anyone. Because everyone brushed him off. Because sometimes I get that. Because sometimes I'm a goddamn nice guy."

I watch him, trying to read his face, his voice. Maybe this is genuine. And maybe it's just a clever performance by a very clever man.

"And sometimes," I test. "Sometimes you're not such a nice guy. Sometimes you break confidentiality. Sometimes you try to seduce one woman with another's secrets."

"That's right," he shoots back. "Sometimes I'm not perfect, sometimes I'm weak. How about you? Are you always honest, strong, brave, wise, the consummate altruist? Always? At least I look at my shadows."

"I wonder." I stand, turn to go.

"I wonder," Heller says behind me. "I wonder what you're really doing here. I wonder why you're looking so hard at me." His voice grows dangerously soft. "I wonder what you're avoiding. What you're afraid to look at."

"Our time is up," I say, an edge to my voice, and walk out.

Out in the street, I still hear his question — despite my brush-off. He got to me for some reason; at least it didn't show. I walk faster now, cutting through the Watergate's large inner courtyard, passing the fountain, the bakery. I grab an outdoor pay phone — I'll call Jed, I'm late for an appointment with him at Headquarters. I hear the coins drop in the slot. I hear the first ring. And then, in the chrome plate on the pay phone, I see a reflection: a man's form and a blue windbreaker.

For an instant, I can see the image in the bright surface. The man is behind me, but at some distance. Something about him is familiar. I turn sharply. The man is retreating.

Jed's voice comes through the line. It is a moment before I can reply, and afterward, in a taxi, I remember nothing of our brief conversation. All I can remember is that Tom's hair is like that man's. And Tom has a blue windbreaker. I've seen it on the back of his door; I've seen him wear it when we've walked by the river. *I wonder what you're avoiding.* Maybe he was watching me, this time, out of concern. *What you're afraid to look at.* Maybe he's watched me other times, and I thought it was Dade. Maybe he has been restraining me on this story for reasons other than concern. *I wonder what you're really* doing ...Outside the cab windows, everything seems to run together like cheap paint. I cannot see anything clearly. I hate looking into that darkness. Even my own. I cannot think. I realize, with a jolt, that the cab has stopped.

I pay the fare and step out onto Indiana Avenue. Time for me to start looking, and looking hard, once more. Jed has said he has something to show me, something "key." Upstairs, in his office, he spreads it before me.

I find myself looking at another photo: an expanse of pale sky with a row of children's faces below. It looks like Sam's work, only now it is a photo of a photo — taken by a Minox camera, on a tripod projecting from a dead man's mouth.

We lean over the enlarged pictures, Jed and I. He called me this morning, as soon as the film was blown up into these three huge photos: enlargements of the photos on Sam's wall. Why that wall? Simple, Jed thinks. The camera was pointed away from the door opposite. The assailant did not want to get caught on film leaving the scene. What Jed doesn't know is if the camera was set off deliberately or jarred into action by the shock. Possibly the attacker only turned the Minox away because it had already started snapping.

But the attacker had overlooked one detail. This detail, I know, is really what prompted Jed's call. The detail is a silhouette: a figure reflected in the glass over that one long photograph, mostly of sky; a tall figure striding toward the door. Jed has studied it. Other detectives have studied it. Crime lab has studied it. Jed wants me to study it — wants me to recognize it.

And I don't. The figure, caught in midstep, could be male or female. It is powerful, tall — but inconclusive. The head is turning to glance back. Around the head: perhaps long floating hair; perhaps only a blur. I think of Zoe's tall, powerful frame; her hair floating in the TV lights. I think of the other figure I saw, blurred by the fountain. The silhouette outside Susanna House; in a dim hotel garage. I look closer at the photo — the vague figure, striding, it seems, into the sky. There is some-thing about the stance, the shoulders, that makes me uneasy.

But maybe after last night everything is going to make me uneasy. Certainly another photo in this series does. It means nothing to the police. It means something, however small, to me. It is simply a photo of Sam, a younger Sam, taken by — who? Wife? Friend? Child? Sam, walking a golden retriever in Central Park. I think of the man recalled last night, greeted on the bridle path: a man with that dog. A man who, I think now, was Sam. To him, we must have looked like the perfect father and daughter, to be photographed .. .

"Look like anybody?" Jed is asking.

My eyes return to the silhouette. "I can't tell yet."

Jed looks vaguely suspicious. I feel vaguely guilty.

"I'll think about it," I say. A promise I can keep.

•

I SEE THE silhouette all the way back to the office. I see it in the car, against the windshield, against the sky. And then, through vast plate glass windows, I see two new sil-houettes. Two silhouettes behind glass in the lobby of the newspaper's huge, boxy building. Two silhouettes I recog-nize, this time, right away. One, small, dark, wiry. One, tall, draped and hooded in a blanket. The guard is just starting to show them out. I move forward, tell him it's okay. He gives me one of those "You reporter" looks. I take Ma'am and Angel outside for more privacy. They have come looking for me because they have news. The kind you show, not tell.

They have come to lead me to another silhouette. The silhouette of a woman down a long steep escalator, in the nearest Metro station. A small female silhouette, past the fare-card machines, past the guard's kiosk, past the hurrying figures — in the dim tunnel to the elevators, a woman like a shadow. Around her swirl the subway's smells: dust and soot and urine. She is caught in subway lighting: flashes of glare, stretches of dusk. In the tunnel, bulbs are burned out. It is a moment before I can see the woman clearly.

The silhouette is Johnice Dade. As I draw near, she becomes more than shadow. I see a worn, faded woman with yellowing bruises on her jaw. Her eyes are a washed-out blue, her face is webbed with lines. Gray threads her dark hair, now cropped short. Her life has aged her, marked her: she looks closer to fifty than mid-thirties. On her left hand she still wears a narrow wedding band; on her feet, rubber thongs. Hands and feet are grimy: that ingrained grime that means a woman is living mostly on the streets. As I approach Johnice looks down, twists the strap of a battered backpack. Then she sees the others; warily, now, she squints at me. Johnice Dade takes a half-smoked cigarette butt from her pocket. She lights it. She waits.

"Safe," says Ma'am, briefly. "Okay."

"Okay," Angel repeats. "You can talk to her."

Johnice exhales smoke. "I ... seen something." She twists the backpack strap.

"Something that ... upset you?" I lean closer.

She nods.

"Something at the shelters?" I ask.

"In the papers — first." The nylon strap twists again.

"Something about — "

"About Dr. Gordon, he was getting this prize." Ma'am and Angel, puzzled, exchange glances.

"I knowed him before I left my husband," Johnice goes on. "His clinic, it was right near our trailer park. Here I am in this city, gone from Fred — and like magic, Dr. Gordon, he turn up."

"You thought he could help you?"

I begin to feel relief.

"He helped us out before, I bring my kids to him, there was lots of times. And me, when I got beat up on, he helped."

My relief grows. Her strap twists.

"I seen him in the paper."

She pauses, as if to add something.

"You saw his picture?"

She nods. Pauses again; afraid.

"Then I see him on TV, that prize, they're giving it to him. And then there's this woman, I seen her one time, dinner, Susanna's — " She breaks off.

"Zoe, she seen her on TV," Ma'am interjects.

"And she's talkin', she's stopped everything, she's — " Johnice takes a breath. "She says he's a pervert."

"And that upset you," I say. "Because Dr. Gordon helped you, your kids?" I study her. "Is there something about Zoe you want to say?"

"About him." It bursts from her.

I find myself gripping my bag.

"No tape recorder on you?"

I shake my head. "I won't even take notes."

"Up home, I take my kids to the clinic — " And suddenly she is in tears. She is in tears there in the dim tunnel, in the dusty subway, and people pass her, their clothes skimming her backpack; she seems for a moment a shadow, a silhouette again. Silhouette of Woman, Weeping. Weeping for my father, it seems. For the man who has been good to her. Maybe it's true: a sick man who got well and made others well . .

And then she speaks again. "Take them to the clinic, it was okay, we get help ... and then one time I take my girls in, they're nine, seven — dog bit their fingers. I take them — and on God, I see — "

Abruptly I feel sick. I stand there smelling dust and hearing trains and seeing the images her words make:

The clean white examining room. Children's drawings on the walls. Bright curtains, bright yellow chair; a doll, a toy truck, a bowl of lollipops. The examining table, steel, covered in disposable white cloth. And on the table, Johnice's little girl. A little girl about seven, looking up at the doctor, and he is leaning closer, closer, This won't hurt, stroking her hair as he unbuttons, with one hand, his white coat. He doesn't know his nurse has been called away; he doesn't see the mother opening the door. But she sees the doctor stroking the child's hair — opening his coat. And then, his pants. She feels numbed, paralyzed, as she sees her child's hands forced to touch him. Then he is pulling the child against him — "He rammed it in her mouth, she's crying, the nurse is back, she's pulling me away from the door, 'Don't you disturb the doctor' — and I'm hollering, I'm fighting her ... my kid, my kid..."

Johnice Dade, outside the examining room, made such a disturbance she was permanently barred from the clinic with her family. When she went home, the kids couldn't quit crying and her husband hit her, hit them, and she about went crazy. She took the kids to her mother's place, and she got on a bus. Johnice had heard about shelters in Washington; she'd heard from four women at a clinic workshop. She had tried to find these women once she reached D.C. But every time she'd picked up a newspaper, one of the women was murdered. Maybe they knew what she knew. Maybe the doctor had come looking for them. Maybe he would come looking for her.

Johnice Dade went underground. "Scared. I been scared the whole time. And — mad, madder than I been my whole life. My whole life, men hitting on me, grabbing ass — now my babies, the same. Mad enough to kill someone, do something, that's why — why — " Her voice drops lower. "I made the bomb threats. I did. And the other threat. To the cops. I heard about the awards, about him getting one, and I went nuts, I called the Kennedy Center, and then the police — damn, I wanted to spoil it, stop it ... couldn't. But then this woman, this Zoe, she gets up, she says it out loud. About him. The truth. Thank you, God, I thought, but then no one believes her, I can tell, just watching the TV. And then he comes on, makes her sound like a nut case, they believe him. I figure if they don't believe Zoe, they'd never believe someone like me, not ever. So I keep low, keep moving. I'm scared he seen me that day, heard me, something. I'm scared every minute ... still scared Dr. Gordon will find me..."

Afterward, I am fighting down sickness and I am taking Johnice to Sidney's office. Johnice Dade needs protection, she needs a lawyer. And she needs to tell this to someone else. Someone who can evaluate her testimony; someone experienced. Someone who is not Karl Gordon's daughter.

I come back on the subway. I come back up through that station where we stood and I listened and smoked and heard those words. I walk forward, drop my fare card in the machine's slot; I take a place on the escalator. It rises slowly, lifting me out of the underground dimness, up toward the light. I stand there on the moving metal step, seeing silhouettes against the blue-white summer sky.

•

SILHOUETTES ON my computer screen. It is blank; I still see them. Figure after figure: from the beginning. The four murdered volunteers:

The young face. The old face. The wife's face. Ola's. All at my father's workshop, this May: I've checked.

Remember, you're like one of my own kids ...

Sam's face; I glance over at his desk.

The runaway's battered face; dead face.

It's all right ... you won't remember ...

My own face, child's face; velvet collar.

Think back on all the tales that you remember ...

Johnice Dade's scared face; bruised face ...

He rammed it in her mouth ...

Tom's face.

I hate looking into that darkness. Even my own.

Zoe's face. Hurt me ...

My father. My girl.

Zoe's face and my father's face: they alternate back and forth, flickering, as that silhouette against the blue-white sky. I light a cigarette; realize there's one already lit in my ashtray. I go through my notebook and the words blur and I set the notebook down. Across the newsroom, I look for Tom. He is in a meeting in the Metro office: I can see him only through the glass wall. He is sitting so that I am in his line of vision. Still, the meeting may go on and on. Words and smoke and glass, just now, separate us.

My phone rings. Jed Jackson. They've found smeared prints on the green mug from Sam's studio — unidentifiable prints, as if someone wiped the mug off. That's all. Call him later. I hang up.

I am still holding out on Jed.

Again, the phone rings. Zoe Heywood. I open my notebook. She is calling, she says, to apologize. Lost control. Bad time. She'd like to explain something, the

phone's fine ... my pen moves, trails off, forms a diminish-
ing line. For some moments after we hang up, I just sit
there looking at the dark computer screen.

.

FINALLY, I CALL Sidney. Johnice Dade has told another
attorney all that I heard in the subway. Sid pauses;
knows this is hard. Afraid of her own biases, she called in
third attorney. He found Johnice's testimony credible,
reliable. Sid hesitates again. Johnice Dade has sworn out
an affidavit. It attests to all she witnessed at the West
Virginia clinic. It also admits to the bomb threats before
the awards ceremony. There is a long silence over the
line. Sidney and I both know it: now the police will have
to be involved.

I put down the phone. On the blank screen now, I see
words: all the words I've written since this story began.
I see the story, in pieces, as it happened, segment by
segment. For an instant it becomes a jumble, a babble, a
tumble of events and details. I wait. Like scraps of paper
the details float down and settle, and now I force myself
to look again.

I open my notebook. Slowly at first, my pen moves.
Faster then, sickeningly fast, the story's larger outline
takes form:

Karl Gordon, M.D. Prominent, visionary physician.
Age, sixty. Peak of career.

Arrives Washington, D.C., two weeks before he is to
receive a coveted humanitarian award: the culmination
of a lifetime's work. With an active lecture schedule
ahead, the doctor settles into his hotel. There he receives
a visit from Zoe Heywood, now a noted humanitarian
herself, the daughter of a deceased friend, and, as a child,
one of the doctor's patients. Zoe does not congratulate

Gordon, on his gifts or his honors. She confronts him with
what is hidden, what she knows from her childhood. A
particularly beautiful child, she was the subject of
pornographic films made by her father, with Gordon's
help, in the doctor's basement room: a room only his
daughter would remember, years later, as she hears it
described on the phone. Zoe was sexually abused by both
men: great men, famed men. Secretive men.

Outraged at Gordon's upcoming award, Zoe threatens
to expose him. To her, it is not only a travesty; she knows
it will perpetuate the dark cycle that marred her own life.
Instinctively, she knows she is safe from Gordon; they
share an almost incestuous bond. The doctor cannot bring
himself to kill Zoe any more than he could kill his own
daughter. And within her safety zone, Zoe can work on
Karl Gordon.

Four of her volunteers, personally trained, have just
returned from a workshop at Gordon's renowned clinic.
Zoe plants in him the fear that these women have found
out about his perversions, which undoubtedly continue.
If the women don't know, Zoe will tell them. The truth
will be revealed publicly, at last — and after so many
years, there will be some kind of justice. Perhaps, then,
for her, the old pain will stop.

After Zoe leaves his hotel, the doctor sits thinking.
Now his dream, his mission, his honor is threatened.
These four women have somehow invaded him and his
Camelot. Now, incited by Zoe, they can take it, destroy it
— so easily. And so he must defend it and himself, at
high cost, he knows. One by one, he murders each woman
by invasion — a kind of rape. The first two are easy. In
the dark, each victim sees the doctor as a friend, as a pro-
tector, as a mentor. Gordon is careful: surgical gloves,
untraceable weapons. With growing confidence, he takes
a greater risk with the third woman; it's almost a thrill,

a test of his powers. He learns of her lunch at his hotel and knows of her physical condition. He acquaints him-self with the ladies' room's logistics, knowing that if need be, his identity as doctor can explain his presence any-where. He does not count on Sharon Welch's strength, but in the end the attack succeeds. He pulls the stall door shut from outside with his belt. There is no trace of his identity. The police are still baffled, and now, Gordon ob-serves, some shelters are watched. He approaches Eighth Street only when he's sure it's clear. Again there is an odd excitement for him, upping the risk, knowing the shelter's top floors are occupied. He does not know his daughter is inside. But he does glimpse Zoe in the kitchen: added incentive..

Here I have to stop. I light another cigarette; go on.

There are some repercussions but none serious. Gordon is unconcerned about Fred Dade and his missing wife. Dade has become a suspect. He has lost control, made himself noticeable around the shelters. At the cathedral, he publicly discredited himself. And Johnice is gone. Gordon does not believe that either one would be taken seriously. His word would hold against theirs; of this he is certain. And there are other suspects now. A runaway dying at Susanna House may cast suspicion on Zoe. There is suspicion around Terrence Heller, who has been at the wrong places at the wrong times. As days pass there seems little danger to Karl Gordon. The police seem no nearer to a solution. This sad mission is complete. With courage he previously lacked, the doctor contacts his estranged daughter. He has kept as close to her as he could: watching her from a distance, clipping her stories, calling her number to hear her voice. He longs to talk with her, to reconcile. How much, he won-ders, does she remember? After their meeting, he knows she recalls only his rages. For these, he is genuinely sorry. For all the ways he wronged her, he feels regret. He is grateful for their reconciliation. He feels blessed: his only child will see him receive the honor of his lifetime.

A bomb scare threatens the awards ceremony. Gordon assumes the threat is made by Zoe — a bluff, he is sure. He is unaware of another warning made to the police but would ascribe it to Zoe if he did know. In any event, the bomb scare is, indeed, a false alarm. Karl Gordon receives his award in a spill of glory. This, the apex of his life, cannot be ruined — not even by Zoe's outburst. In fact, the outburst backfires. Zoe discredits herself and Gordon discredits her further; she herself becomes a suspect. However, just before the ceremony, Gordon has met one more figure from earlier years: Sam Wile, news photographer and old family friend. The doctor always suspected that Sam knew something about him. Wile had been in Central Park on one day when Gordon lost control with his daughter. Sam was walking a dog and carrying a camera; after that, there was an odd distance between the two men. But all these years, nothing had ever been said — until, backstage at the Kennedy Center, Sam invites Karl to his home and mentions a glance at old photos. Immediately, Gordon recognizes another threat; perhaps even potential blackmail.

The next night the doctor visits Sam and kills him, in a way that avenges photographic invasion of privacy. Again, all is done with care. A file is destroyed: the one most likely to contain evidence. Terrence Heller's bill — a suggestive find — is placed in a more conspicuous position, smeared just enough to cast further suspicion on the psychiatrist. The mug is wiped clean of fingerprints; surgical gloves are used for the rest. There are only two slips. Gordon does not realize he has left a snapshot: an innocent one, as they all are — but one that triggers memories in another person who, on some level, knows about him: his own daughter. Karl Gordon has not counted on this, nor on Sam's camera, set off by the attack, recording the doctor's silhouette reflected on glass. Nor does he know that Johnice Dade has come forward and spoken up about her daughters. He could not imagine that she would tell her story to Ola Harris's daughter — and to his own.

As he reads his daughter's newspaper stories, he finds no trace of suspicion. He cannot guess that she has come to remember what happened between them. He gathers that she suspects Heller, an odd bird, conflicted, sexually obsessed — but Gordon does not know that, in the end, he is written off, as merely that. The strongest suspect, Gordon figures, is Zoe. She, he assumes, is in the greatest peril, from within and from without. And so she would remain, if her words were not confirmed by Johnice Dade — and most of all, by his daughter's gradually resurfacing memories. These, he believes, with gratitude, are at rest.

As he prepares to leave Washington, Karl Gordon feels saddened but secure. He has defended his kingdom. He has achieved a kind of public knighthood. Now his clinic will grow faster, and more can be founded on its model. More funding will come; more of the poor will be helped. When Gordon sees his face in theirs, he will know this was worth it; he will be able to heal, to save as never before. And, as never before, he has regained his daughter. He will not have to pass another day feeling her missing . . .

I look at my notebook. The words form a routine report; a journalist's reconstruction. And yet the pages blur in my sight. I look away. My eyes shift to the photos over my head. I see the snapshot of Sidney and me — with Ola's face cropped out. I glance over at Sam's empty desk. For a moment, in the air, I see Sister Joe again,

dead in her car. In that moment, she looks to me like
Nora Callahan. For an instant, I see Meredith Crane's
face again; in that instant, it looks like my own. I look
across the newsroom, once more, at Tom. I try to work
out all the times I saw the blue windbreaker behind me.
The only times I didn't know for certain that Tom was
somewhere else were the last two times. Somehow, I
know it was Tom then; and I know in my spirit that he
was watching out of silent concern, silent love.

I stand up and reach for my bag.

Best to go quickly now.

In moments, I am downstairs in the parking garage,
I am pulling out into the street, I am shaking and cannot
stop. Driving by reflex, I find myself at that small downtown church — my sanctuary. I double-park. As always,
the sanctuary arches over me, dim, protective, maternal.
I move to the candles. My hand trembles as I light three;
my knees tremble as I sit, hard, in a pew. I remember the
evening I felt someone here, behind me. I rise, glance
about. Today, the church is empty. The shadowy confessionals are empty. I slip into one, anyway. On the other
side of the old-fashioned grille, there is only gray air; no
priestly profile, no phrases of mercy. I lean my face
against the grille, feeling its pattern against my cheek. I
take a breath, then jumble the familiar words:

"For I ... Father — " My whisper breaks.

The grille, as I leave, is wet.

■

<31>

N AN," SAYS my father, opening his door. "I wasn't expecting you." He is putting in cuff links. One is still in his hand as he holds the door wide. "But I'm glad — come in, come in, have you ever seen the Marlowe's upstairs?"

I walk into the hotel room's center. It seems a thousand years since I was here last, sneaking in, on the heels of the maid. I glance around; it looks exactly the same. "Lovely." I murmur something like that. I fix my gaze on the bureau: loose change, keys on top. Like the top of his bureau at home. I force myself to count the change; to focus so hard on something, I'll get control.

"Well." Smiling, he puts in his other cuff link, looks at his watch. "I've a meeting here at one, my last, what a relief."

The clock by the bed says noon. It must be wrong. It feels like the day's end; like night, despite the light streaming through the curtains. I met Jed at nine. I met Johnice at ten. The clock is right.

"Have you had lunch?" My father is asking.

Have I had lunch. Any father's question.

"I could order you something — "

"No. Thanks."

I look at the sun on the curtains, the light pooling on the rug. For a moment everything else seems a hallucination.

"We need to talk about dinner tonight," he's saying now. "I've had a few ideas — "

"We need to talk about some other things." I pace to the balcony, look out; watch the curtains.

"Something wrong?" His voice, behind me.

"Sidney has just taken a sworn affidavit from the person who made the bomb threats — at the awards." I turn.

"Really?" He looks interested; he offers a chair.

I remain standing by the window. "She just called me."

"A man?" The cuff links flash gold.

"A woman."

"I would have thought a man, somehow."

I look at him. "A Johnice Dade."

He doesn't react.

I take a breath. "Sound familiar?"

He seems thoughtful. "No ... should it?"

"I think so." A pause. "The bomb threat isn't the only thing."

"Don't you want to sit down?" He looks puzzled; he is ensconced in an easy chair.

I want to sit down. I want to sit down and let him order me up a sandwich. I want to discuss where to go for dinner and I want to drop this; I want to be wrong.

I remain standing. "The bomb threat," I repeat. "That wasn't all she swore to, Johnice Dade. She also swore to something she saw at your clinic. The clinic in Appalachia, she says it happened just a few weeks ago." I watch him. No change of expression. I force myself on. "She says she brought her two kids in, two girls, ages nine and seven. They'd been nipped by a dog, their fingers ... she sat outside the examination room and the nurse got called away. The examination seemed long. The mother got worried. She opened the door to check on her kids." I stop. I am watching him closely now.

He has gone very still, watching me.

I take another breath. "What were you doing to them, Daddy?"

There is a long silence.

"I don't ... understand," he says, finally.

I take a step forward. "What were you doing to them?"

Another silence. Another step. "What were you doing to them?"

His face is calm but alert. "As I remember," he says, "I was examining them for puncture wounds ... in their fingers. They needed a tetanus shot ..."

"Don't. Don't lie to me. Daddy. Please."

"Just the usual procedure ..." He is going on.

I turn away. For an instant I close my eyes. "That's not the way it was." My voice is so sharp, so intense, it startles me. I turn around and face him. "You know that. How many times was it, Daddy? How many children besides the Dade girls? Ten? Twenty? Or was it hundreds — "

"Only the Dade girls." He catches himself. "And that was a misunderstanding — "

"No." My voice shakes. The room seems to open up and spread between us like a field. For an instant he looks very small, very far away, and the carpet seems a vast expanse — acres, miles. And then, abruptly, the space contracts, he is just a few steps away and his eyes are on me and the silence pulls us closer.

"I suppose," he says, at last, "I suppose you've been talking with Zoe Heywood." He takes out one of the cuff links; he holds it in his palm, watching the gold catch the light. "I suppose she's got something to do with this. I wouldn't be surprised if she got to this ... this Dade woman."

"Zoe has said some things. But not everything. Not to the police. Not to Mrs. Dade."

"But to you."

"Yes."

I watch the cuff link flashing in the sun. I remember taking one once from his bureau. Just to have it. To have something of his while he was away.

"Yes," I say again.

"Oh, Nan." My father shakes his head; a slow, sad, reflective gesture. "Zoe ... she's a very troubled woman."

"And why is that, do you think?"

"She was always difficult, even as a child ... her father really struggled, raising her alone — "

"Did he struggle getting her to pose? Making films?"

My father looks at me.

"Did he?" I stand very still. "Did you — Daddy?"

"Films?"

"For God's sake, don't play those games, don't do that to us."

"I don't know what — "

"I think you do. I think you know about the pornography films. Made in the basement room. With Zoe, the child star, the main attraction, I think — "

"Nan." His voice is calm, soothing.

"And not just porn," I push on. "Violence, blood on the floor — "

My father sets the cuff link back in his sleeve. "That," he says, "is a very disturbed projection — I'm sure you recognize it, the displacement — "

I take another step into the room. "I recognized some other things. Yesterday. In Sam Wile's house." I watch

for reaction. I hate this. All the tricks, the ways to surface information — used on my father.

He is careful to have no reaction. I have to go on with
it, then. "I recognized one picture, it was left, overlooked.
A snapshot from 1962. It was a picture of me, Daddy. In
a coat with a velvet collar, it was new that fall. I wore it
to the park with you."

Now, as he is watching me, his eyes sharpen.

"Daddy — I remember. I remember what happened to
that little girl in the new coat, the coat with the velvet
collar. In the park that Sunday, I remember it."

"Nan ..." My father's voice is kind, professional.
"You've been under tremendous strain lately. I know that,
I understand."

"No. No, you don't understand, you really don't get
what's happening here and I don't blame you, I wouldn't
want to either — " I stop myself, turn to the window
again; force myself to concentrate only on the curtains, on
the sun. "There was a missing file of photos," I say,
finally. "The same year that snapshot was taken. Sam
took it. Of me. With you, in the park."

"And why is that so important for you?" He's going
professional on me, he's going psychological. I try not to
listen, I don't answer; just force it out.

"There was film in Sam's camera — the camera on the
tripod. The tripod rammed down his throat."

Turning, I catch a change in my father's face.

"The camera took three pictures of that wall, that wall
of photos. A silhouette showed up on one. That one photo
we always liked, it was mostly sky. And it was framed,
covered with glass. I saw that silhouette in the glass today. I saw it enlarged. And I knew who it was. I couldn't
admit it to myself, to anyone, not then. But I knew. I'd
made myself forget how that silhouette looked. I forgot

for years, I forgot until I saw you turn around one night in a hotel lobby. Daddy — this hotel."

Another silence. Now, abruptly, the space between us seems too close and the room presses in around us. My father stands up. "I can't believe ..." He shakes his head. "I can't believe you'd think I could possibly — "

I move toward him. "Then tell me it isn't true. Tell me, Daddy. Tell me it didn't happen, it never happened. Tell me that isn't you in the picture — tell me this is wrong and it didn't go this way at all. Daddy. Tell me."

I stand in front of his chair. He looks at me steadily; alert, wary, and still he says nothing. He is watching me the way a doctor observes a patient. He seems not to blink; watching, watching. "You're over-wrought, Nan, someone's upset you."

I can feel my fingers press into one palm. I can feel all the hairs on my head. Even my teeth seem to ache with effort, and for a moment I can't breathe. "Tell me," I say, making my voice very quiet. "Tell me you weren't un-nerved when Zoe came up to this room. When she implied that those four volunteers knew — knew about you." I look at him. "And they didn't know, they never knew, right to the end — they thought you were a saint. They admired you till they died. I saw them dead, I saw how they died. Tell me you didn't want to silence them, Daddy. Tell me you didn't. For God's sake, tell me you didn't do that."

"I didn't. Of course I didn't." He shakes his head. "It's a terrible thing, hearing my own daughter — "

"Your own daughter. Daddy. Look at me. Look at us. You know what we did together. What you made me do with you. And not just with me. Not just with Zoe. God — not just with those little Dade girls, I don't know how often. And I know, I know it's a sickness, I understand that now. I could understand that part now, I think — if that was all. But Daddy — God, it's not. Sam is dead. Sam loved us, he never told, he's dead." I press my hands together and still they tremble. "Ola's dead. Ola Harris — Daddy, she was Sidney's mother." And suddenly I have him by his shirt collar, I am shaking him, shaking him hard, and he is letting me and I feel the starch in his collar. "A young girl, going to be married. A nun. A woman with two kids — my God, Daddy, how could you do that? To them? To me?" I let go of his collar. "To your-self."

He moistens his lips, runs a hand over his face. "Look, I know I made mistakes as a father, Nan. I know I failed in a lot of ways. But not these ways. Not this." He looks up. "You don't know me, you never did. You let that Irish woman take you and make you hers, you never let me in. If you knew me you couldn't say these things. You grew up with everything, and you were her kid, not mine.

"I grew up with nothing, and I was nobody's kid. Nobody's, do you know how that feels? I was sickly, skinny, I got knocked around in a tough neighborhood and my parents ran a dry-goods store all hours, I never saw them, it was the store, always the store. You know who raised me? My grandmother raised me, and she wasn't like your Nora Callahan. She was a goddamn Gypsy, Romanian, she told fortunes on the kitchen table. And she cursed me, she spat at me, and she beat the hell out of me — you understand? With her cane.

"That's how I grew up and I overcame it, I decided I'd survive it and help people, and I have, damn it. I've given my whole life to helping people, I worked hard, I worked through school, I learned East Side Manhattan manners. I worked and I never forgot I'd been poor and I never stopped at being rich. But I went to Appalachia and I started a place for kids who have nobody, who get beaten. I'm still helping." He is shaking now; his lips tremble. "I

... have ... helped ... people." He shakes harder now. "I built a place like ... Camelot ... wisps of glory. I built it for them. All those people." His eyes fill. "For them."

"And those four women ..." My voice is a whisper now. "Those women, and Sam ... they might have torn it all down ..."

He takes a shaky breath; his voice is a whisper too. "I couldn't ..." He wipes his eyes. "I couldn't let them do that ... " He sits staring straight ahead.

I kneel before him and take his hands. "Daddy. The police are going to call you in. Or they'll come for you. They'll ask you questions. There's an affidavit now. There are other things. Don't ... don't let it be that way. Go to them ... Daddy, please." I feel tears sting my eyes. "Go on your own. Go as Karl Gordon. The healer. The humanitarian."

He shakes his head. I take his face and turn it so he can look at me. "Please." Tears run down my face now, I taste them, I don't care. "Go and tell them. Go proud. Go as the master of Camelot. His kingdom was falling, remember, and he knew he'd caused it. And he stood. He passed the light to a child and said `Run, tell how it was' — and he went to meet his enemies. His avengers. Go like that, Daddy, please. I'm not asking you to do it for me. I'm not asking you to do it for yourself. Do it for Camelot. For all those people you've helped and healed and saved. For them."

I take his handkerchief from his pocket. I wipe his face. I wipe my own. I press his hands.

After a moment, he presses mine.

Slowly, I get to my feet. And slowly, I walk toward the door. Just as I open it, I hear his voice. "Nan," he says. "Remember."

There is a long pause. "Remember," he says. "There was good." He looks at me and I look back at him and we are still.

"Yes," I say finally. "Yes."

∎

<32>

I DON'T REMEMBER going down in the elevator or going through the lobby or finding my car.

Next thing I remember I am in the car, behind the steering wheel. I start the engine. The car idles. I just sit there. I open the windows, but I can't think, can't drive. Dimly, I hear sounds from the street: voices, footsteps, someone calling a dog. Time seems to stretch and flatten out and still I sit there. Sun flashes from a window; a passerby stares in at me. I don't know how long it is before the car phone rings. I ignore it. It rings again, sounding far off, unreal. Finally, the third time, I grope for it. Jed Jackson's voice is coming through the line — an oddly gentle voice. I don't get it all but I get enough.

"I'll be there," I say; my words sound frayed.

"Hoped you wouldn't."

"Where?"

A pause. He tells me; he'll meet me there — and then I am out of the parking space, into the traffic; the steering wheel slips under my hand, the windshield blurs. I blink;

my sight clears. I try to focus only on the streets, only on the traffic signals.

A string of red lights, green lights, leads me there — there, to a road running alongside the Potomac River. The road, on one side, is bordered by foliage; on the other, by a stone wall that finally curves toward a bridge. Here I slow and stop and pull off onto the shoulder. Ahead, I can see the blue-red flash of squad cars: only two, the first on the scene. I see Jed's Buick. And beyond, flares set up on the cement, burning pink and strange in daylight. My knees tremble as I step out, step forward. I forget to close the door. Stiffly, I keep walking.

The flares surround the shattered glass and twisted metal of a car; a car that has smashed at high speed into the stone wall. I see the sharp skid marks on the road. No other car involved. The collision, in clear weather, in daylight — took only this car, this driver. This car; crushed and compacted, has spun around and faces the long bright road. A cop is already redirecting traffic. His hands seem to move in slow motion. The road blurs.

I walk nearer. Under my shoes there is the crunch of glass. The sunlight flashes from the broken glass as if from ice. Now the car is closer. It is the dark green Thunderbird. I last saw it in the hotel garage. Somehow, I remember how it looked. Holding it in sight, I keep walking. A cop bars my way; I don't know him. But Jed is there — he is beside me now.

"My fair lady."

We look at each other. I step over the flares. Behind me, Jed makes some signal to the others. Vaguely, I see some of the faces. And then I see only the car.

The front end is smashed in, the engine jammed against the front seat, the windshield shattered. The doors have crumpled like foil. The roof has buckled. Compacted by the crash, the sleek car is suddenly small.

And trapped within it is the driver. The steering wheel has been rammed into his chest. Blood runs from his head and flows from his mouth. His eyes are wide open and seem to gaze at me. My father, my father.

I walk closer; close as I can. Directly before him, I stand. I stand and look into those eyes: those wide eyes that cannot see. I stand and do not turn, do not move.

Around me I hear sirens and more cars, more radios crackling. They'll have to labor, getting the body out; they'll need a blowtorch. But for a few moments, they wait. I feel a silent circle of protection form around me. And I go on standing there in my blue dress and my heels, facing the man in the car. Everything seems to recede then: road and noise and even the sunlight.

My father and I are alone together in some spacious expanse. If I put out my hand, I feel, somehow, he would take mine. Suddenly I remember walking with him on a sunlit beach, thirty years ago. I had lagged behind. The surf was rough. He had turned abruptly to see where I was. He had looked at me and I at him and it had been something like this: this endless gaze. But then I had run to clasp his knees. Now I only stand, motionless.

He wanted this. I know it. He wanted this and made it happen. It cannot be proved, even by skid marks; not conclusively. Unless there is a note. And I know, somehow, there is no note. No note and no other cars involved. Just my father and the river and the wall. My father and the light, pure and sharp and piercing, blazing from that shattered glass.

I think of him sitting in that chair where I left him. That chair where he must have decided. That chair from which he must have risen swiftly, decisively. It hasn't even been an hour. He seems to look into my face.

I built it ... I look into his. Yes. For them. I'll think about the rest later.

Someone is behind me now, someone who has been allowed through the protective circle — passed inward, by Jed.

"Nan." Tom touches my shoulders. He holds me against him; I reach up and cover his hands with mine. We stand there together for what seems a long time. Tom has kept his word: he is looking into this darkness with me. And I know in that car, in that bloodied face, he is seeing his own father as well as mine. And Tom knows, as I press his hands, that I am looking into his darkness with him.

This is the darkness that comes in the sun at the height of the day. This is the darkness I want to speak through, before we go. May light perpetual shine upon him ... no, he wouldn't want a prayer. That wasn't his way. My father would want some other word in farewell. I look into his face once more.

Remember ...

In the end, the last words I say to him, spirit to spirit, are the last words he said to me less than an hour ago. There was darkness; there was brutal death. But I am not telling you that now, Daddy. I am telling you something else.

I remember. There was good.

My hand in Tom's, we turn. We walk together over the shattered glass, past the flares, through the circle of police.

■

<33>

Dr. KARL Gordon, 60, pioneering physician and recipient of the National Humanitarian Award, was killed instantly today when his car crashed into a stone wall abutting Chain Bridge ...

I sit in the newsroom writing on deadline, watching the words flash up on the screen. Writing on deadline, as usual.

And not as usual. The city editor told me to go home. The Metro editor told me to go home. No one, they said, expected me to write this story.

I sat down at my desk and signed on at the computer. I would write this story, I would finish this story. And in the end, seeing my face, no one tried to stop me. Tom understood and smoothed it out. And so I sit here, dry-eyed and flat calm, smoking, typing, writing the terrible words. The words I can't not write.

> In the past week, allegations of child abuse have
> been leveled at Dr. Gordon. These allegations in-
> volve his personal and professional life. They
> include statements by Zoe Heywood, director of
> Susanna House, and a sworn affidavit by Johnice
> T. Dade, whose daughters were Gordon's patients.
> The affidavit attests that Dade's children were
> molested by Gordon at his clinic ...

I feel very cold and each word feels like a stone in my
throat. I light another cigarette. It has to be told; told
true. I think of the man sitting in the hotel room chair.
I think of the man pinned in the car. I think of the man
upstairs in the cafeteria. I'm sorry about a lot of things.
Green jello and white bread. A father and a daughter.
I've thought about that more, lately. I think of the man
years ago leaping onto the coffee table, bearing aloft his
dream — a dream he'd protect at high cost.

> Recently, Dr. Gordon was also implicated as a sus-
> pect in the brutal serial killings dubbed by police
> `the umbrella murders.' A growing mass of circum-
> stantial evidence ...

For a moment I remember sitting in my car trying to
breathe. The feeling comes over me again; my chest con-
stricts. I want to open a window, lean back. Instead I
lean forward, toward the screen. I will make this right.
I will write this and it will run and it will be right.

I think of the thin boy beaten by tough kids. Beaten
by his grandmother Anna Maria, for whom I am named —
named for some reason: an attempt to make peace? I
resemble her, I know; I've seen her pictures. Her dark,
long-lashed eyes — like mine. Exotic eyes, with fair
coloring. He must have seen her in me. Perhaps he saw

her, too, in Zoe's different, exotic eyes. And so the cycle
repeated, and must be broken now, by being told. He
would have wanted that, I think — the cycle broken. His
first calling was as healer.

> On June 14, Dr. Gordon was honored for 30 years
> of consistent service to the poor. In 1962, he
> founded the Medical Outreach Clinic in Appala-
> chia, near Parker, West Virginia. The clinic revo-
> lutionized care for the rural poor and has become
> a model for 30 others in this country and abroad.
> Gordon, born near Harlem, in a tenement, worked
> his way through New York University's School of
> Medicine, and prospered. `I grew up poor and I
> never forgot it,' he said in a recent interview, citing
> his abiding desire to help people ...

The screen swims before my eyes. I blink. No shock,
no tears, even now. I look at the wall above my head. A
picture of the clinic hangs there now. A picture of my
father before it. And beside it, the photo of me and Sid —
with Ola cropped out. Across the newsroom I see one of
Sam's buddies cleaning off his desk. We will, none of us,
be who we were.

Perhaps for some of us there will always be pain: For
Sidney, for the Welch family, for Sam's family. Perhaps
for many, there will always be memories of lives saved,
not taken; memories of healing. And for some of us,
perhaps, amid the pain: freedom. Perhaps for Zoe — at
last. For Tom, who is finishing what could not be com-
pleted alone. And perhaps, in the end, for me. For the
woman; for the child in the velvet-collared coat.

> A complex man with strong visions and opinions,
> Karl Gordon often said he felt a kinship with the

anonymous. A man of science, his hero was not a Jonas Salk or an Albert Schweitzer. Instead, Gordon's model was a mystical, semi-mythical king: Arthur of Camelot . . .

For a moment the newsroom recedes. The tap of keys, the ring of phones, the build toward deadline — it all falls away. Around me the houselights have dimmed in a Broadway theater. On the bright stage, the play is reaching its conclusion. The king's realm is crumbling around him; he has brought it down himself. He hands a child a candle: Run, boy, run ... The gravelly voice gives a final command. Ask every person if he's heard the story, and tell it loud and clear if he has not ... And in the dim theater, a father and daughter watch.

The scene shifts now, dreamlike before my eyes. The dusky theater has become a bright cafeteria twenty-five years later. There is reunion, reconciliation — just before another realm begins to fall. And perhaps he knows it. Perhaps he glimpses it even then. You're the storyteller now ... The daughter looks at the pen in her hand; she has forgotten it is there. Didn't the king pass a candle to the storyteller ... she asks. The father gazes out across the cafeteria. Yes. At the end ...

Maybe, somehow, he did know. And, somehow, wanted it stopped: what he could not stop himself.

In a recent interview, Gordon spoke at length about King Arthur. `Great. Glorious. Flawed,' was the doctor's description of his hero. It could also describe Karl Gordon himself. According to a variety of sources, he was seen as a `saint' and an 'ogre.' He leaves conflicting memories behind him: allegations of great harm and testimonies of great healing. His contribution to medical care for the

poor is lasting. His life was complex, a contrast of
light and darkness, even to this reporter — his
daughter who tells his story ...

For some moments I sit there, staring at the words on the
screen. It is 6:00, almost deadline. Behind me, Tom leans
close. "You holding up?" He turns my face so he can see
my eyes. For a moment we just look at each other.
Nothing we can say, here. Nothing we need to.

I nod toward the screen. Tom scrolls up to the lead;
reads over my shoulder, as usual. The long quotes are in
the mid-section. The story rolls, green on black, past my
eyes.

"You'll want that last line out," I say, finally.

He shakes his head. "I want it in."

We go through the piece again, as we have so many
stories; so many leads and lines of type, this past year.
But this story, we know, is not only the final in an important series. It is not only my father's story. It is Tom's.
It is mine.

Someone is standing in front of us; standing over us.
I don't look up, I never look up after six, except for an
editor. This is not an editor; I can tell that much. It's a
woman — Sidney, I think. I glance up.

The woman is Zoe. She stands before me and just
looks. I expect some word of self-vindication. Something
to go in the paper now; just in time. Something from this
woman who's been made to look crazed, jealous, not
credible. I brace — she has a right to this.

But she puts her hand out to me instead. She does not
say she is sorry. She does not speak of fathers and daughters, suicides and survival and shared pain. Her eyes
move over my face. I know she can see the strain there;
the effort at control. I know she sees, in my face, her own.

For a moment her fingers press mine. And then she is gone again. Her perfume lingers in the air.

And then I realize: not perfume.

Flowers.

No freesia, but a gathering of wildflowers not quite in season yet — chosen with care from a florist: marigolds and zinnias and wild carrot and others I cannot name. They are strong and hardy and bright. They lie on top of my computer screen, above the lines of words, in silent, brilliant memorial.

■

<34>

THE LAKE is wide and deep and still. Today it is the blue of ripe berries. We sit at its edge on a narrow strip of sand, our feet in the water: water still cold, in New England in June. The sun, though, is strong. Behind us I smell roses from a trellis: Tom's grandmother built it long ago. Like her and like her sayings, it abides. She is gone; the house is Tom's by inheritance, but rented out. Its tenants, often away, are absent this week, and so he has brought me here.

It is now eight days since my father's death. His ashes repose in a small black box in Washington. Soon I will take them to West Virginia: his request. But not now; not yet. Tom was adamant. First: rest, recovery.

We have rested. We have slept upstairs in the high brass bed, and I have studied the faded wallpaper that runs up under the eaves. We have walked by the lake and talked and not talked and not needed to. We have sat by the fire, that first chilly morning, and before the fire, made love.

Up here I do not try so hard to be brave. I still cry in my sleep, till Tom wakes me and holds me, and I know I will cry for more nights to come. Here it is all right: shock, tears. Tom has cried them with me — tears from years before, unshed after his own father's death. Together, I think, we are starting to heal.

We eat crabs this last afternoon. We pick oat grass from the dunes. We lie in the hammock as we have each evening, watching the sky go plum-dark.

It will be hard to leave, I say. We'll come back, he tells me. We do not know now if the big paper and the fast city and the breaking stories will pull us and hold us; maybe we are more a part of that deadline than we suppose. We do not know yet if a small town and a small paper and a deep lake will pull us — keep us. We are a part of their line, too. But for now, we don't need those answers. We have others.

Two things we know for certain:

We abide.

And we've quit smoking.

§

ACKNOWLEDGMENTS

I remain thankful, as always, to the women of the shelters, for all they have taught me and all they continue to give.

My gratitude to Sister Mary Ann Luby and Sister Nancy Conley, directors of Rachael's Women's Center and Mount Carmel Place, respectively; as friends, supervisors, mentors, and teachers, they remain inspirations and sources of joy. Thanks, too, to Rachael's Associate Director, Thelma Brown, and to Jean Sherry, Susan Shankle, and Karen Stinson.

As ever, special thanks to my friend and agent, Jacques de Spoelberch, for his giftedness, grace, and support. Thanks also to Upton Brady for his editorial insight which contributed much to this project.

Thank you, Molly Sinclair, good friend and gifted reporter for the Washington Post, for all your technical advice — any mistakes here are mine. Thanks too to Sari Horwitz, Washington Post police reporter, for extensive consultation, and to the inspiration of Edna Buchanan, crime reporter for the Miami Herald.

Thanks to Kathleen Dyke for endless patience in reproducing drafts of this manuscript, and to Beek Typewriter & Sons for endless patience with my aging machines.

Thanks, also, to Aux Beaux Champs, for providing the menu for Nan and Tom's dinner out, as well as the inspiration for their restaurant; I appreciate the graciousness of its staff, and the staff of the Four Seasons Hotel, Washington, D.C.

Most affectionate gratitude to my family of loving, steadfast friends, especially during the writing of Deadline: Carol Allchin, Nancy Conley, Nancy Eggert, Hanna Emrich, Shloe Flanigan, Father Thomas P. Gavigan, S. J., Susan L. Hartt, Ellen Holland, Anna Dee Jensen, Sherry E. Joslin, Leslie Lynne Kriewald, Caroline Lalire, Judith R. Lantz, Elizabeth Leland, Monica Maxon, Margaret Money, Ann O'Donnell, Frances Bailey Shoeninger, Carole LaMarca Steininger, Laura Sessions Stepp, Donna Stirling, Jean Sweeney, Melanne and Phil Verveer, and the Carmelite nuns of Carmel, California.

I also wish to thank Hope Dellon, Senior Editor, and Abigail Kamen, Assistant Editor, for the perceptive contributions they made to the final drafts of the novel, and for their help in its final formation.

Above all, my thanks and cheers to Scott Wells, friend and brother, creative catalyst par excellence, first-string "unofficial" editor, brainstormer, and provider of support and laughter.

■

AUTHOR'S NOTE

This is a work of fiction. All resemblances to living persons are coincidental. The National Humanitarian Awards are my own invention; likewise the appearances of celebrities in that scene.

All scenes, events, and situations are also fictive; however, I have worked since 1984 with homeless women in shelters and have drawn on this experience, as well as on free-lance experience at two newspapers.

I wish to note that in June 1988, Ella Starks, a homeless woman, was brutally murdered in Washington, D.C. Starks was stabbed; her umbrella was then shoved down her throat. This incident shook the shelter community, and it remained in my mind. Eventually, the nature of Starks' murder came to influence the development of aspects of this novel.

I would like to add, however, that my experience of shelter work has blessed and continues to bless my life in countless ways — and has not been an experience of danger.

■

Critical acclaim for other works by Marcy Heidish

Novels:

- **A Woman Called Moses**, Houghton Mifflin Co.
  - The acclaimed historical novel based on the amazing life of Harriet Tubman, legendary conductor on the Underground Railroad.
  - A Literary Guild Alternate Selection
  - A TV Movie, starring Cicely Tyson.

Praise for _A Woman Called Moses:_

• **Publishers Weekly:** [Harriet Tubman's] "story has been told before, but never as eloquently, almost poetically, as here...achingly real...a strong narra-tive of a totally committed woman, one who speaks directly to our own desperate need to feel committed — and our wish that somewhere in the world there were more people like Harriet Tubman."

• **The Washington Post Book World:** "Profoundly rewarding...a daring work of the imagination."

• **Chicago Sun Times:** "Marcy Heidish has, almost uncannily, crawled into the skin and very mind of Harriet Tubman....The dialogue sings with poetic beauty."

- **Witnesses**, Houghton Mifflin Co.
  - Historical novel based on the life of lay minister Anne Hutchinson, religious freedom advocate.

Praise for _Witnesses:_

• **The New York Times Book Review:** "....nothing ordinary about her creation of this remarkable woman. The novel abounds in literary grace, employ-ing the voices of the times as though heard this minute."

• **The New Yorker Magazine:** "A striking novel...a compelling portrait."

• **The Washington Post:** "Pure pleasure. Anne Hutchinson is real; thanks to _Witnesses,_ she at last assumes her proper place...in American history."
—Jonathan Yardley, Pulitzer Prize-winning critic.

- **The Secret Annie Oakley**, New American Library.
  - Historical novel based on the life of the legendary sharpshooter.

Praise for The Secret Annie Oakley:

- **Kirkus Reviews**: "An immensely touching and cohesive fictional biography of the legendary sharp-shooter... builds from exemplary research to a fresh portrait of a talented woman in crisis...a class act —as Heidish reconstructs. with color and drama, the choreography of the shows, the tone of the period, and the textures of a haunting past."
- **The Arizona Daily Star**: "Marcy Heidish is an imaginative, amazing writer. She's a magician with words.... Each character has been brought to life with a mere pen stroke; flesh and blood beings that are more than fiction.... A masterpiece of creative writing."
- **The Kansas City Star:** "An unforgettable story."

- **Deadline**, St. Martin's Press.
  - Contemporary psychological novel with a "mystery" as a narrative line.
  - Nominee for prestigious national "Edgar" Award; fine reviews.

Praise for Deadline:

- **Washington Post**: "*Deadline* is a tense, well-turned tale, filled with authentic police and newspaper people. Heidish's taut, punchy style moves the story at lightning speed."
- **Kirkus Reviews**: "The high-tension plot is enhanced by sharply etched pictures, by many vivid characters, and by a crisp, clean, first-person style. Heidish imbues her haunting story and her gutsy heroine with a rare sense of tenderness and poignancy. An impressive mystery by a gifted writer."
- **St. Martin's Press:** "This wire-tight novel probes relentlessly, driving deep into psychological darkness and violent death. As the riveting story reaches its stunning conclusion, we see a complex woman forced to meet the ultimate deadline."

- ***The Torching***, Simon & Schuster.
  -Contemporary literary novel, hardcover and paperback.
    -Literary Guild Alternate Selection; laudatory reviews.
      Praise for The Torching:

  • ***Washington Post Book World***: "Flex your fingers, gentle readers. You're going to be turning pages for the next few hours.... Because of Heidish's skill, we get the full force of her double-whammy...in part due to the grace with which she weaves the present-day and the historical, but also because of her inventiveness at the book's close, the daring way she gets both strands of plot to unite.... Marcy Heidish is a stylish and intelligent novelist to boot, more than up to the dizzying, tale-spinning task that she set for herself here."

  • ***Kirkus Reviews:*** "Shuddery mystery-suspense with supernatural overtones."

  • ***Library Journal:*** "Intricately constructed...A deliciously spine-tingling, multi-layered literary mystery..."

  • ***Publishers Weekly***: "Subtle and gratifying psychological suspense.... Penetrating characterizations ... Heidish impeccably orchestrates the historical and contemporary, the supernatural and psychological."

  • ***Simon & Schuster:*** With this spellbinding tale of mysticism, horror, and history, a gifted, award-winning writer ... here gives us a novel to rival the works of Anne Rice, Alfred Hitchcock, or Edgar Allan Poe — a vivid tale of an eighteenth-century midwife ... sentenced to burn as a witch in the tiny town of Maidstone, Maryland.... The Torching is an unforgettable novel about the power of words..."

- ***A Dangerous Woman: Mother Jones, An Unsung American Heroine***, Dolan & Associates, Publishers.
  - a novel of a self-proclaimed Hell Raiser.

- **Miracles**, New American Library.
  - Historical novel based on the life of Mother Elizabeth Seton, first American-born canonized saint.

Praise for Miracles:

- **New American Library**: *Miracles* is a novel charged with the vitality of a life that saw many changes, and with the power of a love that took many forms...as a lonely daughter of a wealthy, indifferent man; a searching young woman; a con-tented matron embracing a marriage that produced five beloved children; a widow searching for new meaning to life.

- **The New York Times Book Review**: This appealing book, told from the point of view of a skeptical modern priest, moves swiftly through tragedy to triumph.

- **Kirkus Reviews:** Working delicately with a balance of Church hagiography and psychological insight, Heidish provides another strong focus on the root dilemma of female saints and achievers.

Non-Fiction Books:

- **Soul and the City**, WaterBrook Press, Random House imprint.

Praise for Soul and the City:

- "I actually started reading Marcy Heidish's *Soul and the City* on a subway train, and I must say it had exactly the effect she writes about. It gave me peace in the middle of the hurry, the rush, the loud noise of the city." – Rick Hamlin, executive editor of *Guideposts* and author of *Finding God on the A Train.*

- "... a rich and nuanced touring companion to rival any Michelin or Eyewitness guide—usable in any city of the world. Keep it close and...you will meet beauty and holiness no matter where you pause to look." – Leigh McLeroy, author of *The Beautiful Ache* and *The Sacred Ordinary.*

■ *Defiant Daughters: Christian Women of Conscience*, Liguori Publications.

Praise for *Defiant Daughters*:

• *Liguori Publications*: Joan of Arc, Immaculée Ilibagiza, Corrie ten Book, and Sojourner Truth are among those women whom best-selling author Marcy Heidish calls "Defiant Daughters."

This informative, challenging, and entertaining book spotlights the lives of more than 20 spiritual trailblazers and their responses to crises of conscience. They represent different races, denominations, and nations, but all are feisty — often fiery — and always faithful to their callings.

What motivated these "defiant daughters," who gave their all for God? Heidish seeks out the decisive juncture where they took a stand for conscience, regardless of the consequences. This stunning and compelling book will bring you face-to-face with an unforgettable female gallery of "profiles in courage."

■ *Who Cares? Simple Ways YOU Can Reach Out*, Ave Maria Press.

An ideal resource for anyone interested in engaged spirituality.

This practical book is designed to bring out the caring person in each of us. Heidish offers simple, specific ways to practice the art of caring, especially within our immediate circle of concern.

Praise for *Who Cares?*:

• *Cultural Information Service:* "Contains savvy insights and wisdom about service... This is an ideal resource for anyone interested in engaged spirituality."

• *Fredericksburg Free Lance-Star*: "Covers just about every topic imaginable on ways that people can reach out to one another ... [written] in an easy-to-follow simple-style prose."

- ***A Candle At Midnight***, Ave Maria Press.

<u>Praise for *A Candle At Midnight*</u>:

- "...fills a void in the popular literature about depression. ...Heidish recognizes that making one's way through the agony and terror of depression is a spiritual pilgrimage as well. Heidish has constructed a meaningful collection of readings, rituals, and suggestions that have great practical utility. I recommend this book to anyone." – Martha M. Manning, Author of *Undercurrents: A Life Beneath the Surface.*

- "Heidish honors modern medicine and spiritual healing in this compelling work." – Alen J. Salerian, M.D., Medical Director of the Washington Psychiatric Center.

- "A masterpiece!" – Rev. Nancy Eggert, Director of the Shalem Center for Spiritual Direction.

Short Pieces:

- Articles and book reviews published in *Ms.* Magazine, *GEO* Magazine, *The Washington Post*, *The Washington Star*, and various in-flight periodicals.

- "*The Pilgrim Who Stayed*," *GEO* Magazine, about Chartres Cathedral, widely translated into many languages.

- "*The Grand Dame of the Harbor*," about the Statue of Liberty, a highly acclaimed cover story for *GEO* Magazine.

This article is included in a textbook anthology designed to teach writing to college students.